POSSESSED
The Complete Series

COCO CADENCE

CHAPTER ONE

My boss is a fucking asshole.

If he wasn't handing me a paycheck every month, I would be throwing my last pair of unbroken, non-horribly-smelling heels at his face one by one. I love those heels. They're my babies *and* the last ones I have, but damn, I'd sacrifice them for a good cause. This man needs a right smacking.

Let me explain. I've never been very fond of my boss. He's an obnoxious asshole who tramples all over my privacy, as well as personal time. As his assistant, he expects me to be there for him 24/7, ready for any order he has to give me.

I could've gotten used to it if it wasn't for the fact that he ignores the shit out of me. I'm only there when he needs me, and that's it. Conversations? Don't happen. Chatting like a normal human being? Not in it. Social interaction, you know, asking about my week or saying 'you look cute in that dress,' not by a long shot. A little kindness goes a long way, but not with him. Unless I fish for it, but no way in hell am I going to stoop that low.

I often wondered if he treated his previous assistants the same way, but then I realize that might be why I got the job in the first place ... because they all left. Of course, this job pays too well, so I've made it my personal ambition to stick with him for as long as I can muster. As long as the cash keeps flowing and I can pay my bills, I'm happy. Maybe it's also the fact that I consider staying some sort of achievement, despite the cocky asshole sitting in the chair in front of me.

I've learned to deal with his aloofness over time. I treat him with equal stuck-up bitchiness by not giving him an inch of emotion during our brief exchanges, but not to the point of actually getting fired. I might get the sack now, though, because I'm about to shatter glasses with my voice.

"What?!" I yell.

"Oh, c'mon, it's only for a couple of months."

He's referring to his latest crazy request. He wants me as his wife. His fake wife. As in, pretending to be married.

Leo fucking King, the CEO of *W*, a women's magazine, wants me—a big, curvy fake redhead—to be his wife?

This assistant job was just pushed to a whole new level of crazy.

"No. Oh, no, no, no," I say, frowning.

He raises his eyebrows in that same annoying way whenever he won't take no for an answer. Oh, hell no. Shit's about to hit the fan.

"You haven't even thought about it," he says.

"I don't need to think about it," I say, shaking my head. "Are you crazy?"

He smirks. "Maybe just a little."

"For thinking I would actually do it, yeah!"

He lowers his eyebrows with a faint smile on his face. "Oh, c'mon, Samantha …" The way he speaks my name, like he owns it, gives me goosebumps. "You're not even a little curious?"

"What? No, what would I be curious about?" I mumble, but some little voice in my head tries to pry my lips open to ask for more information. I drown the fucker in Pumpkin Spice Latte from Starbucks. Sugar rush and coffee keeps me on the saner side. Need as much of that shit as I can get to deal with this asshole.

When he opens his mouth, I'm slurping up my 'heroine' for the day, and I'm totally not prepared for what he says.

"What it would be like." He raises one cheeky eyebrow, slowly.

I cringe, trying to keep the laughter inside. I fail. Miserably. So badly, I spout my coffee all over the floor.

My bad. I'm not sorry. This dude … really?

"Sorry, I couldn't – I'll clean it up later," I mutter, still recovering from my outburst. I want to laugh but pressing my lips together so hard it hurts seems to do the trick.

"You'd better," he muses, clearing his throat. "You seem very amused."

"You're right, this is hilarious. As a matter of fact, I've never enjoyed any moment with you as much as these two minutes. This is amazing, Mister King, this prank … you've taken this asshole routine to a whole new level."

He smiles, not even slightly amused; it's more of an 'I'll punish you later' smile. "Except this isn't *Punked* and we're not on MTV."

"You're not serious, are you? Because if you are, I'll need to leave for like ten minutes."

"You're robbing me of more time with you?"

Robbing him? That's a laugh. I squint. "So I can get some more coffee so I can drown this day away. Besides, it's not like you *want* more time with me. I know you want me to agree, but throwing me a bone isn't going to work. I'm not that easy."

"Such a shame," he says, licking his lips, which distracts me momentarily.

To any woman, he would be an eye-fuck. Like those guys you see on those runway shows and you just wanna lick them. He's like that – chiseled jaw, kissable lips, sparkling brown eyes, scruffy stubble, sleek suit. Who knows what more he's hiding underneath? Except, he's a jerk, so thinking of it only makes me want to hurl. Or at least, I force myself to remember that I should. Nothing pretty on the outside can mask the ugly on the inside. I try to keep that in mind every time he has me distracted with his handsomeness; I shroud myself in loathing, just for the sake of my honor.

"… You assume too much, Miss Webber. Throwing you a bone is the opposite of what I want to achieve."

"You want me to run out of this office then? Because you're achieving that in a minute." I chortle. "You can ask me a lot, but being your wife is at the bottom of my list of things-I-have-to-do-for-my-boss, and that list is a mile long."

"Funny," he muses. "You're so funny."

"You, too," I retort.

We're so not funny.

This is so not funny. Not in a million years.

If he's actually serious, that is – which I still doubt because what in the effing hell? Who would ask something like that? And why?

Now he just sits there, staring at me, his hands folded on the table, and I'm seeing his serious face in action. I've only heard of it in rumors before, the impact it has on people he wants to get shit done with, and I've always assumed they were exaggerating. They weren't. This look rips panties off. Those eyes are like cracking whips, forcing you to beg for mercy.

Oh my god, how am I ever going to work my way out of this without losing this job? I'm starting to get this feeling, like I don't even have a choice in the matter, because he keeps his eyes on me at all times, his fingers strumming continuously.

This is happening, whether I like it or not.

Oh, dear.

Well, I'm not going down easily. If he wants to pin me down and make me do something I know I'll regret, I'd better get as much out of it as I can get. Time for some big girl panties and overrated confidence. This fat girl has some demands up her sleeve, and she isn't saying 'yes' for anything less.

"Okay, so let's for a second assume you are serious about wanting me to be your wife. What's the reason behind this request? Because as your assistant, I'm supposed to be 'working' for you in this office, not in your home, so if you require my assistance there I'm afraid you'll have to think of some kind of reward. Hypothetically speaking, of course. Because there is no way in hell I'd ever agree with this."

"Oh, Samantha… you have no idea how much I require your assistance. For example, there are plenty of times I'm dying for some 'personal' assistance at home … and if it was in the contract, I'd definitely make use of your 'assistance.'"

The way he says 'personal,' in that low voice of his, has me momentarily frozen in place, eyes peeled.

"Hypothetically speaking, of course." He smiles slyly. "The reason will be explained once you agree. And as for a reward, I can think of a few things …" He frowns, and while he cocks his head to check for someone passing through the hallway, he bites his lip.

Oh, sweet lord. This is too much.

His eyes find their way back to me again. "I could give you anything you want … anything you desire. You'd just have to ask." He smirks. "Hypothetically speaking, of course."

"You're bribing me now?" I place my coffee on the table and cross my arms. "Hypothetically speaking."

"I would call it a proper incentive."

"Not good enough," I say.

This guy has some nerve. After all that ignoring, I'm having a hard time believing his interest or innuendos are real. I know this man, and I know he thrives to tease. He's never given me a glance, though. Not once. It's like I don't exist, at least not as a 'sexual interest' to him, whatever the hell that means, because I have no clue what he likes. All I know is that I was never 'it', and it bugs me that he throws it into our conversations right this very moment. It's so out of the blue, I can't help but associate it with just another cheap trick at getting me to agree.

"What kind of reward are you looking for then?" he says, rolling back his chair.

As he stands up, I take a deep breath to keep my posture. I feel weak in the knees as he comes toward me. His vibe has always been so overpowering as if he's trying to claim the very air we breathe. Everything. Doesn't matter what, he needs to control it.

Now, even my decision.

"I want a raise," I boldly state.

He smirks. "Oh, you'll get a rise out of me all right."

Somehow, that statement heats up my cheeks like nothing else he's ever said before. Goddammit.

"Miss Webber, is it that you enjoy taunting me or do you just *want* to be punished?" He squints. "I must say, you are extra sassy today. I like it."

He tries to touch a string of my hair, which hangs in front of my face, but I block his hand and avoid it. Sweep across the floor like a ninja. Out of the danger zone where snakes bite my ass.

He takes a deep breath and then sighs. "All right, I'll give you a raise." He laughs, clearing his throat afterwards.

This has to be a cruel taunt because he keeps mentioning raise and I keep glancing at his package every time he says it. I swear to god, these treacherous eyes should be gouged out.

"Hypothetically speaking, of course," I add.

Suddenly, the amused look on his face disappears. "This isn't a game or a joke, Miss Webber. As my assistant, it's your job to supply whatever I want you to supply. Now, I want you to be my wife. I won't take no for an answer."

I cringe. "What? You're not even giving me a choice?" Somehow, I knew this was going to happen.

"You have a choice, but if you want to keep your job, I suggest you say yes."

My jaw drops. "This is ridiculous." I look around. "Where's the camera?"

"For the last time, Miss Webber. This isn't a joke. I need you to become my wife for a few weeks. It's not much, and you won't get any other strange requests from me other than this."

"It can't get any stranger than this," I interject. "You're going to extort me?"

"I wouldn't call it that …"

"But it is …" I shake my head. "This is insane. *You're* insane."

"You have no idea …but thanks for the compliment," he muses to spite me. "The point is, I need you for this, and I'm willing to double your salary."

I stare him blank in the face. "Triple."

"Fine." He holds out his hand. "For as long as I need you, you'll be my wife."

"Pretend-wife." I swallow.

"As real as we can both muster up."

"That's going to be hard, and I don't mean for me."

He smirks. "There are a lot of remarks floating through my head right now, like other things that are *hard*, but I'll spare you. For now."

He didn't spare me one bit.

"Ha-ha," I say. "If I do this, I want it on paper."

He squints. "Aw, you don't trust me, Samantha? You, out of all people."

"Trust is earned. You just wasted it all by giving me no choice in the matter."

"I know what I did, but I promise you it'll be worth it. I'll make it so you won't regret this."

I sigh, closing my eyes. "I'm crazy for doing this …" I hold out my hand. "Ignoring that little voice in my head right now."

"Keep ignoring that voice, Miss Webber. It makes life easier. Does for me."

"Ha, like you ever have such a thing."

"Oh, I do. For instance, there's this thing in my pants that keeps pointing in all directions, but if I let it make all the decisions, this company would be down in the gutter pretty quickly."

Not just this company but this conversation, too. Holy damn.

"I didn't have my second coffee yet, Mister King, can we spare the dick talk for later, after lunch maybe?"

He laughs. "I'll take that offer."

I sigh loudly; tired of all the sexual innuendos he's throwing at me. I hold out my hand. "Let's get this over with."

He shakes my hand, and I know that I just made a deal that'll kill me.

It'll definitely kill my career, all right, if I don't manage to keep this quiet. The chances that this comes out is about fifty percent, which means I have to get as much out of this as I can before someone blows the whistle and exposes us.

An assistant and her boss, getting it on? That's hot news. Definitely wrecks any chances to be taken seriously.

A boss pretending to be married to his assistant? Well, that just makes headlines. Tabloids sniff this juicy news out like dogs on the hunt, and I know it'll ruin him if this is ever exposed.

Which is why I'm adamant about finding out what exactly is it that drives him to do this. What the reason is for this charade. It has to be a good one since he's willing to risk it all.

This isn't just risking his own company; he's even risking my career.

I think I need to spike my coffee today. And maybe the rest of the week. Or month.

Fuck it; I'll need a whole bottle of whiskey to get through this day.

CHAPTER TWO

Fifteen minutes ago

FROM: doritoslover@gmail.com
TO: mrawesome@hotmail.com

Hey, are you there? I could really use some of your snark right now. Or a spicy pep talk, whichever you think is more appropriate.

Xx
S.

Thirteen minutes ago

FROM: mrawesome@hotmail.com
TO: doritoslover@gmail.com

Whose head should I bite off? Oh, wait, you didn't ask for a shark. Never mind.
Tell me what's bothering you. I want to know.
Spice comes after.

A.

Eleven minutes ago

FROM: doritoslover@gmail.com
TO: mrawesome@hotmail.com

I freaking hate my boss right now. Like, I want to jam his own foot in his mouth and make him gag on his own stench.

He's such an asshole sometimes. Never talks to me, and then out of the blue he starts making these sexual comments, although they weren't very literal. It got to me. I HATE that he made me blush. Goddammit … The nerve this man has to ask me all these things and think I'd agree, even putting my job on the line. Ugh! *Makes strangling gesture*

Xx
S.

Ten minutes ago

FROM: mrawesome@hotmail.com
TO: doritoslover@gmail.com

I understand how you feel. Bosses are a species of their own. Raging beasts. Must be a lack of sex. I tell you, a man without sex is like a man without a brain. I know so from experience, trust me.

Don't think about it, S. He probably didn't mean to make it difficult on you. He's just out of options, and you're all he has. Think of it as an honor, something only you can do for him. And then make him remember that he needs you. If someone's gonna be nasty to you, you be even nastier.

Talking about nasty … I know exactly what you need to take this off your mind. Are you interested?

A.

Eight minutes ago

FROM: doritoslover@gmail.com
TO: mrawesome@hotmail.com

I don't want to bother you with my shit. I'm sorry; I don't know what made me do that. Please ignore my rant. I think it's the hormones. And that man. Basically, a combo of both. Damn hormones …

I am interested. Very much. What do you have in mind?

Xx
S.

Seven minutes ago

FROM: mrawesome@hotmail.com
TO: doritoslover@gmail.com

Don't be sorry. You can talk to me about whatever is on your mind. I don't bite.
Hard …

I want you to make me hard. That's what I have in mind.

Playtime starts now.

A.

Six minutes ago

FROM: doritoslover@gmail.com
TO: mrawesome@hotmail.com

Yes, Sir.
What do you want me to do? I am at your disposal.

Xx
S.

Five minutes ago

FROM: mrawesome@hotmail.com
TO: doritoslover@gmail.com

Join me on the app.
I will give you instructions there.

Your boss made you blush, so now it's time to top that. Blow off some steam. Literally.

I expect you to be online within two minutes or else punishment will ensue.

A.

Four and a half minutes ago

FROM: doritoslover@gmail.com
TO: mrawesome@hotmail.com

Is that a challenge?

Three minutes ago

FROM: mrawesome@hotmail.com
TO: doritoslover@gmail.com

Don't tempt me, S.
Punishment isn't meant to be fun, and if it is, I'll make sure to

never do that again.

You're very cheeky today. I suspect it's because of your asshole boss, so I'll ignore this one slip-up, but don't push my buttons again. I realize you need to vent, but we'll do it in a different way. My way.

Come online. NOW.

A.

CHAPTER THREE

I close the browser on my desktop and grab my cell phone to open up the app. Mr. Awesome is already online, which makes me all giddy for some reason. I know what's coming now, I just don't know how yet. We talk, I blush on camera, he gives me sexual assignments to please him, I get off, he gets off. Conversation done. Rinse and repeat.

We've been doing this for some time now, and I have to say it really helps to deal with all this craziness at work. I like this dynamic – two people who don't know anything about each other getting each other off online – a perfect way to destress. Plus, I love to be dominated by him. It's just the way he does it that gets me so aroused; I swear, I haven't come this hard since I've known the dude. And I'm only fucking myself now, so god only knows how good it'd be to actually have sex with this mystery man.

But what the hell am I thinking? It's not like we'll actually meet. He's told me from the beginning that it'll never happen and that I shouldn't count on it. It was one of the rules we discussed prior to engaging in this hot affair; no addresses, no names, and definitely no attachments. It's all loose and fun … and totally sexy … so up my alley. Who cares about the stigma? As long as it doesn't hurt anyone, I'm having fun with him doing what we do.

I could use the distraction, and Mr. Awesome knows exactly what I need, which happens to be what he needs, too. He always needs me, which is why I enjoy talking to him so much. It's nice to be *needed*, once in a while, in the sense of actually being attractive and knowing someone else likes to see you and hear you talk. Yeah ... I'm an addict to Mr. Awesome's demands, for sure, but I don't regret a thing.

Mr. Awesome: Are you ready?

S: Yes, Sir. Please, let me know what you would like me to do.

Mr. Awesome: Take out the pink dildo you hide in your desk and go to the bathroom.

S: Yes, Sir. Can I add: the bathroom is unisex. Not just women will be there.

Mr. Awesome: Not important. Tuck it in your purse and go to the bathroom. Lock your stall door and put lid down on the toilet. Tell me when you're seated.

Licking my lips, I take out the dildo, careful not to be seen. I check my surroundings first before slipping it into my purse, making sure nobody is close. Nervous, I get up and walk to the bathroom. I walk inside and stop to listen if I hear anyone, but not a sound is made. I walk to the stalls and look under some of them, but I don't see anything. I don't have much time, so I go into my own stall quickly and lock the door, reminding myself that I'm alone in here. Time for some action before anyone comes in.

S: I'm here.

Mr. Awesome: Good. Now spread your legs. Wide. Let your skirt come up all the way until your panties are exposed. And then slip your fingers into your bra and touch yourself. Rub them softly until they're nice and peaked. Tug them at least thrice. Then tell me how you feel.

I do as he says, spreading my legs until my skirt crops up and then some. I slip my fingers into my shirt until the buttons explode and start playing with my breasts. My nipples are eager to pop, easily teased into arousal. Tugging them hurts a little, but the pain only gives me pleasure, making my pussy thump. I can already feel it getting wet.

S: Oh, it feels good.

Mr. Awesome: Tell me what you're doing. Pleasure yourself. Give me all the details.

S: Yes, Sir. I love my fingers all over my nipples, straining them to the limit. I'm desperate to touch myself. Can I, please?

Mr. Awesome: Are you wet for me, princess?

S: Oh, god yes, Sir. I'm dripping.

Mr. Awesome: Send me a picture. I'd like to enjoy as well.

Slamming my lips, I flip out my breast and hold out the phone to take a picture. Then I press send. It's not embarrassing anymore; instead, it riles me up to know he's looking at my nipple right now.

Mr. Awesome: Imagine me licking those rosy nipples of yours. God, you're beautiful, princess.

S: Thank you, Sir. I love to hear that.

Mr. Awesome: Your boss is crazy for not saying that to you every day. You always make me hard just by talking to me.

S: I'm glad I can do that for you.

Mr. A: Do some more for me, princess. Hot. Naughty. Show me. Pleasure yourself until the brink and then stop. Send me some pictures along the way.

S: Yes, Sir.

I tease my nipples until I'm hot and bothered, then slide down to my pussy to give it some attention. I slide my fingers up and down and push them into my panties, feeling my own wetness. My clit is thumping from his commands and the sheer pleasure it gives me to follow his demands. I love doing this, just letting go at the moment with a stranger.

I send another picture of my hand inside my panties.

Mr. Awesome: Tease. Send me more. I'll show you mine if you show me yours.

Now that's a challenge I'll gladly accept.

I take off my panties and slide my fingers into my wetness, then take a picture. Biting my lip, I play with myself while taking a whole set more. I'm getting so turned on – my breathing is ragged and my heart rate is picking up. Flicking my clit, my body is ripe with need, ready to let all of it out.

Mr. Awesome: Such a nice, wet pussy. Is it ready to be fucked?
S: Yes, Sir. I'm ready for you.

He sends me a picture.

He's holding his cock. My eyes almost fall out of my eyes. He's hung, and dammit, it's making me drool. If it wasn't for the bad lighting, I would've stared at it longer, but I can't hold back anymore. I have to touch myself just from seeing that.

Mr. Awesome: Want more?
S: Oh, god yes.
Mr. Awesome: Beg.
S: Please, Sir, give me more.
Mr. Awesome: If you're a good girl, I might send you more than just a photo.

Oh my god, does he mean an actual clip? Oh, Jesus, yes, I've been waiting for this day.

Mr. Awesome: Someday.
S: Way to blow my excitement.
Mr. Awesome: Aw, poor you. Will it help if I let you come this time? I'll make you blow something else, though.
S: Yes, it might.
Mr. Awesome: Good girls do what they are told. Take out the dildo and put it in your mouth. Take some pictures. I want you to suck it, hard. Make it wet.

I do as he says, taking out the dildo and licking it while I take some pictures. Having something in my mouth makes me so goddamn horny. Some see it as being devalued as a woman. I see it as empowerment. I love to do this, knowing this man is getting off on the things I send him; it gives me power, which makes me feel good, too.

He sends me another picture of him jerking his cock. God, I love this, it's making me drool over the dildo.

Mr. Awesome: Keep slipping your fingers down that pussy. I want you dripping before I let you do anything else. I'm rock hard, and I want you to make me come by being a dirty girl. If it's wet, slip that pink cock into your slit. But don't come.
S: Yes, Sir. I'm so wet. So goddamn wet. I want to come so badly.
Mr. Awesome: Don't. Come. Understand?
S: Yes, Sir.
Mr. Awesome: Who do you want?
S: You, Sir. Always, only you.
Mr. Awesome: Then please me and I will please you. Make me squirt my cum all over the floor and I might give you what you want.

I take the dildo from my mouth and slide it up my pussy, the fullness of it overpowering. I love how it feels when I slide it up and down, toying with my clit at the same time. I'm on the verge of coming, but I know he won't allow me yet, which only adds to the thrill of it. I can't help but moan, and once it comes out, I immediately slam my lips shut praying nobody heard me.

I send him pictures of my pussy and how I slip it in, my lips while I bite the bottom one, my wetness spread on my fingers, my nipples strained to the limit. God, I'm so fucking horny, I don't even feel bad for doing this at work.

Mr. Awesome: That's it, princess. Show me what you got.
S: Please, Sir, can I come?
Mr. Awesome: Not yet, princess, not yet. Take out the picture I sent you and look at it while you pleasure that pussy. I want you to imagine it's deep inside you, riding you from behind. Can you taste it yet?
S: What?
Mr. Awesome: My cum. Imagine it dripping into your mouth as you suck me dry.
S: Oh, god yes, please. I need it. I can't keep this up, please

Sir, please allow me to come.
Mr. Awesome: hmmm …

Another picture is sent.

It's his cock again, but this time a white jet spurts from the tip right when he took the blurry picture. Oh, holy hotness. Now I'm not just a bottle redhead, but literally a redhead. My cheeks feel like they're on fire.

Mr. Awesome: Now you can come.

Oh, fuck yes! Gazing at the picture that he sent me, I flick my clit. I imagine what he would taste like, how he would feel inside me. I push the dildo in and out, heightening my pleasure until I'm at the brink … and then I fall, so hard. I come and come, my body flooding with ecstasy, my muscles contracting and relaxing at the same time. After the orgasm subsides, I take a deep breath and text him back.

S: Fuck, that was good. Just what I needed.
Mr. Awesome: Glad I could be of service. You've gotten me in quite a bit of trouble, too, with those hot pictures. I couldn't control myself. Now, I have to clean myself up again. I hope you thoroughly enjoyed that.
S: Yes, I did.
Mr. Awesome: What do we say then?
S: Thank you, Sir.
Mr. Awesome: You're welcome. Are you feeling better now?
S: Ugh, you have no idea! I feel like I can sit behind my desk again without having the urge to throw a brick through his window into his room.
Mr. Awesome: I love your feistiness.
S: Funny, he says that too, except that I hate it when he does.
Mr. Awesome: If that means you like it when I do, then I'm fine with that statement.
S: I do. I like this.
Mr. Awesome: Good. I'm glad you do because I wouldn't want my princess to feel unappreciated.
S: Thank you, Sir.

Mr. Awesome: Don't spend the day cranky. He's not worth it. And if you feel the urge to strangle him, remember these words: bad princess, bad.

I chuckle from his comment.

S: Yes, Sir, I will. Thank you.

Mr. Awesome: You're welcome. I'll contact you for our next session. Or you may contact me if you wish to do so. Have a good day.

After blowing out another breath, I put my phone back into my purse and take out the dildo. I'm not sure if I'm still alone, so I decide to tuck it in my purse first. I'll wash it in the sink once I'm sure there's no one here.

I pull up my panties, which were shoved down, and pat down my skirt, checking myself before I open the door.

Right as I step outside, the door opposite to me opens as well. I freeze. My eyes widen as Leo King steps out of the stall with a huge smile on his face.

Oh, dear fucking god … please create a hole in the ground so I can jump to my death. Thank you.

How long has he been there? I try to hide my embarrassment by averting my eyes, hoping he didn't hear anything. I swallow away my nerves and immediately make a walk toward the sink.

"You spent an awful lot of time in there, Miss Webber." He walks after me.

"Maybe I did, so what?" I open the faucet to try to ignore his voice … as well as the flush growing on my face. God, why is it so goddamn hot in here?

He stands beside me and puts his hands under the water. "I could've sworn I heard some noise. It sounded like … a cry …"

I frown, raising an eyebrow right after. "I wasn't crying; if that's what you're suggesting."

He smiles. "I'm glad you weren't."

"Don't feel flattered. It takes much more than what you say and do to make me cry."

He raises an eyebrow. "Oh … claws, Miss. They're sharp today."

I sigh, gazing back at the mirror to clear my face of the hairs that are sticking to my forehead. Somehow, all I can think of is that dildo in my purse and imagining he can see straight through the fabric like he has some kind of x-ray vision or something. Just thinking about it makes me shiver. That's some scary stuff, my boss, the peeping tom.

"No, no, wait … that sound … it was more …" He leans in. "Like a moan."

I stop breathing. My eyes widen as I stare at myself in the mirror. His eyes briefly meet mine, and I swear I see a cheeky smile spreading on his lips. However, before I have a chance to take a really good look, he's already turned around to dry his hands.

"What are you getting at, Mister King? Are you trying to intimidate me? Scare me?"

"Absolutely not," he says, dryly drying his hands.

Yes, I totally thought of that, and I'm keeping back the sniggers as I think about how stupid it sounds.

"I'm just very curious as to what you're doing in there."

"In this case, curiosity *will* kill the cat, *Leo*."

He laughs. "You don't have to tell me. I know what I heard."

My heart is practically jumping out of my chest, and I swear I'll see it walk right down the hallway within a minute, along with my pride.

"I recognize that sound all too well."

"What do you want, Mister King?" I ask, holding my hands underneath a different dryer.

"You already know what I want. I want you to be my wife." He steps toward me. I try to ignore his body as it looms close.

"Pretend wife," I say.

"Right. Well, in order for that to be successful …" He leans in, and I swear to god, I think he smells me because I hear him sniff. "I need to know everything there is to know about you."

I turn around right, facing him not even inches away. "And you think knowing how I smell is going to do the trick?" I laugh. "Because as far as I know, married people don't go off telling people how stinky their spouses' armpits are."

He smirks, licking his lip. "I never said you smelled bad."

"You didn't, but I find it incredibly weird that you even want to know what I smell like."

"I'd like to grow accustomed to you in every way possible."

I raise an eyebrow. "Oh, now I'm interesting all of the sudden?"

"Excuse me?" He frowns.

I shake my head. "Forget it. Just … let me know what you want me to do. Also, I'd like to have it on paper that you'll give me a raise."

He nods, briefly closing his eyes. "I'll do just that, Miss Webber."

"I'd like to know how long this is going to last, what's expected of me, and exactly what the limits are. I want to have a say in it all. And I want to know why."

"Why what?"

"Why are you doing all of this?"

He sighs. "Fine. Whatever you want, Miss Webber." He nods, rubbing his hands. "Right, we'll talk about this tomorrow then."

"What?"

He steps backwards, gazing at the door. "I have some more urgent matters to attend to right now, like a model completely flipping out over a bad Photoshop job, but I'll make sure to discuss the perimeters of this assignment with you, okay? Tomorrow!" He holds out his thumbs.

"Okay," I say.

"Oh, and before I forget," he says while opening the door. "To make this all believable, I need to know *everything* there is to know about you. So make sure to tell me all about those filthy minutes you just spent in there, because I need to know all about what makes you and your body tick and explode."

I gape at him.

"Bye!" And then he walks out the door.

CHAPTER FOUR

The next day...

I barge into his office first thing in the morning. "So? Let's hear it."

He turns around in his leather chair. "Close the door, please."

I kick back to close the door, never taking my eyes off him. "Spill it."

He playfully raises a brow. "Oh, so feisty ... I love it!"

"Stop playing games, Leo," I say, stepping forward. "If you want me to do this, I need to know why because I'm not putting my hands on it if it's anything illegal."

He laughs. "Relax; you make it sound like I'm trying to avoid immigrations or something."

"For all I know, you could be."

"Samantha ..."

Oh, here we go again. I roll my eyes at the sound of my name.

"You know me better than that," he says. "Besides, do I look like a foreigner to you?"

"With that tan, you could pass as one. Tell me, where do you get sprayed? I should visit that salon some time." Okay, that's just snark from this shark, but I needed to bite something today.

He laughs. "I like this ..."

"Yeah, right," I scoff, crossing my arms.

"I do. I mean it," he says. Suddenly his smile his gone and his eyes zoom in on mine. "Sit down."

The way he says 'sit down' has me shivering. He just used a very low, assertive voice.

I sit down in the chair in front of his desk and wait. Taking a deep breath, he grabs a few papers lying on his desk and places them in front of me.

"Your requested raise."

I read the document, but the further I get, the less I understand. This mentions work hours outside of my regular ones, extra workload, as well as special requests. Basically, he's describing why I am getting a raise, but none of them are real. Nothing on here states his actual request.

"But this ..."

"I'm not going to put our agreement on any official document, so this will have to do. Do you want that raise or not?"

"Yes, of course, but—"

"Then this will suffice. Now, do you have questions?"

"Yes. I'd like to know why we're doing this so I know what I have to prepare for."

"Nothing special. Just to visit my parents and a few clients."

"What?" I say, my jaw dropping. "You want to fool your parents into thinking we're married?"

"They're easily fooled, especially considering they haven't even met you yet."

"Why? What in the world have you done?" I ask, frowning. "As your personal assistant, I need to know what I'm getting myself into."

"You make it sound like you have to keep tabs on me."

"It's not easy being your assistant."

He licks his lips. "If it was easy, you wouldn't be getting a raise."

"My point exactly."

"Which is also why you will do your very best to make sure this raise is not uncalled for." He smirks.

"You're the one with ludicrous requests."

"Oh, it can get even more ludicrous if it were up to me."

"No, thank you." I clear my throat. "My ludicrous bucket is full." I frown. "What is the point in deceiving your parents? Why go through all that trouble?"

He sighs, licking his lips. "I can't get rid of your incessant questions, can I?"

"You'll be rid of me if you pay me one million dollars." I place my pinky near my mouth.

He laughs. "If I paid you that, you'd be out of a job."

"Exactly."

"Oh, excuse me, Miss Webber, would you like to be fired?" he muses.

"No, but if I'd get a million dollars, I sure as hell wouldn't work for you."

"Oh, ouch." He grins. "Whatever have I done to deserve such hatred."

I shrug. "Hmm, part assholeness, part obnoxiousness." I smile.

"Aww, you hurt me, Miss Webber." He places his hand on his heart.

"Aww … want a cookie now?" I say, raising an eyebrow.

"You really love me so much, huh. I can tell," he says. He leans forward over his desk. "Tell you what, I promise I'll work on the asshole part if you promise me you'll do your best as a pretend wife."

I squint. "And you think there's actually something you can do about that?"

"A man can always try, that has to count for something."

"What about the obnoxious part?"

He leans back in his chair. "Nope, sorry, but that's just part of my awesome personality."

I roll my eyes and shake my head. "Fine. Let's get to the point already. What happened that you have to lie to your parents about this."

He grabs a pencil and starts fiddling with it. "Right. Well, you know I went to Vegas this last weekend."

"Please don't remind me. I still have to clear out your phone of all those pictures that can't see the light of day. As well as mine."

"Oh, I sent them to you?" He laughs. "Goddamn, I shouldn't have drank that much."

"Nope, and I warned you, but you wouldn't listen to me, as always."

"I don't listen to anyone, you know that, Samantha."

"You should, though."

"Should I listen to you then? Or should you listen to me?" He leans forward again with a big smirk on his face. "Because as far as I know, this nameplate here means that I'm the one in charge." He taps on the metal nameplate that's on the front of his desk. "See that? What does it say?"

He's just doing this to taunt me. He just loves to see me snarl. Goddammit, I won't be provoked that easily.

"I know what it says," I say through a slit between my teeth.

"Say it." His command is so direct that I immediately respond just because of the fierceness of it.

"Leo King, CEO of *W* Magazine."

"Exactly. I don't listen to you, you listen to me."

"No wonder this Vegas trip worked out so wonderfully. You know so well what to do when you're drunk. Even then, you base your decisions on your amazing intellect. I'm but a humble assistant there to serve you."

The smile builds on his face. "Just what I like to hear."

"I'd like to hear what happened that causes you to want me to be your pretend wife, though. After all, you know so well what to do in these situations, and I'd like your advice." I blink a couple of times.

"Well, if you'd listened to me from the start and actually let me talk, you would've known by now."

"Oh, my god. Just get to the point already!"

His eyes widen. "Such brashness." He grins. "Just the way I like it."

When he sees the annoyed look on my face, he sighs.

"Right ..." He clears his throat. "I was there with a good friend of mine, and on the day after our little drinking party, I ... sent a text to my parents stating that we had gotten married."

"What?" I say, with a scrunched up face. "You did what?" Now I'm the one leaning forward in my chair.

Oh, Jesus Christ, how are we ever going to fix this? As his assistant, I'm not in full panic mode.

"So, my parents think I'm married now. To that friend."

"Leo ...." I sigh. "What have you gotten yourself into?"

"Now, I know what this sounds like, but it'll only be for a while that you have to pretend to be my wife. Until things simmer down and I can explain it all."

"Tell them you're not. Let's start telling the truth now before this gets out of hand."

"Oh, no. Definitely not. My father has been pushing me for years to get married."

"So? Who cares? Do they still wipe your ass after you took a shit?"

"No?" He laughs.

"Then why do you care what they think you have to do?"

"Because this is my father's business, and he gave it to me explicitly stating I had to get married soon. As in, this year. Otherwise, they would basically kick me out of the family."

"Oh …"

He clears his throat. "Yeah …"

I didn't know it was that personal. "I'm sorry."

"Don't be. I can handle it."

"But what about that friend? Can't she explain it to them?"

"She doesn't want anything to do with me," he says. "Trust me on this."

I have no clue why, but it must have something to do with the fact that he basically put her in the middle of this.

"Okay … so you want me to pretend I'm that friend."

"They don't know what she looks like, so it works perfectly."

"Right …" I nod a few times, slamming my lips together. "You know how stupid this all sounds?"

"Totally, insanely stupid."

"The biggest nonsense of all times."

"That's me."

I want to wipe the smirk off his face.

"And you think I'm going to succeed at this how?"

"I'll give you a list of things that'll tell you all about me. What I like." I can't ignore the certain sparkle in his eyes. "You have to give me a list as well."

"That's absurd; you think I can get to know you through a list? And that you'd actually know me that easily?"

He cocks his head. "I think it'll be easier than you think."

I chuckle. "Well, that'll take you a while then because my list is a long one."

"You mean the things-you-hate-most list?" He lifts a brow.

"Oh, ha-ha. If I had such a list, you'd be at the top."

"Good. I'm always at the top. And on top." He licks his lip, biting his bottom one shortly. Somehow, that makes me squeeze my legs.

"Besides, I think I know more about you than you think … more than you probably know about me." He winks.

"I doubt that," I say.

"I know about your bathroom incident."

"That wasn't an incident, and it sure as hell wasn't any of your business."

"Ouch, Miss Webber. Retract those claws, they damage my reputation." He smiles. "I'll be gentle with your dirty secrets. You can trust me on this."

"I doubt I can trust you with anything, let alone tell you my secrets."

"Oh, I assure you, I'll treat them with care, as with anything else that becomes *mine*."

The way he says mine creates goosebumps all over my skin. Why is it that every time this man talks I get the feeling he's trying to either dry-hump me with his words or make a fool out of me?

"Don't think I'll tell you anything that can damage *my* reputation," I say. "If this is for a job, I'll stick to professional details only. Things that matter."

He grabs his pen again. "Anything matters if it involves you." Placing his hand under his jaw, he leans on the desk, twirling his pen in the other hand. "I need to know *everything* there is to know about you."

"As if they'd ask about personal stuff."

"You have no clue how personal it can get when you're near me. Or my family, for that matter." He seems so very amused by all of this.

I pick up the list he placed on the table, desperate for some distraction. "How long do I have to study all of this?"

"Two days."

My jaw drops. "What?"

"Do I speak Chinese?"

"What do you mean 'two days'?"

He lets go of his chin and starts playing with his pen with both hands. "We're going to visit them in two days' time."

"Oh, my god, you have to be kidding me."

"I wish I was, but unfortunately, we're not that lucky. My parents want to see you. Now."

"You mean 'your wife.'" I make quotation marks with my fingers.

"Let's not forget that part."

"Oh, I'll never forget that part, Miss Webber. You need not worry."

"For all I know, you'd make this permanent."

"If I was, you'd know."

There's a slight hint of amusement in his eyes that makes me want to slap him across the face. How dare he even suggest I would marry him? That I would actually be with him for longer than is needed in order to keep my job? And how dare he make me think about all those things that involve 'marriage' and how he'd 'let me know' that I was his? Goddammit. Put your bitch-mode on, Samantha. He keeps making me blush, and I can't have that. This fucker deserves some arse-kicking.

The phone suddenly rings. He keeps his eyes focused on me, not moving a muscle.

After a while, I ask. "Aren't you going to pick up?"

"This conversation is far more important."

"You don't even know who it is."

"Does it matter?"

"Maybe." I swallow. Then I quickly reach for the phone before he can stop me and pick it up. If he's not going to do it, then I will. I'm his assistant, here to catch him when he's throwing himself off a building again. That also includes when he makes stupid decisions like this.

"Hi, this is Leo King's office, Samantha Webber speaking."

Suddenly a beeping noise ensues.

I look up and find Leo pressing his finger on a button that immediately cancels the call.

I sigh out loud. "That could've been important."

"*This* is important, too." He points his finger between the two of us. "You might not see it, Miss Webber, but this is very, very important to me."

"Oh, I see it all right," I say, putting down the phone. "Clearly."

"I don't think I've been clear enough. When I say I don't want to pick up the phone, I didn't mean you could do it for me."

"Sorry that I put your best interests first, *Sir.*"

His eyes narrow when he hears that word; his lips twitch, not quite forming a smile.

"Hmmm …" It sounds like he's humming or … moaning.

I swallow away the lump in my throat. Dammit, I can't think about stuff like that. Jesus, why'd I have to say that word? I've only given him more fodder to feed me with, and I don't mean the good kind. He'll tease me with this, I'm sure of it.

"I will see you tomorrow, Miss Webber."

"I thought you wanted to talk some more?"

"No ... never mind. I just remembered I have things to do." He clears his throat. "Regardless, you will do this for me."

"Is that a question or an order?"

He smiles. "Do you have to ask?"

"I suppose not," I say, getting up from the chair.

"Stop."

I cease in the middle of my movement.

His eyes skim my face, then down my body, passing my cleavage as well as my skirt. Shit, now I'm flushing again. Why is he looking at me like I'm some kind of juicy beefsteak? Hmmm, although thinking about that makes me hungry now. Damn.

"What?"

"Shhh," he interrupts.

I raise an eyebrow, slamming my lips shut as he keeps engorging my body with just his eyes. Briefly, I glance down at my own outfit, suddenly overcome with the urge to prove to myself that I did actually put on some clothes today and that I'm not naked. Nope, no skin showing. Phew.

When he's done, he looks up at my eyes again with a big smile on his face. "You can go now."

I frown. "What ... uh ... was that?"

"Nothing. I just have to think about something." He blinks. "I'll call you if I need you. Bye, Miss Webber."

I scoot the chair back, still confused about what the hell is going on, but I'll take this as a sign to leave quickly before he comes up with more excuses to keep me here.

Whatever is going on, it's totally weird, even for him, and that's saying something. He's always weird but never this weird. It's like he's suddenly discovered I'm a woman or something. That, or he was blatantly checking me out.

Nah. I'm going crazy.

Time for some sweet ... dark ... delicious ... Snickers.

CHAPTER FIVE

FROM: mrawesome@hotmail.com
TO: doritoslover@gmail.com

I'm horny. Let's start our game.

A.

FROM: doritoslover@gmail.com
TO: mrawesome@hotmail.com

Whoa, not even a 'hi'? What's up with you?

Xx
S.

FROM: mrawesome@hotmail.com
TO: doritoslover@gmail.com

Sorry, Princess. Tough day at work. Wanna play? If you're up for it, of course.

A.

FROM: doritoslover@gmail.com
TO: mrawesome@hotmail.com

I want to see more of you before I say yes.

Xx
S.

FROM: mrawesome@hotmail.com
TO: doritoslover@gmail.com

More of what? My cock?

A.

FROM: doritoslover@gmail.com
TO: mrawesome@hotmail.com

Cock is always good, but I'd like to see your smile. That would be nice. Any smile would be nice right now …

Xx
S.

FROM: mrawesome@hotmail.com
TO: doritoslover@gmail.com

Never mind.

A.

I frown, gazing at my screen. Jesus, did he just blow me off because I didn't want to participate in his game without him showing me more? Is a picture of his lips so hard to do? Men …

Shaking my head, I sigh and close my laptop. I was serious when I said I would play if he showed me some more, but I was really in need of something … sweet. Just once, a guy who doesn't want to use me would be nice.

I think Mr. Awesome had a very bad day because he normally never acts like this. At least not to me. I hope it'll blow over soon; otherwise, I'm afraid I can't continue our little affair. I don't do dipshits, and I certainly am not interested in a one-way-please.

Groaning, I flop down on my bed and close my eyes. Guess I'll have to do the job myself tonight. This lust isn't going anywhere if I don't make it go away, and I have the perfect toy sitting in my closet. Time to make use of my good old fantasy.

I just have to ignore the fact that it was Leo who got me this annoyed and riled up at the same time.

***

The next day…

My phone buzzes, waking me up way too early for my comfort. It's Friday, one of my two days that I have off from work, and now is the time Leo decides to text me. While wiping the sand from my eyes, I check his message.

Check your mailbox. I had something delivered to you today. Let me know when you have it. It's important.

"Yes, Sir," I reply in the air, but then immediately shut my mouth because I know I sound ridiculous talking to myself. Guess there's no such thing as a day off in Leo King's book.

I scoot up from the bed, put on a robe and a pair of slippers, and then make my way outside. I speed walk down the path to pull open the mailbox and quickly take out whatever's inside. There's no package, however. I return to my home with all the papers in my hand. Just before I close the door behind me, something hits the back of my head. It all drops to the floor, and as I turn around I put my hand on my head to check for injuries. The newspaper boy just flew by on his bicycle. I guess he forgot I'm capable of throwing back a brick. Too bad he's already too far ahead.

"Little shit!" I yell, which he hears, but then he sticks out his tongue, only angering me more.

I swear, one day, I'll be charged with assault for strangling both him *and* my boss.

Sighing, I start picking up all the mail, when I notice there's a peculiar one sticking out. Something handwritten without an address on it. If this is from Leo, he sure went through some trouble to keep this far away from any official system. He actually got someone to deliver it straight to my home. Talk about invading my privacy.

Shivering, I go back inside and open his envelope first. Inside is a fucking credit card.

Oh, my god.

Samantha: What is this?

Leo: I want you to go shopping today. Get yourself some nice new clothes.

Samantha: I can't pay for this. Please, don't send me this.

Leo: Relax, it's on me. Don't worry about paying me back. I put it on the business tab so it's all deductible.

He didn't just say that, did he? Jesus, he put 'buying clothes' on the business tab?

Samantha: It's not really 'work', so that's illegal and you know it.

Leo: Who cares? Just buy something nice for yourself. Go out shopping with your friend. Spend as much as you like.

Samantha: Okay, but you gotta promise me this isn't some kind of trick. I'd hate to be indebted to you for the rest of my life.

Leo: It isn't a trick; you have my word. If there's anyone indebted, it's me. I owe you some, so take it. I will not accept a refusal.

Samantha: Okay, but if you're lying and I end up in jail, you

know whose ass I'll be scribbling on my cell wall.

Leo: *laughing* I can't wait for you to come after my ass in that imaginary vendetta. If you wanted to have my ass, all you had to do was ask.

I'm ramming the touchscreen buttons with my fingers now.

Samantha: Sorry, but I'm way more content with my own ass than your flat one, thank you very much.

Leo: I am, too. With your ass, that is.

Samantha: Are we going to talk about my lady humps now, or are you done?

Leo: I'm never done talking about lady humps. Especially yours. They're so round and ... full. Has anyone ever told you that?

I roll my eyes. What is he trying? Why is he so onto me now? I don't get it. It must be some kind of cruel joke. That, or I'm really losing it because Leo King cannot genuinely be interested in me. Can he?

Samantha: Yes, actually, I've been told plenty of times that I have a fat booty, and I'm not afraid to show it.

Leo: I know you're not afraid to show it. You're not fat, though. I'd like to consider myself a connoisseur on the topic.

Samantha: No wonder you spend so much time in that tiny office of yours. You must be inspecting booty all day long on your computer. I figured you were the type. No wonder I'm left doing all the work.

Leo: Ouch, Sam ... you hurt me...

Sam? Sam? Since when did I become Sam? This is getting way too personal. It's making me flush.

Leo: My ego, that is. There is only one booty I check out regularly, and it's not via the internet, trust me.

Samantha: Enough talk about booty. I don't want to think about how I still haven't done my workout for today.

Leo: Say that again when you're back in my office later.

Back in his office? I'm guessing this isn't going to be a free day at all.

Samantha: Why?
Leo: I can help you with that.

Staring at my screen, I swallow away the lump in my throat. He did not just say that.

Samantha: Can we stop playing this game? I'm your personal assistant, and you're my boss. Let's stick to professional talk only.
Leo: If that's what you wish.

Somehow, this little voice inside my head wants to say 'no, that's not what I wish,' but that would go against my rules. The rules that I'd love to ignore, for once, if it wasn't for the fact that I know he's a giant dickhead and that this can't be real. I won't allow another man to break my heart just because he finds it amusing to do so.

I'm not someone's play-toy, and I refuse to even pretend to be one.

Samantha: Yes. I have to go now.

That statement creates an unwanted pout on my face. Goddammit, why do I feel this way? Why do I have to like talking to him? I shouldn't, he's an arse, and yet I can't stop smiling and blushing when he makes those comments about me.

I wonder where my old boss has gone and if I can have him back. Hating him was much easier, having clearly defined limits.

Leo: Good. You go dress that big booty up. I can't wait to see. Good luck!

Goddammit. There goes my heart again, fluttering like it can afford to be hurt.

I guess professional is long lost with us. Or should I say lust?

I guess shopping isn't all I'm going to do today ... to the bar it is!

CHAPTER SIX

"That looks amazing!" Stephanie says.

"You think?" I ask, looking at myself in the mirror.

"Like a celebrity, I'd say," she says.

"Stop it." I laugh, punching her in the shoulder.

"What? You gotta admit you look fab in that dress, hun."

I turn around. "But doesn't it make my ass look like it's Kim Kardashian's?"

She sniggers. "Maybe, but that's a good thing."

"Why? Who on earth would consider that 'professional'?"

"If professional was the reason we went shopping, you wouldn't have brought me to this store, hun. Stop lying to yourself."

"It *is* only for work."

"Uhuh … keep telling yourself that. I know better." She folds her arms.

I blush. "What? Can't I look nice for once?"

"No girl dresses up like that," she points at my dress, "for work." She makes quotation marks with her finger. "Unless she was trying to screw her boss."

A blush appears on my face.

Her eyes widen. Oh, shit no.

"Omigod, you are trying to screw your boss."

"No! Oh, no. No, no, no." The more I say no, the redder my face becomes.

"Oh my god, you have to tell me!" she screams.

"Nothing. There's nothing to tell. He wants me to dress more ... sophisticated. That's all."

"My ass, he does. If he wants you all glammed up, that means you're in business, hun. Oh my god, who is it?" Stephanie asks. "Your new boss or something? No, you have got to be kidding me. It isn't that Leo King dude, is it?"

"Um ..."

"Oh, holy shit, it is! Samantha! You are one lucky-ass bitch, you know that?" She wraps her arms around me, squealing like a high school girl. "I can't believe it." She slaps me on the back. "You did it, girl. Good job. That is one fine-ass man."

"I didn't do anything, and he isn't fine at all. He's a huge prick."

"Who cares? If he has money, I'd say go for it. You can cross that one thing off the perfect-man list. The others will soon follow."

"Off *your* list, you mean."

"Whatever. You know as well as I do, you need a man as well as the money, and this is the perfect combo. It's only a plus."

"I'm telling you, we're *not* dating and this isn't a thing. This is purely for work."

She shrugs. "Maybe for you, but not for him. If you're doing this for him, that means he *wants* you to do it, and that means he's interested. For sure. All men want a big, fat tush to enjoy."

I pull the dress down further. "You don't know that. Besides, he just wants me to look this way for a special event."

"Right ..."

The way she says right sounds unconvincing, but I decide not to get into an argument. She'd only ask for more details, which I'm not even allowed to discuss or else my job and 'reputation' might be in danger. Ugh.

Suddenly, my phone buzzes.

"Hold on," I say, as I walk back into my stall and take my phone from my purse. It's a text from Leo.

Leo: You done yet? Come to my office when you are. I don't expect this to take longer than a couple of hours, and you've been gone for about four of them now.

Samantha: I specifically remember Friday as being my day off, as well as tomorrow.

Leo: Days off are retracted until further notice.

Samantha: What? You can't do that.

Leo: I sure can. This is a special contract, and I require your assistance 24 / 7. You'll regain your free days afterwards.

Samantha: Get that on paper. With your signature.

Leo: Get your lady-humps back here then, and I *will* give it to you.

I'm getting all flustered here in this stall, but I'm not sure if it's his text or this dress choking the life out of me.

"Is that your boss? It is, isn't it?" Stephanie says.

Suddenly, she pulls the curtain back, exposing me. I feel watched, so I quickly tuck the phone back into my purse.

Her eyes narrow. "It was him …"

"He just wants me to get back to work."

"Ha, perfect! You can show off that delicious booty in this perfect dress then."

She drags me out of the stall, and I can barely grab my purse.

"Wait, my clothes!"

"I'll grab them while you're on your way out, don't worry. Just go pay and get the hell out of here. You just got a booty call!"

"What? No, it's not like that. At all."

"Uh-uh. Then make it happen, hun!" She pushes me to the cash register as she bounces on her feet. "Be back in a sec, going to grab your clothes."

She's already gone before I can reply.

I pay for the dress by bending over backwards across the table, completely embarrassing myself as they have to scan the tag and remove it for me. I quickly pay and scurry out the door, when Stephanie comes up behind me, scaring the shit out of me for the second time when she starts screaming.

"I'm so excited!"

"I'm glad one of us is."

"Oh, cheer up, I'm sure he's not that much of an asshole. This is a good thing. A good opportunity."

"Right, but he is, and I'm not so sure about all that. But we'll see."

"Good, see? You can do it!" she says. "I'll get back home and cheer you on from the sidelines. Prepare my magic voodoo shit and stuff."

I laugh, shaking my head. "Say a prayer for me while you're at it."

"I'm gonna text you in an hour, okay? You have to let me know how it went."

"Thanks for coming along, Steph," I say as I walk to my car and she walks to hers.

"Don't mention it, just keep me updated."

"I will!" Not. It's not like I don't want to, I'm just not allowed. Which is a perfect excuse because I'm not waiting to walk around with a gigantic red face all day.

Stephanie can get a little excited when it comes to fresh man-meat. She likes to eat them whole, plenty a month. I don't know how she does it. Or how those men even deal with her.

Or maybe I'm just not used to anything.

***

I arrive at work, and people are looking at me like I'm some kind of alien which, of course, makes me squeeze my butt cheeks as I walk to my desk and pretend nothing's different. Don't ask; I have no clue why I do it. Must be the nerves.

I drape my coat over my chair and gaze at Leo's office. He's lowered all the blinds, not giving even a peek inside. I wonder what in the hell he's doing in there. For all I know, it's something that can't even stand the light of day.

Preparing myself for the worst, I knock on his door and say, "Leo? You there?"

I hear some rummaging, something dropping to the floor, a loud noise, and then his dark, but quavering voice.

"Yeah, come in."

I slowly open the door, afraid of what I'm going to find. It sounded very much like he wasn't prepared for me, even though he asked me to come to his office. I wonder what's up.

It doesn't take long to find out.

My eyes widen at the sight of his neat suit. My, my, if handsome existed, it would be strutting around this room right now.

"How do I look?" he asks as I peek through the door.

I'm momentarily baffled, and I think he catches me staring at him because there's a huge smile on his face.

"Good, right?"

"Yeah ..." I mutter, trying not to think about how delicious he looks.

"You're wearing that?"

"To my parents, yeah. You think it's okay?"

"Of course." Damn, this assignment just got a whole lot harder. He cocks his head. "Did you succeed?"

I raise an eyebrow. "In what?"

He laughs. "Tell me you didn't just waste four hours doing nothing?"

"Oh, right, the shopping." I almost forgot because of my drooling. Bad Samantha, bad. I clear my throat. "Um ..."

"C'mon in. I want to see what you bought," he says, winking.

I lick my lips, suddenly very aware of this dress plastered around my curvy body. Gathering some courage, I step further inside. His eyes skim me, starting at the bottom all the way to the top, slowly taking me in. He's taking his time sucking up this image of me, which makes me wonder what in the hell is going through his head.

"Is it any good?" I ask, focusing on the dress instead of his eyes eye-fucking me.

"Oh ..." he grunts. He seriously grunts. "Yes."

I stare at him with raised eyebrows, not able to utter a single word.

"Close the door behind you," he says.

I do as he says, but then when I turn my head back to him, he's right in front of me. Instinctively, I take a step back, but I'm already against the door, and there's no way out.

"It's more than just 'good' ..." he murmurs, licking his lips.

Oh Jesus, why did I look at his lips?

"You look like someone who should have dressed like this way long ago."

My lips quiver. They never quiver. Goddammit, Sam, get your act together!

"And what's that supposed to mean?" I say, swallowing away the lump in my throat.

He keeps inching closer. I keep trying to push further back into this door, but unfortunately, it's not made of rubber.

His voice turns raw, laden with testosterone. "It means I think you look ... sexy."

Oh my god, I think I just died.

"Don't look so surprised." A smirk appears on his face. "Just because I'm an asshole, doesn't mean I'm not a man."

"I never thought you'd—"

"What? That I could ever think a woman like you is sexy?"

"I didn't say that …"

"No, just you. I know what you're thinking." He takes a pluck of my hair and tucks it behind my ear. It feels like I'm dreaming, and I'm almost tempted to pinch my arm just to prove to myself that I am.

"Contrary to what you may think of me, you know nothing about my tastes," he muses. "And my taste right now is you."

My lips part. "W-What?"

"Oh, it's purely for professional reasons, Miss Webber. If we're to make a convincing couple, we'd have to kiss some time."

He comes closer and closer, keeping his gaze on me at all times, even though his lips are moving forward. Yep, they're definitely coming toward mine. Oh, dear lord. Is he actually going to kiss me?

Why am I wondering how good it would feel? Why am I actually hoping he will?

"Uh …" I mutter.

"Let's start now," he whispers.

And then he presses his lips onto mine.

CHAPTER SEVEN

His kiss is sensual, and so very … seducing. His lips are warm and tantalizing, heating my body like fireworks are exploding inside me. I let him explore my mouth with his, gently pecking while nipping at my lips as well. It's so good, oh my god, I can't even begin to describe it. His kisses are sex on a stick.

He pushes me further up against the door, even though I thought I couldn't go any further. I was wrong. His hands find their way to my face, cupping me with gentle care as he swipes his tongue over the seam of my mouth, coaxing me to open. He kisses me softly, licking the tip of my tongue but never driving further inside. It's like he's holding back, but at the same time, showing me what he can do. Expertly moving his tongue, he drives me insane. It's like he's a master at this.

Oh god, I think I just died and went to heaven.

I'm supposed to hate him. Remember, remember, Samantha! He's a douchebag who wouldn't even look at you before, and now he has his tongue marking you as his. Somehow, I can't resist, can't push away the temptation to keep kissing him back, despite the voice in my head calling me a stupid girl. I shouldn't be kissing him, and yet I am.

And then he stops.

Just like that.

Secretly, I wish for him to continue.

My lips are parted and swollen, buzzing with sensation as he withdraws. A giant lopsided grin forms on his face as he looks me in the eye.

"We should practice that some more," he murmurs, gently caressing my cheek. "We're not convincing enough, yet."

"What?" I mutter, feeling like the ground underneath my feet is quaking.

"If we wanna convince my family that we're a couple, a married couple even, we'd have to do this more often."

"Right …" I whimper from his hot breath blowing against my sensitive lips.

I'm not even registering what he's saying, still locked in that fantasy where Leo King just kissed me because he wanted to. Because at that moment he couldn't do anything else than kiss me.

Except, I'm lying to myself, and I know I am.

Wish I could live in that lie for one more second, but he has to slap me out of it like it amuses him.

His hand leaves my face. "Our act needs to be polished."

"Act?"

"The walk and talk, you know, how we behave toward each other. It has to be genuine."

"Except it isn't."

"Right." He winks. "Which is exactly why we should practice more."

I sigh, slamming my lips together. "I get it. You just kissed me because you want to see how I do it. Because you think I won't be able to do it when we're around your family."

"Oh, no, I have no doubt you can do it. I just wanted to see if it could really work."

"And? Can it?" I fold my arms, frowning. "Was our fake kiss to your satisfaction?"

"Very much." He smiles broadly, annoying the hell out of me.

I knew I shouldn't have expected anything else from him.

"Is that all for today?" I say, grinding my teeth.

"For now, but I'm sure I'll need you again later." As he turns around, he glances over his shoulder and I catch him licking his lips. "Be sure to drop by often, so we can fake make-out."

I barely manage to stop myself from growling as I turn back around and open the door.

"Oh, and Miss Webber ..."

I'm about to scream 'what?!' across the room, but I bite my tongue.

"Go home early. I want you to pack your bags."

"Why?" I ask, gazing at him over my shoulder.

"We're leaving today."

CHAPTER EIGHT

Later that day…

He forgot to mention the fact that he had to book an early flight because his mother accidentally gave him the wrong day for the family gathering, which is apparently tomorrow during lunchtime. So, I had to grab my stuff as quickly as I could, which of course turned out to be a disaster. Half of my clothes are missing, and I didn't have any time to eat. Luckily, I managed to grab a quick bite in a fast food stance at the airport. While I was stuffing my mouth, I almost choked when I noticed we were entering a private jet.

And now I'm sitting here in my chair, still amazed at the fact that Leo King has his own private airplane. I shouldn't be surprised, and yet I am. I've never been in one of these, but damn, it's nice for a change.

I'm sitting in a seat close to Leo so I can still hear his requests if he has any, but far away enough not to be annoyed by him. We're both fiddling with our tablets, ignoring the other completely. He's been quiet ever since our kiss. Of course, I can't stop thinking about it, which in turn makes me think he thinks about it, too. But that's ludicrous because Leo fucking King has better things to think about. I should totally *not* be thinking about how good it felt to have his lips on mine. Totally. Jesus. It was good.

Shaking my head, I focus my attention on the email that just landed in my inbox.

FROM: mrawesome@hotmail.com
TO: doritoslover@gmail.com

Please accept my apology for my behavior the other day. It was not appropriate and there is no excuse. I do not wish for our mutually beneficial relationship to end in murky waters, so I'll make it clear now that I do want us to continue what we have going here. But only if we keep all private information to ourselves. That includes our faces.

Let me know how you feel. I have a special surprise for you if you agree to keep playing with me.

A.

FROM: doritoslover@gmail.com
TO: mrawesome@hotmail.com

I accept your apology and thank you, I appreciate it. I thought you were having a bad day, so it's fine … as long as you keep talking to me and sending me delicious commands, I'm all yours.

I promise I won't ask for anything else again.

Xx
S.

FROM: mrawesome@hotmail.com
TO: doritoslover@gmail.com

Open Attachment: Your_mouth.avi

Good. I've included something for your eyes only. Watch it. Then go to the nearest bathroom with your vibrator and watch it again. And again. And again … You get the picture.

Oh, and one more thing: No coming.

Enjoy.

A.

Biting my lip, I open the file on my tablet. I could use a little distraction, especially after that hot kiss from Leo, so I'm all for a little play right now. However, Mr. Awesome doesn't know I'm on a plane so this could get a little tricky. There's only one toilet, and it's a small cubicle with barely enough space to move your ass around, let alone my big ass.

Gazing up from my tablet, I check to make sure that Leo hasn't seen me get all excited because I obviously don't want him to know what I'm about to do. He briefly gazes up at me for a second, raising his eyebrow in that daring way he usually does. God, the amount of panties he could twist just by giving that look.

Too bad my panties are already in a twist because of the assignment Mr. Awesome just gave me. I see it as a way to relieve myself of all the stress I keep inside, not to mention the arousal. That kiss keeps swirling in my head, and I want to rid myself of its memory. It was too hot to be fake. I gotta cool down.

With my purse in my hand, I get up and place the tablet on my seat.

"Where are you going?" Leo asks. "We still have some things to discuss."

"We can discuss it in a minute. I'm going to the ladies' room."

"No such thing."

I chortle. "What in the world makes you think you can stop me? Your discussion can wait."

"Oh, I don't mean it like that. I just meant that there's no such thing as a 'ladies' room' on a plane. A toilet, sure. But it's nothing more than that."

I roll my eyes. "Well … thank you for that very useful information, Mr. King. I'll be sure to remember that." I clutch my purse in front of me.

"Hmm … I do hope so. It's right over there." He points to the back with an amused look on his face. "Gotta pee that badly?"

"What?"

"It looks like you're clenching your legs."

I lift an eyebrow. "I'm not clenching anything."

He grins. "Keep telling yourself that."

"If I was, I wouldn't tell you, no matter if I have to pee or not. I'm going to the bathroom now," I say, as I walk through the aisle.

"You wouldn't even tell me if you didn't have to pee?"

"I don't think I should answer that question," I say.

"Aw, why not?" he teases.

"Because it isn't very professional."

"I agree," he muses. "But that's what makes it so fun!"

"I'll see you in a minute, Leo. Or not."

"It's Mr. King for you. Leo King …"

The last thing I hear as I enter the cubicle is his laughter. He sure does seem to enjoy torturing me today. I should think of something to torture him with instead, but I can't think of anything because I'm not as much of a sadistic evil motherfucker as he is.

Or maybe I just don't want to waste any time on him when I have Mr. Awesome's video to watch. I'm curious about what he sent me.

I take my phone out of my purse, open the email, and download the video. When I open it, my jaw drops. It's a video of him stroking his cock. There's no sound, but by god, just looking at him jerking off on camera is getting me all heated up. I hold my breath as he goes faster and faster, minutes flying by. I can't take my eyes off him. All I can think of is wanting to be there with him, seeing him do it in person, and then taking over. Instead, I watch him bring himself to the brink. All I see is his hand rapidly stroking his length, his veins throbbing, and delicious drops of pre-cum dripping down. His cock bobs up and down in his hand, and I can feel my pussy throb as his grip tightens and his speed increases even more. He brings his hand to the base, holding his breath. Then jets of his seed spurt out onto black sheets. It keeps coming and coming, and my lips instinctively part as I watch him shoot it all. I'm wet by the time the video comes to an end.

Jesus Christ, that was beyond hot. That was on fire.

Oh god, I wish he had put an audio under this. I could beg to hear him moan. I wonder what my name would sound like in his voice.

I grip my shirt, trying to catch my breath, which is apparently quite shallow. I feel like I just watched someone in private, even though he sent me this on purpose. It's so freaking naughty ... I love it!

The title is also very appropriate: Your_mouth.avi. I guess he figured I was the kind of girl to sit below him and lick it all up as he comes. God, he knows me so well, even when he knows me so very little. It's funny.

I take the vibrator from my bag, and I start up the app on my phone.

S: Jesus that was hot.

Mr. Awesome: I hope you enjoyed that little show. I would give you more but ...

S: But what? Please, tell me.

Mr. Awesome: Oh, you know how much I like you begging.

S: What can I do to see more?

Mr. Awesome: I think you have to earn it first.

S: Damn.

Mr. Awesome: For starters, what should you call me again?

S: I'm sorry, Sir. Your video just gave me hot flashes, I completely forgot.

Mr. Awesome: As long as you remember who's in charge. Want to earn more cock? You can start by getting yourself off on that vibrator, but I want you to watch that video while you do it.

S: Yes, Sir. I will thoroughly enjoy myself.

Mr. Awesome: And two more things: a) you're not allowed to come, and b) keep your mouth open while you pleasure yourself.

S: Yes, Sir.

Mr. Awesome: Ten minutes at the very least. I want you soaking and wild, without a chance to relieve yourself. Feel your own desperation. Be nice and wet until I contact you later tonight.

S: Okay, Sir. Thank you, Sir.

I close the app and open the video again, pushing up my dress. I slide the vibrator inside my panties, open my mouth as he instructed, and turn it on. I'm already wet, so it slips and slides easily. I hope the sound isn't too loud, but at this moment, I don't think I care if anyone hears because I'm so turned on. The vibrating brings me to the brink easily, but I know I must continue for at least another seven minutes. It's torture, pure torture I tell you, but it's worth it. Watching him stroke his cock is making me delirious with need, and how he comes over and over again has my mouth wide open, ready to receive. God, I wish it were real. For a second, I almost forget I was supposed to stop myself from coming, but I regain control quickly. When the time to please myself comes to an end, I'm left with a swollen clit, soaked panties, and a mouth so hungry for cock and cum I could grab Leo and suck him instead.

Oh, god, what am I thinking?

Swallowing away my lust, I take the vibrator out and wash it in the tiny sink.

A sudden knock on the door has me jolting up and down.

CHAPTER NINE

"Samantha?"

I was so totally into what I was doing that I forgot I wasn't alone on this plane. Dammit.

"Yeah?"

"Are you okay?" It's Leo.

"I'm fine. I'll be out in a second."

I swiftly pat my dress down and freshen up before I open the door. I squeal when I find Leo staring right at me. I'm petrified as his lips curve into a smile.

"Had a nice … break?" he asks with emphasis on the 'break' part.

"Don't scare me like that," I say, sighing.

"What were you expecting? With all that noise, I had to find out what was going on."

"I don't know what you're talking about."

He leans forward, coming dangerously close to my lips again. "I think you do." His hand reaches toward my face, and for a second I almost think he's going for it again, but instead he grabs a loose strand of hair and tucks it behind my ears.

"Do you like bothering women on the toilet?" I snarl, lifting an eyebrow, trying not to come across as intimidated.

"No." He grins. "Just you."

"Oh, fuck off," I say, frowning, trying to walk past him.

But he places his hands on both sides of the door, trapping me in.

"Is that the way you talk to your boss?"

"You're asking for it."

"I'm not asking for your metaphorical fuck you. The regular one ... now that's a whole different question."

I fold my arms. "What do you want, *Leo*?"

"Getting personal, are we?" he says, cocking his head.

"It doesn't get any more personal than stalking a lady on the freaking toilet."

"True." He licks his lips. "Hmmm ... have I ever told you how good you look when you're all flushed?"

My lips part in shock. "What?"

"You're blushing."

"No, I'm not," I quickly retort.

"Yeah, you are." There's a cheeky smile on his face. "I can't help but wonder if it's because of me ... or because of something else."

Gasping, I lean back to gaze in the mirror, but I only see a bit of redness on my cheeks. Nothing special. It's not like my entire chest is radiating, which has happened in the past.

Suddenly, he steps inside with me.

"Hey!"

Before I can push him away, he's already grasped something off the sink.

Something that belongs to me.

Something I accidentally left there when he interrupted me.

Oh, god.

Oh, shit.

Oh, fuck no.

My eyes widen. "Give that back. Right. Now."

"Or what?" he taunts, biting his lip. "You gonna throw yourself at me?"

"I might. Give it to me." I hold out my hand.

"I think I'll prefer the throwing yourself at me part. We can use a little extra practice in the marital fights."

My hand shoots out to grasp his, but he holds it up in the air, far away from me.

"Dammit!" I say, standing on the tips of my shoes, but it's no use.

He slowly opens his hand to reveal what's inside. My vibrator, of course. And he holds it between his index finger and thumb like it's some kind of magical bullet that can destroy anything.

"Leo …" I growl.

He holds it in front of him. "This belongs to you?"

"Yes, now hand it back."

He smiles. "Interesting …"

Before I have a chance to grab it, he turns the bottom part around, turning it on.

Oh, holy shit.

The grin plastered on his face is both humiliating and infuriating. I'm contemplating on whether to kick him in the balls, punch him in the throat or just blatantly jump from this plane to escape embarrassment.

"This explains a lot."

"Oh, fuck off. Do you take pleasure in torturing me?"

"As a matter of fact, yes, I do find it very … pleasuring to torture you like this."

"Screw you …" I grate my teeth.

He laughs. "Oh, Samantha, you are way too punishing on me. I'm not as cruel as you think I am, even though I might come across as such."

"Definitely. Are you done laughing now?" I say as I hold out my hand.

"Not sure, it depends on if this little thing got you what you wanted … Did it get you off?"

I frown, licking my lips. "I'm not even going to answer that."

"You don't have to," he muses. "I can see it on your face."

"Can you see something else on my face, like the angry redhead whose about to punch you if you don't give that thing back?"

"I can definitely see something else … especially the desire to finish what you started."

He leans forward again, causing me to arch my back as he towers over me. "Is this what you enjoy, Miss Webber? Spending some time alone during work, pleasuring yourself?"

"I don't need to answer that," I snarl.

"Oh, but you do, since you work for me, and you're basically wasting valuable time here."

My jaw drops. "Excuse me?"

"Oh, don't get me wrong, I'm all for a little enjoyment at work, and I would definitely not discourage you from doing exactly that."

Now I'm flushing even more.

"But to use *this* thing?" he says. "And then not come?" He shakes his head. "There are much better ways."

"Like you know all about that …" I say.

"That's exactly my point. I do."

I've had about enough of his smugness and my own flushed skin.

"Right," I snort. "I didn't take you for a man who cared anything about what a woman wants."

"You took me wrong then."

Wow, the way he says it, all dark and with a low tone, covers my skin in goosebumps. So serious all of the sudden …

"Whatever," I say, clearing my throat. "It's not like you know me. At all."

I try to push past him, but he places his hand elsewhere, trapping me once again.

Let's change that," he says. "I think it's time we got to know each other a little better."

"We can go over our notes when we're seated again. Can I have my thing back now?"

"It's called a vibrator, Samantha. Don't be scared of the word. I'm not, and I certainly don't mind you using one. However, I can definitely recommend a few better ones …"

I'm a bit stumped for words, uttering nonsense with my lips half-parted.

"It's okay; you don't have to say anything. I'll take care of your needs."

"W-what?" I mutter.

"Well, as my wife, I should take care of your needs, don't you think?"

"Um … I guess. But you don't know anything about me. You don't know what I need. And what I definitely don't need is another asshole in my life."

He makes a sort of 'tsk' sound. "You keep saying that word, but you're wrong about that part. You don't know anything about me, either; nor what I need. Does that make you an asshole, too?"

"No, but that's not what I mean, I–"

"For example, I might've been thinking for ages about how good it would feel to have a certain beautiful, curvy woman in a tight top and skirt walk into my office, go to her hands and knees, crawl under my desk, and suck me dry. After which I would drag her out, bend her over my desk, and fuck her senseless."

My mouth has completely dried up, and my breath is faltering.

He blinks as a quick smile appears on his face. "Of course, that's all hypothetically speaking. Fantasy is fantasy." He grins. "Because what boss would fuck his employee?"

I can't stop the whimper from coming out.

He leans in. "Did you know?"

"W-what?" I murmur, my lips quivering as he comes so close I could almost taste him again.

Goddammit, why does he do this?

"That's what I like."

I shake my head.

"Thought so."

And then he backs off and turns around. Just like that.

I'm left partially leaning forward, expecting a kiss, which didn't happen. I can still smell his intoxicating aftershave as he walks through the aisle with a confident stride and an ass so tight I could squeeze it.

Oh, fuck me, I'm screwed now.

CHAPTER TEN

We go over and over each other's letters, making sure we don't miss anything. We even quiz each other. I now know he enjoys his steak medium-rare, has at least one glass of wine every day to relax, and likes to take long showers. He enjoys anything that has to do with women (of course, that's a no-brainer), loves dressing well, and enjoys fishing from time to time (I didn't see that one coming). He also likes to play video games in his spare time (I definitely did not see that one from a mile away), and he sometimes likes to gamble (no wonder he was in Vegas).

He dislikes girls who make everything difficult (I think that remark meant for me specifically, but whatever), hates loud music (I might use that against him sometime), men who behave like pigs (I snorted reading that one), his sister (ouch), his parents (more ouch!), bad writing, and obligations. Ha, I guess we have one thing in common.

Well, it's nice to know all this, but I still don't know shit about him, and neither does he. It's just not possible to write your whole damn life on a little piece of paper, let alone know yourself well enough to be able to explain it to everyone.

I think it's wiser to stick to the important stuff like who our family is, where we went to college, what we do for a living. For instance, I know his sister's name is Emily, that he has a brother named Adrian and another named Christopher, and that his parents are Tricia (short for Patricia) and Frank. If I can only remember not to call his brother

Christopher … Leo told me that he hates it; he prefers Chris.

I hope I don't screw up.

I'm getting worked up over nothing, but damn, my job depends on this and I can't mess up. My armpits are already sweaty by the time the jet has landed. We leave the airport in a personal limo that Leo has arranged for us. I don't know how much time we spend driving toward his parents' house, but the closer we get, the more anxious I feel. I tell myself to calm down, but when I spot Leo peeking at me with a lopsided grin on his face, I get the urge to make them pull over so I can run far away.

It's stupid, I know. He'd never let me leave.

I snort to myself, thinking not even bad jokes are going to save me from this. It's happening, whether I like it or not. So I better put my big girl panties on, pretend I'm the nicest fucking wife he could ever have and get it over with.

And then I can go back to being the snooty assistant I've always been.

I'm surprised to find out his parents actually live in an estate far from the city center, close to the edge of a forest. Their land is huge, and it takes us a minute to drive from the gates up to the house, which is also enormous. It reminds me of those castles the queen of England owns, except his mother isn't the queen, and this is ridiculously unbelievable. Completely in awe, I let him escort me out of the car, but then he comes to a stop a few feet away from the door. He pulls my hand and turns me toward him, narrowing his eyes.

"Do you remember everything I told you?"

"Yes, I think …"

"Don't worry about it. Just relax and act natural."

"I'm about to meet your parents, it can't get any more absurd than this," I say.

"Oh, yes it can … wait until you meet them." He chuckles. "Or worse."

I frown. "Worse?"

His lip curls up into a smile. "I'm glad it's just them and not my entire family."

That makes my pupils dilate. Oh, god no. I don't even want to think about it.

"Well, let's just get this over with. The sooner it's done, the faster

I can get back to being just your assistant," I muse, as I take a deep breath.

"Hmm … pity," he hums.

"What?" I glance over my shoulder at him.

"Oh, nothing." He walks to the door. "Let's just go inside."

He rings the doorbell, and the moment his finger leaves the button, my heart begins to race. Some guy in a suit opens.

"Leo, how nice to see you."

"Hey, Dave," Leo says, and he leans in close to my ear, whispering, "Our butler." His hot breath creates goosebumps on my skin, but there's no time to linger. The butler is already holding out his hand.

"Come in; the Kings have been waiting for your arrival." He looks at me. "May I take your coat?"

I smile nervously as I let him take off my coat and step inside the hall. It's so high, and there's a white staircase in the middle, leading up to what must be at least fifteen rooms in three different hallways. Expensive wooden paneling covers the walls, and the marble on the floor is so white and clean, I could eat from it.

"Oh my …"

"Leo?" I hear a faint voice coming closer and closer. A woman in a dark red dress steps out from a room with a gentle smile on her face.

"Hello, Mother," Leo says, smiling.

She walks toward him and gives him a short hug. "Oh, Leonard," she says. "It's been too long."

"Leonard?" I repeat, making a face, swallowing back a laugh.

Leo shoots me a look with narrowed eyes that could kill. I almost choke on my laughter.

When she releases him, she looks at me and says, "So you must be … the girl." Her shoulders rise, and she makes a short squeaky, happy-fake sound before hugging me so tight I can barely breathe.

"It's so good to meet you," she says.

"Her name's Samantha," Leo says. When his mother releases me again, he grabs my hand and squeezes it softly, cocking his head to give me a fake, love-struck smile. "My Samantha."

His father comes up to me, rubbing his grey stubble. "Frank."

"It's so nice to meet you," I say.

"Yes, it's such a shame Leo hasn't told us anything about you,"

Tricia says.

"For good reason," he sneers.

"Oh, Leonard, now is not the time to start arguments."

"Yeah, Leonard," I say, winking. "Your mother is just trying to be polite."

She smiles at me with a smug look on her face while Leo grinds his teeth. I can almost hear him seethe; the hissing is quite unmistakable. I chuckle. This is going to be fun.

CHAPTER ELEVEN

This late dinner is horrible, horrible I tell you.

Why? Well, it took me exactly five minutes to slam-dunk a tiny piece of potato into Tricia's wineglass. Add that to the fact that I mumbled while introducing myself to his brothers because they were so goddamn sexy, and I've just made a complete fool out of myself. I keep stumbling into everything, tripping over the rugs, bumping into people; I even accidentally poked Emily with my elbow. That didn't go well with her. She seemed livid, throwing her napkin on the table and groaning as if she went totally mad. She refuses to look at me now. I get why Leo hates her.

"So, where did two meet?" Frank asks us.

"Oh, Vegas."

"Vegas ..." he repeats.

Leo kicks my shin and flashes a look at me.

"Oh, no, I mean, we got married there." I laugh it off, getting red as a beet again. "We met at his office."

"Oh, interesting."

"Yep, she was one of my models."

"Oh, really? You model?"

"Uh ..." I look back and forth to Leo, getting lost in this maze of lies. He shrugs and nods. I guess I should go with it.

"Plus-size," I say.

"Yeah, the magazine is looking to expand its base."

Tricia smiles. "That is wonderful. Well, I'm sure you two had a great time in Vegas. Do you have some pictures? I'd love to see them."

"Oh, no, not yet," Leo says, coughing. "They're still at the photographer getting processed."

"Oh … well, I must say, I was rather stunned when I heard the news. I would've loved to have been there during the exchange of the vows," Tricia says, taking another sip of her wine.

"Yeah, I would've loved to have you there, too, but this was a spontaneous act … of pure love." Leo looks at me, sighs, and puts on an unprecedented performance. It almost makes me laugh out loud.

"I can see you two are very fond of each other," Frank muses.

"Very much …" Leo repeats, gazing at me.

"Well, let's leave those lovebirds to eat," Tricia says, chuckling to herself. "After all, they must be hungry after that long trip." She looks at me. "Is it to your liking?"

"Oh, very much, Mrs. King."

"Nonsense, call me Tricia." She laughs. "I'm not that old."

"Of course," I say with a blush on my face.

I continue eating in the hopes that they won't ask any more questions that'll embarrass the hell out of me.

Adrian keeps throwing me weird glances from across the table, and it makes me feel so awkward. I'm already red as a tomato, but I know it can get worse. It can definitely get worse.

I lean to the side and whisper to Leo, "Hey, is there something stuck on my face or something?"

"No, why?" he says.

"Is it my teeth then?" I say, flashing him a smile.

He laughs. "Well, you do look ridiculous. Maybe that's it."

I shove him quietly under the table. "Shut up. I'm trying to do my best here."

"I can tell," he muses, drinking his wine. Something tells me that he's being sarcastic in a not so funny way.

"Do you want me to get up and tell everyone the truth?" I whisper-yell.

"Do you want me to fire you on the spot?" he retorts.

I growl.

"You two seem like you're having fun." Suddenly Adrian draws my attention back to him. He raises his eyebrow in a cheeky way and smiles at me. God, so smug, he reminds me of his brother. With his tan skin and brown hair, they almost look like twins.

"Jealous, much?" Leo asks.

"On the contrary, I'm quite glad I don't have any of that." He leans back.

"What's that supposed to mean?"

"He's allergic to women," Leo jokes.

"Hey!" Adrian laughs. "I'm just waiting for the right one."

"Yeah, right. You just wanna jump in and straight out of the sack with them."

"Leopold! Watch your language," Tricia says, frowning.

"Sorry, Mother," he says, clearing his throat.

Adrian leans forward across the table. "He's right, though. No way I'd let myself get tied down this quickly. No offence."

"None taken," I say. "You wouldn't get a piece of this regardless of your preference."

"Oh, ouch," he says.

Leo laughs, wrapping his arm around my shoulder. "Good one, Sam."

"I would be hurt by that comment if it wasn't for the fact that I honestly do not care. And not because you aren't a nice piece of ass."

"Adrian!" Now it's his father yelling. "What is up with you two?"

"Sorry, Dad ..." Adrian totally ignores him, keeping his focus on me. "You're quite the catch. I mean, you're pretty, you seem nice, and you're smart, as far as I can tell."

"Thank you," I say, blushing.

"But my brother caught you first, which is what I'm trying to say. I don't steal." He smiles and leans back again. "I'm happy for my brother that he finally found someone to share his ... *thing* with. Whatever that is." He smirks, and then they both burst out into laughter as if it's some sort of subliminal joke I'm totally not getting.

"What's so funny?" Emily asks. "Last I recalled, our brother isn't the one to like any type of spare time, let alone spend it with a girl. He's too busy playing with his magazines."

"Hey, don't talk shit about me with my girl here, all right," Leo says. "You don't know what I like to do in my spare time because you don't care."

"Hey, let's all calm down, okay?" Chris pitches in. Finally, he speaks up. He's been silent the entire night. I wonder if it's because of me or if he's always this way. "We don't want to give Samantha over here a bad impression of our family by acting like a bunch of little kids."

"Says the guy who plays with bikes all day," Emily says.

Chris throws her a look, and she stares right back at him as if they're trying to engage in an epic staring contents. Wow, awkward. This entire dinner is just awkward. I wish it would be over soon.

"Guys, please …" Leo says, sighing.

"Oh, please, don't pretend like you actually want to be here," Emily says to Leo, squinting.

"Hey, I just want to talk with my brother, all right? Nothing wrong with that. It's just dinner. Let's just talk … act like a normal family. Please?" The way he pleads with her tugs at my heart.

"So you're just gonna ignore that whole thing? You're just gonna let it go?" Emily spits.

Leo nods. "People change."

"Chris doesn't." She throws her fork down. "Chris never changes. Once an asshole, always an asshole. One dinner isn't going to change that."

"What is wrong with you?" Now his father even joins the conversation. "We are trying to have dinner here, and all I hear is squabbles. You are all adults. Behave like one."

"Yeah, what is your problem, Emily?" Chris muses.

"Really? You're gonna pull that crap on me now?"

"Can you all please just stop?" Tricia asks.

Everybody's stopped eating now. For a dinner, there sure isn't a lot of eating going on.

"No, just no," Emily snaps. "You think just because some time has passed, I'm suddenly okay with sitting in the same room with that guy again?" She points at Chris. "Have you all forgotten what he's done?"

Her face is growing redder by the second while I'm trying to make myself invisible. Too bad it doesn't work.

"I'm done pretending we're all good," Emily says. "I'm done sitting here, having to be nice to the new girl when I have so many other, way better things to do." Emily scoots back her chair. "God, why did I even come here? It was a mistake."

In a fit, she walks away.

"Emily …" Tricia gets up and follows her out of the room.

The rest of us are quiet, sitting here like a bomb just exploded, and I feel like I'm about to burst into tears from the stress.

"Well, this was fun," Frank says, throwing his napkin on the table. Then he sighs.

"I think I'll just … excuse me," Chris says, and he gets up and leaves, just like that. I don't know where he's going or if he'll be back, but this is one disaster dinner, all right.

I frown, feeling very bad about the situation. I look at Leo, who seems to have pissed off his father because they're engaging in an epic staring contest. I swallow away my nerves and tug Leo's suit.

"Do you mind if I go …? You know," I sigh to myself, holding my stomach. I feel sick. Like, really sick, and it's getting harder to breathe.

"Are you okay?" he says.

"Yeah, yeah … I'm fine," I lie, and I scoot my chair back.

"Take a break. The bathroom is to the left."

I nod, and then glance at his parents. "Excuse me for a second."

With a red face and a bloated feeling, I hurry to the hallway and find the bathroom after trying three doors. When I'm inside, I take a deep breath and then walk to the sink, opening the faucet to spritz some water on my face. As I look up to face the mirror, I want to slap myself for not keeping it together while being here.

A sudden knock on the door draws my attention. "Samantha?" Leo's low, seductive voice sends a chill up my spine. The good kind. "Are you okay?"

CHAPTER TWELVE

I clear my throat. "Yeah ..."

"Do you mind if I come in?"

Frowning, I pat my face dry with a towel before replying. "Sure."

He opens the door softly, stepping inside with a gentle smile on his face, one that I haven't seen before. I lean back against the sink, biting my lip. He comes closer and looks down at me with sultry eyes that somehow became a lot more difficult not to look at.

"Are you sure everything is all right? I know my family can be ... difficult."

"Don't worry about me," I say, sighing. "I'll be fine."

Suddenly, he cups my face, tilting it to look up at him. "I do worry about you. You're forced to lie for me." He frowns. "I'm sorry my sister is being such a bitch about this. I wish it could've gone better, but she had to go and ruin it again."

"There seems to be a lot going on that I don't know about," I say.

"Yeah, she and my brother have a ... problematic history.

"Obviously." I laugh, trying to shake it off, but it's not working. "Sorry."

"Don't say sorry." He tucks a strand of my hair behind my ear. "It's not your fault."

"I know. I just want to do this right, but I keep running into moments where I have no clue what to say. And then I stammer and trip. And your sister is angry with me, too."

"Don't say that," he says, leaning in even closer. "She's not angry with you, not at all. She's just taking it out on everyone because she can't stand to be around my brother. Don't take it personal."

I look up at him, my lips parting because I want to say something. I want to tell him how stupid this is, how I'm so not good at lying, how afraid I am that this is going to fail.

But then he does the weirdest thing. He grabs my face with both hands and leans in to press his lips on mine. This sudden sign of affection leaves me awestruck, and my brain stops thinking about all the problems and consequences. There's only him and his soft, wet lips kissing mine with pure need. Oh god, I'm losing it, losing myself at the moment. His fingers grip my face tight as his lips eagerly explore my mouth. His tongue darts out to lick the top part of my lip, and it's such a rush that I instinctively wrap my hands around his neck, pulling him closer.

Leo momentarily takes his lips from mine, and I'm left wanting desperately for him to continue. It's as if I've finally been allowed to eat the most delicious desert that's been dangling in front of me all this time.

"Wha–"

"Shhh …" he whispers, and then he leans in to kiss me again.

Oh, fuck me, I can't say no to this. His lips are rougher with every passing second, sucking at my bottom lip, licking the rim of my mouth, probing me to open up. His hand lowers from my face to my shoulder, and then down my back to squeeze my ass firmly. It makes me gasp, and when I do, his tongue finds its way into my mouth to lick me. His hot kisses have me lost in delirious, heating up quickly, my blood pulsing with desire.

He growls into my mouth, which sets me off like a bomb, my pussy thumping to the sound. He shoves me up the sink, his tongue eagerly exploring my mouth. As I get more and more turned on, his hand moves up to my head to grip my hair tight as his lips trail a path down to the side of my neck. I moan as he plants kisses everywhere, alternating soft pecks with nibbles and licks, causing me to quiver.

And then the door opens.

I squeal as I stare straight at Adrian, a self-indulging smirk building on his face.

Leo immediately stops, his hands still all over me, as he gazes at his brother with his mouth open. Then he backs away and clears his throat, straightening his suit.

"Well, seems like you too are eager to get it on. Couldn't wait until you got back to the hotel, huh?" He winks. "Hey, don't let me stop you. I'll find another bathroom." He makes a move to close the door again, but Leo says, "Ah, no worries."

I frown as he steps away completely, leaving me breathless.

"No, it's fine," Adrian says. "Sorry for interrupting." He chuckles.

"Oh, stop laughing, asshole," Leo says. Then he returns his attention to me. "Let's get back to the dinner table, shall we?"

"Uh …" I stammer for a second. "Yeah … I guess."

Leo grabs my hand and drags me out of the bathroom, stopping in front of Adrian.

"You gonna let us pass?"

"Of course, I just wanted to enjoy the moment for a little longer. It's not often I catch my brother putting his hands all over a girl."

"Ass," Leo says. "You'd better not tell Mum about this. She'd be pissed if she knew."

"Knew what? That you soiled her pretty bathroom?"

"Shut up." Leo shoves Adrian, and now they're both laughing while I'm so terribly confused.

I don't get it. One minute he can't stop touching and kissing me, then out of nowhere he wants to leave. What is up with him?

"What was that?" I ask.

When we're a little further away from his brother, he says, "Just a little distraction."

I wince. "For who?"

"You. Me. Him and my family."

"I'm confused."

"My brother saw it, no way in hell he's going to keep quiet. Especially now that I said that he can't tell her, which is exactly what I want. It's a sure way to make them believe we're a couple."

"Oh …" I mumble. "Is that it?"

He glances at me shortly, a look of confusion flashing on his face, but then his parents call out his name and he's lost in the game again.

We'll have to talk about this sometime. I'm not going to let something like this slip through my fingers again. Once we get back to the hotel, he's going to tell me exactly what in the hell that was and if it was anything more than just part of the play. I won't take no for an answer.

CHAPTER THIRTEEN

When we get to the hotel, the huge double bedroom in the suite he booked is a welcome sight. I'm beat and about ready to crawl into bed and snuggle my pillow like it's a giant marshmallow. Hmm … god, why did I think about that? Now I'm hungry again.

Leo throws his keys on the table as I throw my purse on the couch and sigh. A nice, warm bath would be great before I go to sleep, but first there's something else I need to do.

"So, are you ready to talk now?" I say.

"What?" he asks.

I put my hands on my side. "Well, I'm not just going to let you do that to me."

"What are you talking about?" he frowns.

I roll my eyes. "Have you already forgotten? Right," I scoff. "Of course. That's typical."

"Sam, explain. I'm not up for games right now."

"Me, neither," I hiss, throwing him a glance.

"I don't understand what you're getting at. Honestly," he says, rolling up his sleeves.

"Of course, you don't. I should've realized that. Sorry I even started this." I sigh and turn around, taking off my coat.

"What? Can you just stop and tell me what the hell it is you're talking about?"

"I'm talking about you and what you do."

"What do I do, exactly?" he says, shrugging.

"Really?" I turn around and make a face. "You're going to pretend you don't know?"

"No, because I don't, and it'd be nice if you'd just tell me what the hell is going on."

"This. This is my problem. You don't *know* what's going on, that's the problem."

He shakes his head, chuckling to himself.

"Are you laughing? Is this funny to you?" I say. "Never mind." Grinding my teeth, I turn around and look at myself in the mirror standing in the corner so I can take off my make-up.

"Sam ... c'mon, you're angry at me for not knowing what you're angry for."

"Exactly."

He sighs. "That's kind of childish."

"And your games aren't?"

"What games?"

"What you did in the bathroom!" I yell, making a fist.

"What I did ... Oh." He nods slowly. "*That.*"

"Yes, that. And all the other times."

"Sam ..."

I can't help but turn around to face him again. I want to look him in the face when he tells me he did it all to fool his parents, and that none of what I'm feeling is real. "No, don't Sam me. I just want to know when this is all done. When you're finished playing around."

"I'm not playing around, but this is important to me."

"Well, I'm done," I say. "I can't do it anymore. I can't pretend to be your wife. I was horrible at it anyway. I mean, look at me. Do I look like wife material to you? I was a bumbling mess."

"No ..." He cocks his head and smiles at me. "You did fine. Is that what you're worried about?"

Somehow, I can't stop this boiling anger from bubbling up again. "No."

"Then what is?"

"Just the fact that you don't realize, that you can't see it ... ugh!" I blow out some air. "You make me so angry sometimes."

"I can see that," he says, laughing again.

"It's not funny!" I grab a pillow and throw it at him. "You are such an asshole."

He catches the pillow and throws it on the bed. "Is that what you really think of me?"

"Yes! You're a fucking asshole!"

He looks me in the eye, his face all serious and stern. "Tell me what else you think."

"You're a liar, an asshole, a bastard, a manipulator, and a pig!" My face is turning red, but I don't care anymore. I'm letting it all out. All that pent-up frustration from having to work with him is coming out, and right now I don't give a shit about the consequences. Screw everything.

"Say that again, I didn't hear it quite well," he says, cocking his head to the other side.

"You're an asshole, Leo! A complete and utter prick!"

"For kissing you?"

"Yes, for fucking kissing me!" I yell. "How could you do that? When you know …" I choke up.

"When what?" He raises an eyebrow.

Suddenly, I get the urge to just stomp to the other end of the room where he's standing and smack him in the face. Maybe it would knock some sense into him.

But I don't even need to because he's already walking toward me instead. When there are only a couple of steps left, he stops. "Could you repeat that?"

"You know you're an asshole for doing what you do, Leo. Admit it. You know damn well what you're doing."

"And?"

"And … I hate you for it," I spit. "I hate it."

He narrows his eyes as I breathe in and out; wiping my hair to the side, which is all messed up. God, I'm messed up. Oh, god. What in the hell did I just do? I just signed my own resignation and handed it to him on a platter. Oh, I'm so stupid.

Right when I'm about to smack myself in the face, Leo stomps forward, saying, "Fuck it."

And then he grabs my face with both hands and smashes his lips on mine.

CHAPTER FOURTEEN

His kiss is intense, so deep; I'm at a loss of words. My brain just goes blank. He is rough and soft at the same time, desperately clinging to my lips, and I don't even want him to stop. His kiss has me mesmerized to the point of completely freezing up. As his lips roam mine, his tongue dips out to lick the rim of my mouth, coaxing me to open. Instinct makes my lips part, allowing him to lick the roof off my mouth and my tongue, blowing me away. I'm lost in him, lost in this kiss, and I lost my brain.

Oh, fuck me. What the hell?

My lips unlatch from his with trouble as I push him away a little. "What …" I mumble.

"I can't stand it when you call me names," he whispers against my lips. "Makes me want to do this." And then moves in for the kill again. He kisses me harshly, his hands drifting down my body to my ass to cup it and squeeze it. I moan into his mouth, surprised, my eyes opening up.

"Wait," I murmur, pushing him back a little. "No."

"This is what you want, isn't it?" he asks.

Hot flashes shoot through my veins as he says that. I don't know how to respond. At times, I hate him, like when he uses me to gain something. When he acts like a total dick. And other times, I want to screw him so badly … ugh, what am I thinking?

"But that kiss … in the bathroom …" I whisper as he kisses me again and again.

"What about it?"

"It was only for show, right?"

"Look around you," he says, and my eyes drift from left to right, trying to understand him. "Do you see anyone here?"

I shake my head.

He bites his lip so seductively it makes my head spin. "Screw the rules." And then he plunges in to kiss me again. He presses his body to mine, sucking on my bottom lip as he drags me even closer. His hot kisses take the air from my lungs while he grabs my ass tight and cups my face with spread fingers. They drift to the back of my head to grasp my hair and push me even closer.

"Fuck …" he whispers as our mouths unlatch to breathe. "I can't stop. I won't."

He's smothering me with kisses, not giving me an inch to breathe. He lets go of me, only to take off his own shirt, dropping it to the floor. Only his tie is left hanging around his neck. What appears underneath has me gasping for air. He's ripped, six-pack and all, a delicious V-shape disappearing into his pants. He's muscular as hell, and it's making me even more hot and bothered.

"Holy crap …" I mutter.

He flashes a cocky smile, smashing his lips onto mine again. He pulls me along toward his bed, tugging the zipper on my back. The dress falls down, but I don't even realize it because his kisses are just that good. It's hard to admit because I hate how he treats me, but at the same time, I can't get enough of this. Fuck no, I don't want it to stop, either.

Next thing I know, I'm on the bed in just my bra and panties, and he's crawling on top of me like a real lion.

"I don't understand …" I murmur as he starts kissing my legs. I look down at him, getting flustered when I realize he's looking at my partially naked body, which isn't all that flattering.

"Isn't it obvious?" he says, dragging his lips up my thighs, making me moan. "I want you."

He leaves a trail of kisses up my stomach and to my chest, hovering close to my face. I feel myself getting red again.

"Oh god, but why? I don't understand. I thought you said—"

"Shh." He places a finger on my lips. "Enough talking for today."

Leo removes his finger and replaces it with his mouth.

Well, that shut me up all right.

I don't know why I'm letting him ravage my body and talk to me like this, claiming me as if I can't say anything back … oh, who am I kidding, I can't. This is what I've wanted all along, ever since he started teasing me, and oh boy, it's so not what I expected. It's even hotter than I imagined. I'm not prepared for the exquisite sight of his rippling body as he leans up to unbuckle his belt.

"You've been such a fucking distraction all this time … I'm not going to hold back any longer."

"Hold back?" I whimper, as he loops his belt through the holes.

"And you call me an asshole?" He raises a brow. "I've seen the way you react to my flirting. You want this. Badly. So bad, you're even angry at me for not giving it to you."

"What?" I exclaim.

And then he grabs my wrist and pins it above the bed. "You heard what I said."

He wraps the belt around my wrist and pulls it tight. "What are you doing?" I ask, my heartbeat rising.

"Doing what you want," he says. He bends over until his forehead touches mine, his fingers grasping the bed tight. "Your emotions are all over the place, Sam. I think it's time I got them under control."

With a smirk, he pushes himself back up and undoes his tie, strapping it to my other wrist and tying it to the other side of the bed. I'm not sure how I feel about this, if I should tell him to stop and get the fuck off me so I can yell at him some more, or if I should just let it go and let him do with me what he wants. My traitorous body already knows what it wants as I press my legs together to prevent myself from feeling my own pussy. Goddammit.

For a second, he licks his lips, glancing down at me from under his eyelashes as if he's admiring the view. "You know, I've dreamt about the day I could tie you up like this."

I make a face at him. "I bet you have."

His lips curl up into a smile. "And I bet I'm not the only one in this room who has."

He lowers himself on top of me and hovers close to my lips, daring me to see if I'll bite. Maybe I will. I kind of like where this is going, I admit.

"Stop playing around, Leo," I say.

He taps my nose. "It's Mister King to you."

I squint. "I'm tied up on the bed, half naked, and you're telling me to call you what I've always called you before?"

"I like it," he says with a cheeky grin. "In fact, there are a lot of things I like that you probably don't know about me."

He kisses my cheek and drifts down to my neck, leaving marks everywhere, making it difficult for me to breathe and think right.

"Like what?" I say, gasping. "That you're a pervert?"

He chuckles, and then takes my earlobe into his mouth to suck and gently nibble on it. "You and your filthy mouth really make me want to be harsh on you."

"Try me," I jest.

He whispers into my ear, "I like it when you play hard to get."

His hand drifts down my body, over the swell of my breasts, causing me to suck in a breath, but he doesn't stop there. His hand slides all the way down my belly toward my pussy, and when he cups it I gasp and moan.

"Is this what you were thinking about when I kissed you in the bathroom?" he whispers coyly into my ear. "Do you want me?"

"Uh-huh …" I moan, unable to stop myself anymore. When he starts rubbing, I'm done for.

"You're a very naughty girl, you know that? And the problem with me is that I cannot resist."

I moan again when he pushes down with one finger, sliding across my clit. My panties are already soaked.

"But the things I like might scare you, Sam," he whispers, and I open my eyes again, seeing him eye me from the side. "I love the sight of a woman tied up just like you are right now. It makes me want to do so many … nasty things to you." Those last words come out with a groan, seeping into my pores as my body turns to liquid underneath him.

"Are you scared?" he asks, his fingers floating across my lips. "Do you want me to stop? Say it now, before I can't control myself anymore."

"No," I whimper as he plants another kiss on my jaw.

"You have me in a cinch, Sam. Right now, this is what I need. Especially after today. But you need to know you can always tell me to stop. The safe word is pear."

"Pear?" I ask. "Why?"

"If you're afraid, use it. Like I said … there are things I like that you don't know about me, and this is one of them. I enjoy complete and utter control, Sam. This is what I get off on."

My heart flutters from his words.

His hands slide down my arms, tickling me, setting my skin on fire. "You look so ravishing …" he growls. "I could almost eat you up." He bites in the air, making me squirm as he leans in to lick my neck and collarbone. "Is this what you need?" he asks, his hand sliding underneath the fabric of my panties. "Is this what you've been thinking about? When you saw me? When I first kissed you? When you came out of the stall on the airplane?"

"Oh, yes …" I mutter, lost in delirium as he toys with me. His fingers feel so good, and I've been fantasizing about this for so long, I can hardly believe it's real. I want to slap myself for wanting him, but I do, and I can't stop myself from enjoying this. It's impossible. Holy shit, he sure knows what to do.

Suddenly, he pulls away and hovers on top of me, kissing my chest while he fumbles with the clips on the back. "Wait," I say.

"Shh," he says. "No talking unless I ask you something."

"I just feel …"

"What? Uncomfortable?" he asks, frowning. "Tell me if you want me to stop."

"No, it's not that. It's just that I'm a little nervous." I giggle, but then stop myself, because I sound like an idiot. "Ah, forget it."

"No," he says resolutely all of the sudden. "Whatever you're thinking, I want you to stop it, right now. There's nothing to be nervous about when you show me your body. It's what I want, and that is the only thing that matters."

"Okay … but—"

"Stop." He grabs my chin, making me focus on him. "If we do this, you don't talk. You don't think. Just let go and enjoy. I don't want to hear anything but your moans and gasps, understood?"

I nod, a bit shook up by the fact that Leo is really into this controlling thing. I didn't expect him to be like this, which makes it all the more difficult for me to say no. I actually want this.

He smiles. "Good, because I'll have you wet and begging before this night is over."

I swallow away the lump in my throat. Oh, fuck me, this is just too hot to deny.

Before I know it, my strapless bra is off and flung through the air, and Leo has buried his face in between my breasts. I moan when he cups them and starts playing with my nipples, tugging and teasing me to my limit. He covers one of them with his mouth and sucks, causing me to moan.

"So sensitive ..." he murmurs, tugging with his teeth. "I bet you must be quivering by now. Do you like it when I'm rough?"

"Yes," I say. "I've always quite liked it but never had it like this, though."

"Like how?"

"Tied up," I say.

"Hmm ... I guess we're both hiding who we truly are then." He winks. "You've been deprived of good sex, Sam. Let me give it to you."

CHAPTER FIFTEEN

He kisses my stomach and goes down, pulling my panties with his teeth. When they're off, he chucks them off the bed and pushes my thighs with his hands. "Spread your legs, Sam. I want you wide and wet."

I do as he says without saying a word. It's oddly satisfying as well.

He plants a kiss on top of my vulva, and then slides down toward my pussy, blowing hot air on me, causing me to buck my hips. His fingers play with me, and then his tongue darts out to play along. I moan out loud as he licks and sucks, playfully teasing me to the edge.

"I must say, I never imagined you'd be so easily persuaded to let me fuck you."

"I'm not," I say. "I have no say in this at all."

"Ah-ah." He slaps my inner thigh, causing me to squeeze them together. "No talking."

"You're mean," I say.

He slaps my other leg, and I growl.

"I can get a lot meaner if you don't behave," he muses. "I told you I like the control. I expect you to do as you're told if you want me to give you what you need."

I huff and puff, trying to come up with an honest reply, but I can't. My brain has turned to goo, and all I can think of is having him fuck me senseless tonight. I'm losing my mind.

"Such a delicious pussy you have," he says, chuckling against my skin. "If I'd known you tasted so good, I would've eaten you long ago."

I want to say 'fuck you,' but then I want to say 'fuck me,' as well. Goddammit.

He laps me up sensually and slow, causing sweet bliss. I'm desperately holding onto the tie and belt, building toward a climax. He's pushing me to my limits, toying with me like he knows exactly what to do and how to do it to make me scream. I'm teetering on the brink, desperate to fall over.

"Oh, god … I'm going to …"

"Come? Do it. Come for me, Sam."

"Oh, fuck," I whisper, and then the waves start coming like there's no tomorrow. My body convulses, my pussy clenches, and I can feel his fingers and tongue everywhere as I come apart from his touch.

When the orgasm subsides, his body rises above mine, and he licks his lips with a contented smile. Then he jumps off the bed and barges through the room to search his bags.

"What are you doing?" I ask.

When he has what he was looking for, he holds it up for me to see. A condom.

He quickly unwraps it and drops his boxers just as quickly, and holy shit, what comes bouncing out widens my eyes and makes my jaw drop. He's huge! Like, he could fill me to the brim and then some.

I swallow, my mouth watering as he strides toward me with confidence. Not a second does he wait to climb on top of me, leaving kisses everywhere. He only leans up to put the condom on his hard-on, and then immediately comes back down to kiss me again. His mouth is hot and full of lust. I kiss him back with equal desire; I can't help myself. His hands are all over me, grasping my waist, cupping my face. When the tip of his cock touches my entrance, my pussy begins to thump again.

"Are you ready for me, Sam?" he asks.

"Oh, god, yes," I moan into his mouth.

He pushes in slowly, and it feels so good that I gasp. He fills me up so tightly, I can feel everything, even the slightest movement. I love how he feels, even if I can't touch him with my hands. Just the feel of his body on top of mine and his cock sliding into me … god, I could come again.

He rocks my world slowly, teasing me until I start to bite my lip from excitement. His thrusts are calculated, sensual, and increase in speed at just the right time. He never takes his eyes off me, his lips hovering dangerously close to mine but never touching. I lean closer to steal a kiss, but he won't let me. The cocky smile on his face accompanied by him biting his lip has me bucking my hips in rhythm. I'm lost in his eyes, his beautiful body, and the way we're both coming closer to the edge. I can feel it from the way he moves and hear it from his sexy groans that he's about to come.

"Fuck, I want you to come, Sam," he murmurs, his tongue darting out to lick my lips.

"Yes, oh, yes, I'm so close," I say.

"Do it. Come for me, Sam."

I don't need to think twice, my body does all the work. His thrusts push me over the edge and into another delirious orgasm. My body falls apart underneath him, my muscles tightening around his thickness. He pulsates inside me, a loud moan escaping his mouth, and then he fills me with his warmth. Three more thrusts and he's thrust all his energy and cum into me.

He plants a deep kiss on my mouth, cupping my face with his hand, one that has my head spinning and leaves me wanting more when he stops. He briefly gazes at me with sultry half-mast eyes, and then leans back to take off the condom and chuck it in the trash. Then he drops down next to me and undoes the belt and tie around my wrists. When I'm free, I rub my wrists, but he takes me into his arms and presses me into his chest. His body is warm and comforting as I lay my head on his chest. He smells exotic and so good. God, I could sniff him up for hours. I love the way he feels, and even when we're both naked, I don't feel any shame for my body. I'm actually grinning.

Dammit. I'm really into him.

When I raise my head to ask him something, I notice his eyes are already closed. When he starts to snore, I realize it's too late to talk about what just happened. I chuckle to myself. What an easy sleeper.

It doesn't take long before I too fall into a deep sleep, huddled in his arms, listening to his steady heartbeat.

CHAPTER SIXTEEN

I awake to the sound of zippers going up and down. I pat the bed with my hands, but there's nothing next to me, and the bed is growing cold. My eyes are glued together, but when I open them, I notice Leo is no longer lying next to me. I should be surprised, but I'm actually more concerned with the fact that the sun is already out and I'm still in Leo's bed. I slept with Leo fucking King last night.

Holy shit.

What have I done?

I sit up straight and see myself in the mirror standing in the corner. Immediately, I rake my fingers through my hair, trying to make myself look less of a mess. However, it's no use because my make-up is all over the place. I hope he likes witches because I look like one right now.

As I gaze around the room, I notice Leo's already dressed in his suit, up and running, packing his clothes. Confused, I frown.

When he looks up and sees me, he says, "Morning. I got the help to pack your bags for you."

"What?" I mumble, yawning.

"Don't worry, they're trustworthy. I paid double for the room."

A maid scurries in and out of the second bedroom, the one I'm supposed to be sleeping in.

Well, this is not how I pictured the morning after having sex with Leo fucking King.

"What's going on?" I ask.

"We're going."

"What? Why?" I make a face. "I thought you still had business with your family."

"No, we have to leave. Get dressed." His monotone voice makes the hairs on the back of my neck stand up.

"Excuse me?" I say.

"We're leaving," he says, eyeing me. "Why aren't you out of bed yet?"

"Well, this is nice," I scoff, sighing out loud. Frowning, I slam the blanket, watching him continue packing like nothing's going on. And here I was, hoping that this liaison somehow meant that he'd still be here when I woke up, that he'd eat breakfast with me, that he … I don't know … that he'd want more from me than just sex. God, I'm so stupid. I slap myself on the head.

"How could I not see this coming …" I mumble to myself.

"What?" he asks.

"Nothing," I mutter.

I shouldn't be disappointed because I could've seen this coming if I had only kept my brain in the game. But, of course, I had to let myself get carried away. Why on earth did I let him fuck me? I should've realized it was never more than just a fuck to him.

Throwing the blanket off me, I quickly grasp my clothes and put them on before he turns around and sees me naked. Like hell I'd let him enjoy that again.

When I'm done, the packing is finished, even without my help. Leo hurries out the door and says, "Are you coming?"

I don't get what all the fuss is about, but he sure is in a hurry. "Why do you want to get out of here so quickly? Bad memories?" I jest.

He makes a face. "Huh?"

"Never mind …" I say. He clearly doesn't get it. Well, we'll talk about this on our way home all right.

Along with all the luggage, a thundering cloud of silence hovers over us when we get into the elevator. Awkward doesn't even begin to describe this, and I'm so glad when the doors open. When we walk into the lobby, a woman standing near the entrance smiles at Leo.

"Oh, Leo! Did I make it in time?"

She's long and thin, with curly blond hair, wearing a tight red dress and matching high heels with black soles. I recognize that brand, and it's nothing cheap.

"Oh, no ..." Leo drops the suitcases, the look on his face going from resolute to pure misery in a snap of a finger.

The woman walks toward us, having only eyes for Leo as she gets up close and gives him a kiss on the cheeks. "Leo, hun, how are you?"

"I was fine without your interference."

"Tsk, such attitude." She winks at him, which makes me wince in disgust. "So, where's the party?"

"You're too late, Marilyn," Leo says.

Party? So, she knows about the fake marriage, too? Or am I missing something?

"Oh, well, that's unfortunate. I would've loved to meet your parents," Marilyn says.

Leo grabs her by the arm. "What are you doing here, I thought you said ..." Leo's voice diminishes in volume with each word.

I clear my throat because I've had enough of them ignoring my presence.

"Leo, who is this?" Marilyn asks.

"I'm his—"

"Assistant." He gives us both a fake smile.

"You brought your assistant?" she scoffs. "Well, that's new. I thought you'd be rid of this one by now."

I don't know if I should feel offended by her comment or if I should punch Leo for giving her that idea in the first place. What on earth is going on?

"Who are you, exactly?" I ask.

Marilyn gazes at me with an annoyed look on her face. "Darling, you're just the *pretend wife*. Don't act like you have the right to ask me that."

"What?" I scoff, my jaw dropping. I can't believe this woman.

"Ah, she's—" But before Leo can finish his sentence he's interrupted by Marilyn.

"Me? Well, I'm his *real* wife."

CHAPTER SEVENTEEN

"His *real* wife?" I repeat in shock.

My fingers can't keep a strong hold on the suitcase as I'm caught off guard by her comment. It drops to the floor, and with one of the zippers broken, some of my panties come tumbling out.

Embarrassed as hell, I duck to pick them up when Leo does the same. As he attempts to pick one of them up, I say, "No!"

"Let me help you," he says, but I shove him aside.

With a flushed face, I stuff them in my suitcase and stand up, breathing out loud as I gaze at Leo. "What in the hell is going on?"

"Long story, darling. Too long for you to know," Marilyn says.

"What? How dare you ..." I mutter.

Marilyn makes a face, but before she can respond, Leo says, "Lyn, you're only making it worse."

"Lyn?" I scoff. "Well, I guess I should've known I wasn't the only girl you gave a nickname to." I'm disgusted by what's happening here. His *real wife* showing up? Like, who the hell is she and why is this happening?

"Your real wife? Seriously?" I say.

"Yes, it's the truth, if you doubted my statements," Marilyn muses, smiling obnoxiously. "Am I really too late, Leo?"

"Yes. Why the hell are you here, Lyn?" He grabs her arm.

"Because I wanted to help," she says.

"No, you said you didn't want to do it, and now all of the sudden you're here? What is going on?"

She shrugs. "I changed my mind."

"On what?" I yell. I look explicitly toward Leo, as I don't want that woman interjecting again. "You still haven't told me what the fuck is going on."

The whole lobby is looking at me right now, and I feel shitty for shouting, so I shut my mouth immediately.

"Okay, remember when I told you I got drunk and married a friend?" he says, frowning. Then he cocks his head, aiming it at her. "That's her."

"Hi," she says, waving as if she's all cute and stuff. Oh, fuck off.

"She's your wife ..." I mutter.

He bites his lip and mulls a bit before saying, "Yes."

My jaw drops. Quiet for a second, I just stare at him, unable to speak a proper syllable. "Your ... wife... You mean you're still married? To *her*?"

"Technically ... yes," he says with an apologetic face.

"Don't be so surprised, darling," Marilyn says. "I mean who doesn't want to be married to this?" She laughs, but it doesn't feel like a joke to me.

"Lyn ..." Leo says. "You're only making it worse."

"Yes, Lyn, this isn't right. Did you know your husband asked me to be his pretend wife?" I say, making a face.

She folds her arms. "Actually, I didn't, but this just makes it all the more fun."

"Fun ... Fun?" I'm fuming right now. "You call this fun?" I direct my attention to Leo. "You have *got* to be kidding me."

In a fit of rage, I waltz right past him. I can't bear to look at his face right now. What I want to do isn't legal, and I'm sure as hell not ending up in jail for this asshole.

"Sam, wait," Leo says, walking after me. "Let me explain."

"What's there to explain? You have a wife. Explains enough, doesn't it?" I spit.

"No, it doesn't, and you're getting this all wrong."

"Oh, *I'm* getting this all wrong?" I scoff.

"I didn't mean it like that. If you stop running, I can tell you what's going on."

"No, thank you. I think I've seen and heard enough." I stomp forward.

"Stop," he says, standing in front of me. "C'mon."

"No," I say, frowning. "Now get out of my face before I throw my panties at you."

This makes him laugh, which pisses me off. "I'm sorry, that was bad," he says.

"Yes, it was. Just like everything about you," I snap.

"Ouch …" he says. "Sam, please, let me explain."

"What's there to say? You're married! I thought you'd already annulled the contract and that you wanted me as your pretend wife only for a little while until you could tell your parents the truth. Wow, was I wrong there." I roll my eyes. "Jesus, you're really good at fooling women."

I clear my throat and walk past him. "Now, if you'll excuse me, I have a plane to catch."

"Wait," he says, grabbing my hand. "There's way more to it than that. You haven't given me a chance to—"

"To what? To tell me how I was only used for show? How your real wife could show up at any time to take over? Like, seriously, what is this? Are you for real?"

"It's not like that, at all. I wanted you to be my pretend wife because she refused to come with me to meet my parents."

"Oh, so you got me to play the role instead? How chivalrous."

He frowns. "I got myself in some deep shit, all right, but that doesn't mean that I did this to hurt you. That I don't care about you."

"Say that to the woman you married in the first place." I point at Marilyn. "Because we both have no fucking clue what's going on. And now you've cheated on us both."

"Cheated? What, no, you're taking this whole thing way out of context," he says.

"Really? I'm taking it out of context? Because I seem to remember you were the one who fucked your fake pretend wife, knowing that you still had a real wife on the side."

The look on Marilyn's face right now is priceless.

I wince. "You're disgusting. Now let me go." I jerk my hand free and turn my head. The annoying twitch in my nose is starting up again, and I don't want to feel it. Just like I don't want to hear his irritatingly sultry voice.

"Samantha!" he yells, but I ignore him. "Where are you going?"

"Home," I say. "Without you."
And then I stick my middle finger up in the air.

CHAPTER EIGHTEEN

I got home alone by buying a ticket out of my own pocket. I couldn't stomach the thought of having to sit next to that asshole, so I wasted a bit of money on this. Anything was better than the thought of being close to him right now. He can stick that second ticket up his ass for all I care.

I regret ever kissing him.

The worst part is that I actually believed it was more than just a fling. Boy, was I wrong. Of course, it was only sexual gratification for him. He used me. How could I be so stupid to fall for it?

My suitcase completely falls apart as I throw it on the floor and sit down on my bed. For a second, I stare at myself in the mirror hanging above my cabinet, blowing off steam. The more I look at myself, the angrier I get. I can't believe I let myself get carried away like that.

Sighing, I drop down onto the mattress and stare at the ceiling. That prick doesn't deserve any more attention, and yet I can't stop thinking about how fucking angry I am at him.

Guess that guy really did a number on me.

Fucker.

I'm not going to waste another second thinking about him, so I take my phone from my pocket and open the app Mr. Awesome and I use. I could really use some distraction right now, and I know he can give it to me without any fuss. I haven't heard anything from him since yesterday, despite him saying he'd contact me before the night was over. He sure left me hanging in the airplane. Well, it's not like it mattered because in the end I got what I wanted ... I got much more than I bargained for.

S: Hey, are you there?

I stare at my phone for a while, but no answer seems to come in. Instead, it rings, which makes my heart explode. I breathe a sigh of relief when I notice it's Stephanie.

"Hey," I say as I pick up. I can't hide my mood, though, and of course, she notices.

"Hey girl, what happened? Had a good time?" she asks.

I groan, not knowing how to answer.

"I take it that's a no then," she says. "What did he do?"

"Ah, it's not so much what he did, but mostly what he didn't do."

"Do you want me to punch him in the face?"

I laugh. "No, you're not the one who deserves jail time."

"Oh, Jesus, he really did a number on you, didn't he?"

"Ugh, he's such an asshole." I roll around on the bed.

"So you did have sex with him."

"That is none of your business," I muse.

"But you did. I knew it."

I blush, even though there's no one here. "Shut up, it was just ... sex."

"Of course, it is. That's why you sound so depressed."

"I do *not* sound depressed ... Do I sound depressed?"

"Yes, like a girl who just got her heart stomped on."

"Hmm ..." I frown because she's actually right, but I don't want to admit it. I don't want to even think about it because the thought of being used almost brings me to tears.

I sniff.

"Aw, girl, don't cry," Stephanie says.

"There's something in my eye."

She laughs. "Your finger, yeah."

"Oh, you and your stupid jokes," I retort. "Not helping."

"I know, but he's a dick and whatever the fuck he did doesn't mean he gets to make you cry. Do not let him make you cry, Sam. He's not worth it."

"I know. Thank you," I say, swiping away a tear.

"I think it's time I got my ass to your place," she muses.

I laugh. "Ugh, I could so use your snark right now. Seriously. You do not want to know what he did."

"Tell me all about it when I get to your place. I'll be there in five. And make sure you have plenty of pillows."

"Why?"

"So I have something else but my phone to throw."

I laugh so hard that I snort. She never fails to amuse me and keep my mind off *him*.

***

About thirty minutes later, Stephanie knows all about what he did.

"What a pig!" she says.

"I know, right? And the worst part is that he practically tried to hide it from me."

"Pfft, I should've known something was up when he told you to go dress shopping. With *his* credit card."

"He used me. For his own gain. And then he had sex with me, and I let him. It's like the cherry on a giant turd mountain."

She giggles but quickly stops when she notices that I'm not laughing. I can't help it, I'm so not amused. All I want to do is grab my belongings, go to his house, and throw everything in his face. Even if it costs me a fortune, the bastard deserves it.

"Well, let's stop talking about him then. He doesn't deserve the attention."

"No, he doesn't," I say, grabbing my laptop. "Unless it's negative. And I have the perfect thing in mind."

"What?" she asks as I pull up my document and start typing.

"Well, I'm expecting to lose my job after all of this."

"But you did what he asked! Even if it went against everything you stand for. And he hasn't even paid you."

"I know, but that won't stop him from trying to rid himself of this problem called 'me' as soon as possible. He has a tendency for picking the easiest route."

"Asshole," she says.

"But I won't go down without dragging him with me."

"How?"

"I'm going to type out this entire fucking story, and then laugh my ass off at my own stupidity."

"Hey!" She shoves me. "You're not stupid."

"I had sex with him. Of course, that's stupid."

"You were following your vagina. We all do that sometimes. And then we learn from it."

"Bad vagina, bad!" I say, and we both laugh. "The power of cock was strong this time."

She snorts. "Well, I hope that part was good at least. The fucker might be an asshole, but if you got good sex out of it, then that's at least one thing he can't take away."

"It was good all right, which is why I hate him even more," I growl. "More material for me to write about."

"So what are you going to do with the story then? Publish it? Let the world see your 'stupidity'?" She makes quotation marks with her fingers.

"Maybe ..." I hum. "If he's going to fire my ass."

"But what if he doesn't?" she says.

"Then at least I got it off my chest and got a fat paycheck with it as well. There's no way in hell that I'm not going to get paid for the shit he pulled. I have it on paper."

She holds out her hand for a high-five. "You go, girl!"

My phone suddenly rings again and both our eyes zap toward it like a hawk zooming in on prey. Of course, it's Leo.

When I move my hand to grab the phone, Stephanie pushes me and snatches it away. "No, nu-uh."

"I wanted to press decline."

"Of course ..." she jests. "I know you're dying to hear his excuses, but I'm not letting him hurt you again." She turns off my phone and places it on my nightstand. "Ignore that fucker. Write your story, get it off your chest ... and then we're going shopping."

I smile, grinning when she holds up my purse and takes out his credit card. "Time to put this baby to use."

"You're evil," I say.

"I know. Don't you just love it?"

"He's gonna be so pissed when he finds out."

"If he finds out."

"He will," I say. "He's not stupid."

"I'll take all the blame, baby." She slaps my bum. "Now go type so we can get to the mall quicker. I'm not letting you off the hook until you promise me that you'll stop giving him the time he doesn't deserve from you."

"Fine, fine, I promise," I say, when she pokes me.

"Good. It's girl-time now."

CHAPTER NINETEEN

Later that evening...

Stephanie and I got wasted. After shopping, we paid a visit to a few bars and let me tell you, the fine pieces of man-meat I found there surely had me distracted in the nicest of ways. Too bad none of them wanted to take me home. I'm sure I hung on their lips, sometimes quite literally, but I don't think they liked the smell of liquor. Oh well.

As I drop down on the bed, sighing, trying to ignore the zinging thrill running through my veins because of all the alcohol, I think about how much I want cock right now. There, I said it. And not just any cock, although any could suffice, but I'm sure I would be thinking of someone else's cock if I was fucking someone right now. And that someone would always be Leo.

Goddammit.

I roll myself over my bed, giggling when half of my body flops to the floor. My balance is lost now that I'm so drunk I can barely control my muscles. I don't even care that I'm still thinking about Leo, despite my best attempts to get over him as quickly as possible. I thought any man would do to fill the void, but guess what? My vagina has a mind of its own. And it wants some right now.

Luckily, there is one last remedy to my problem.

I pick up my phone and turn it back on again. About ten missed calls from none other than Leo King. Frowning, I'm contemplating whether or not to even return his calls. He doesn't deserve it, hell no, but the fact alone that he attempted to reach me multiple times shows he cares. Or he's terrified that I'll go public with this.

I smirk to myself. Yeah, that would ruin him completely. And me. Do I care? I'm not sure.

All I care about right now is my hunger for pleasure. I guess alcohol has this unwanted effect on me. I should've remembered that before I started drinking with Stephanie in the first place. God, that girl removes all my natural reservations and together we crash and burn. But it's fucking fun to do, though.

I should do what she said. Ignore him completely.

Yes. And contact Mr. Awesome. Because I really need *his* cock right now.

FROM: doritoslover@gmail.com
TO: mrawesome@hotmail.com

Hey.
Was wondering if you had some time on your hands?
Because otherwise I'd like to have you in my hands.
Like, right now.

Xx
S.

FROM: mrawesome@hotmail.com
TO: doritoslover@gmail.com

Hey …
Quite direct today, are we?
Are you that eager to play?

A.

FROM: doritoslover@gmail.com
TO: mrawesome@hotmail.com

Yes, well, since you left me hanging yesterday, I figured I'd take this into my own hands.
Quite literally.
I want something in my hands right now … ugh.

Xx
S.

FROM: mrawesome@hotmail.com
TO: doritoslover@gmail.com

I'm sorry I left you hanging. Something came up business wise that I couldn't ignore. My sincere apologies. I will most certainly make up for it, although you should never expect such a thing. I will offer you my playtime now, for both our enjoyments, only because that is my choice. And also because you so obviously seem to need it.
Before we start, I want to ask you: is there anything we should talk about? You seem to be acting rather disorderly.

A.

FROM: doritoslover@gmail.com
TO: mrawesome@hotmail.com

Nothing to talk about, since my boss means nothing, so nothing's bothering me. I just had a few drinks and want some fun. Can you give it to me?

Xx
S.

FROM: mrawesome@hotmail.com
TO: doritoslover@gmail.com

Nothing's changed then, I see. Whether that's good or not I'll leave up to you. I will not tell you what to do with your private life. I will only tell you what to do with that pussy of yours. I'm definitely up for some fun.

Come on the app.

A.

I immediately close the email to open the app and wait for him to come online.

Mr. Awesome: Take a picture of your tits and send it to me.
S: All right, Sir. Hold on a second.

I whip out the camera and hold it in front of me while I pull up my top and shove down my bra. Flipping out my boobs, I take a couple of pictures until I find the perfect one to send to him.

Mr. Awesome: Thank you. Your tits look magnificent. I bet you imagine me tugging them until you moan.
S: Oh, God yes, Sir.
Mr. Awesome: You will appreciate what I'm going to do to them now then.
S: What then, if I may ask?
Mr. Awesome: You may, but I won't answer. You'll just have to see.

For a second, it crosses my mind that he might actually send that picture all over the internet. He wouldn't ... right? I mean, he doesn't feel like the type to do that. Plus, it's not like anyone can see my face, so nobody knows it's me. That, and I'm too tipsy to care.

Mr. Awesome: I want you to take that dildo you have and smear some lube over it. Ride it. Prep yourself with your fingers too, Princess. You cannot come until I say you can.
S: Yes, Sir.

Smiling like a lunatic, I fetch my dildo and lube and rub it and myself. It feels so good to give some much-needed attention to myself and not to anyone else. I'm not thinking about anyone else but me right now. Nope. Just me. No Leo.

Dammit.

S: Having a hard time picturing something sexy while doing this, Sir. I want to enjoy myself, but my brain keeps distracting me.
Mr. Awesome: Turn it off then. I will give you a picture you'll remember.

I check the picture he just sent me and, oh boy, is it hot. His cock in all its glory, held by his hand, and right underneath it is my picture. My boobs. Right on his desk. Holy shit.

Mr. Awesome: I'm going to enjoy myself all over your tits. Want more, Princess?
S: Yes, please.
Mr. Awesome: Use the dildo first. Send me a picture of your filled pussy. Then I might.

I do what he asks, circling my entrance with the dildo before pushing in. I'm already wet and willing, and it feels so good to have it inside me, even if I wish it was a cock instead. This will have to make do.

I start pleasuring myself, which makes snapping a photo all the more difficult but fun at the same time. I love this time with Mr. Awesome. It's so thrilling to do it with a stranger. Plus, it takes my mind off … other things.

Shaking my head, I push away the thought of 'other things' and focus on the task at hand. I'm getting quite flustered, especially at the thought of what Mr. Awesome is doing to my picture right now. I quickly send my pictures to him, hoping he'll send something back.

Mr. Awesome: **Your pussy looks so good. I can imagine burying myself deep inside you.**
S: **Me too, Sir.**
Mr. Awesome: **Would you like that, Princess?**
S: **Yes, Sir, but you know that won't happen. You don't want this to be more than anonymous sex.**
Mr. Awesome: **Right.**

It's quiet for a while, but then suddenly I get a message. What he sends blows my mind. It's a movie clip of his cock, and when I press play, I get so turned on I almost explode right away. He's blowing his load all over my tits.

Mr. Awesome: **Coming all over your tits felt good. I hope you enjoyed watching that.**
S: **Oh, my God, that was hot.**
Mr. Awesome: **Good. Now I want you to come while watching it.**
S: **Yes, Sir!**

It doesn't take me long, nor is it hard. All I have to do is visualize his body, his physique, him coming all over me instead of a picture of my tits, and I'm done for. I come apart and drop down on the bed, pulling the dildo out of me. For a few minutes, I just lie there, staring at the ceiling, letting the silence sink in.

I should feel happy because endorphins are flooding my body, but I'm not. This feels wrong. Bad, even. Like I'm not supposed to enjoy this. I hate being alone.

I get up and clean the dildo then text Mr. Awesome.

S: **It felt good for me, too.**
Mr. Awesome: **Did you do as I told you?**
S: **Yes, Sir. I came because of you.**
Mr. Awesome: **What do we say then?**
S: **Thank you, Sir.**
Mr. Awesome: **Good. Is there anything else you want to do**

or talk about?

S: Well, that's unlike you, Sir.

Mr. Awesome: You're correct, but in this case I have something to make up, so I am free to talk if you wish.

I sigh and mull around before making a decision.

S: No, I'm fine. Thank you.

Mr. Awesome: All right. We'll speak again soon.

S: Yes, Sir. Thank you again.

Mr. Awesome: My pleasure. Literally.

I smile then put my phone away. Even though I am in the mood to talk to someone, I don't want it to be him. I barely know him. He can't console me. He can't hold me and comfort me. He can't take me out for a drink or come dance with me in a pub. Well, he can, but he won't because of the rules …

Guess I'll have to think about this later, when I'm sober.

***

The next morning…

I get up from bed with a hangover and some coffee, and I grab my laptop. Then I start typing away about my experience with Leo King. The words flow out like a river, and I feel unstoppable. Invincible even. Just penning down how horrible he is makes me grin because I love being an evil bitch for once. Besides, it's not like anyone will see this.

Yet.

Suddenly, my doorbell rings, and I'm pulled from my thoughts. I check the time, which somehow flew by. Looking at myself in the mirror, I pat down my hair and clothes until I look presentable. I double check if I really put the dildo away last night before opening the front door.

The face that appears behind it makes me scream out loud.

"Wow, I must look like a grizzly bear to you."

CHAPTER TWENTY

I almost have a heart attack right there and then.

"Leo?" I gasp.

Leo's raised eyebrows and plastered on smile immediately make me growl.

"What in the hell are you doing here?" I say. How did he get back from his parents so quickly? Did he follow me home? "Never mind, I don't even want to know. Bye."

I attempt to close the door, but he places his foot between the door and frame.

"Wait; I'm not here to be a bother."

"Well, you *are*," I snarl, trying to shove the door in his face. However, he's quite persistent, holding on to the wood. "Let go of my door, Leo."

"I know you don't want to listen to me, but you have to know that I'm sorry. It's all one big mistake."

"Yeah, tell that to the woman who told me she's your real wife. How many do you have? Five? Do you tell all of them they're just faking it?" I make a face when he laughs.

"No, it's not at all like that. She is my wife, yes, but only on paper," he says.

"Oh, so you collect them like trophies? Is that it?" I wince.

"No, stop putting words into my mouth." He sighs. "I'm sorry. I'm an asshole, I know."

"Damn right you are. Now, tell me why you're here because I'm really not in the mood to talk."

He chuckles. "Damn, you're so feisty."

I sigh out loud. "Leo…"

"What?" He leans in. "I like it."

"And you think that I give a shit right now? Smooth talking won't get you out of this mess, mister."

"No … but you should know that I *do* give a shit. I give *a lot* of shit. And I'll try to smooth talk my way out of anything; you know me." He smiles so seductively with his eyes half-mast, eyeing me up like he wants a piece of this ass. Well, he ain't getting any.

"I know, which is why I won't let you use me for your own pleasure again."

"What?" Now he's the one making the face. "You really think I …?"

"You used me," I reiterate, getting up in his face. "Which makes you an even bigger asshole than I could've fathomed."

"Hmpf." He steps back. "If that's how you think of me." His voice is laced with regret, although I'm not sure if it's because of what he's done to me, or that he got caught.

"I came to apologize, but you don't seem to want to talk to me, which is okay. I understand." He rummages in the pocket of his coat and takes out a check. "I wanted to give you this."

I frown as he hands it over to me. "What's this?"

"For the expenses. Traveling back must've cost you."

I look at the paper which says about a thousand dollars. Jesus Christ.

"I can't take this," I say, pushing it back into his hand.

"You have to. I'm not letting you pay for your flight back home. That was on me," he says, refusing to take back the check.

I sigh, swallowing away the lump in my throat. Then I tuck the paper in my pocket. Leo's already turned around and is walking down the path. I feel like I should say something, even though I hate him so much right now. Some part of me also wants to believe in the good part of him … even if I can hardly see it right now.

"Thank you," is all I can muster up.

He waves back at me, and then steps into his car, throwing me a final glance before driving off.

Why do I feel so wrong about this?

CHAPTER TWENTY-ONE

Two days later

With a heavy heart and a heavy ass from eating all the chocolates I had stored in my emergency cabinet, I get myself to work. Papers have piled up and my inbox has my eyes rolling into the back of my head, looking at the sheer volume of replies. I hope Leo will still pay me extra for doing what we did, plus this extra work I now have from not being able to answer all the phone calls and emails that I had when I was away. Being his assistant doesn't pay well, and I'm not sure I want to keep this job after what happened. Of course, no way in hell am I leaving before he gives me a big, fat paycheck to take home.

On top of that, I just noticed my natural dark brown hair is growing back. Eew. Better get a dye job quickly, I do not want to lose my redhead factor. It's about the only thing that looks good on me.

Suddenly, an email pops up on my screen that I can't ignore.

FROM: mrawesome@hotmail.com
TO: doritoslover@gmail.com

Are you up for some play? I have something filthy in mind.

A.

FROM: doritoslover@gmail.com
TO: mrawesome@hotmail.com

Sorry, but I'm too busy with work right now. Another time?

Xx
S.

FROM: mrawesome@hotmail.com
TO: doritoslover@gmail.com

Suit yourself. No promises.

A.

I frown. Well, isn't he a joy. God, what is up with all these men and wanting to get a piece of me? I'm going to give them a piece of my mind, instead, if they keep going like this. What happened to being civilized? Or at least pretending to be. That would be better than nothing. Well, if they're not going to be then neither am I.

I click away the email and right then the office phone rings.

"Leo King's office, Samantha speaking."

"We need to talk."

It's Leo, and I immediately feel the urge to chuck the phone at his office. However, that wouldn't be productive … or legal.

I sigh. "What do you want, Leo?"

"I want you in here. *Now.*"

"Is it about work? Because otherwise you can suck it."

"Don't tell me about sucking anything, Miss Webber, because you know damn well that it makes me think of other, less talkative things to do."

I make a face. "As if."

"If you don't get your round ass in here right now, I will fire it." I can hear him tap his fingers on the desk through the phone.

"You wouldn't," I growl.

He hums. "Maybe."

"Asshole. After everything I did for you ..." I hiss through the phone.

He chuckles. "Keep saying that, Miss Webber. You know I like it."

"So, now we're back to last names only? You really do go through girls quickly."

"Insult me more because it only turns me on."

"What do you want?" I ask, tired of these games.

"Was I not clear enough? I want you. In my office. Right now."

And then he slams the phone down before I have the chance to rebut again. I stare at the microphone with my mouth open, a disapproving sound leaving my lips. I'm going to give him such an ass whooping if he's really going to fire me. There's no way in hell I'm losing out on all that money he promised me. No fucking way.

My chair rolls back a few as I shoot up and waltz into his office, slamming the door shut behind me. "What?"

His eyes light up like a fire has been lit. I feel like gasoline. We're surely going to explode.

He gets up from his chair. "We need to talk."

"About what? That you're a pig?"

He raises a brow. "Does it make you feel good to call me names?"

"As a matter of fact, yes," I snarl. "It does."

"Continue, then. Please." He smiles. "Don't keep it all inside. Let it out. It's good for you."

"I don't want you to tell me what's good for me," I growl, huffing. Why does he make me so angry? I feel like I could scream.

"You want me to give you more fuel to hate me, but I won't." He chuckles. "It can't get any worse than this."

"I doubt that. You've been lying about that woman, so who knows what more you've been lying about."

"Not much, actually. And technically, I didn't lie about her. I just didn't tell you. There's a huge difference there. I don't like lying, I just like hiding things."

"Oh, you call that hiding?" I cross my arms. "Deliberately keeping information to yourself to benefit you but not the other? I call that straight-out lying." I take a deep breath. "But who cares, I mean, you got what you wanted, right?"

"Sam." He frowns. "Don't say that, it's not at all like that."

"Whatever. As long as I get my payment. I'll be out of here before you know it, and you can get a new assistant again. Some new ass for you to conquer," I sneer, cocking my head. "Now, if you'll excuse me, I have *real* work to do."

He walks to me and grabs my arm when I'm about to open the door. "Wait. I'm not finished yet."

"What do you want from me, Leo?" I jerk my arm free.

"First, let me apologize. I dragged you into this and it's my fault you're feeling this way, however—"

"I don't want to hear your excuses, Leo. It won't help." I frown. "You ... you made me believe that ..."

"Believe what?" he asks, leaning in further.

"You kissed me. And then ... I thought it was only for show because you kept saying that, but then you kept doing it, and somehow we ended up in bed together."

"Uh-huh," he says, placing his hand on the door behind me.

"We had sex, Leo. I thought you liked me. I thought it was because you genuinely wanted me."

"Who says I don't?" Now he places his other hand on the door, trapping me between his arms. Shit. I can't get away now.

"Your *wife* came to our hotel, Leo. The *real* one. You used me for your own sexual pleasure."

He winces, frowning like he's confused. "Is that what you think this is? That I just used you for sex?"

"After all of this ... How can I not think that? You've been using me all along."

He bites his lip, gazing straight into my eyes with those flaring, needy, gorgeous eyes of his ... and oh, God, I'm doing it again. I see only the good side while there is plenty of bad in that devilish man. *Stop it, Sam!*

He leans in even further, making it hard for me to breathe as I'm pushed against the door and I feel his body against mine.

"And here I thought you kind of liked what I did back there in the hotel," he murmurs, licking his lips.

"I didn't say that I didn't," I murmur, feeling his hot breath against my skin. It's hard to keep my cool … and my resolve.

One of his hands moves to my waist and pulls me closer. "And you think my concern to pleasure you was only for my own satisfaction?" he muses with half-mast eyes.

"That's how it feels …" I gasp when his hand moves to my ass and squeezes it.

His head moves to my ear. "Tell me how I can persuade you that your feelings aren't correct …" he whispers.

My lips shudder and my breath comes out in hitches as he places a kiss on my neck.

"Because, contrary to what you believe, I didn't just have sex with you because of my own horniness, Miss Webber." He places another kiss right below my ear, causing goosebumps to scatter on my skin. "This isn't just a one-time fling. At least, it doesn't have to be." His hand moves to my front, down my dress and curls underneath, crawling up my thighs. I'm having a hard time forming any coherent thoughts right now, let alone a sensible response.

"But you used me as a fake wife while you had a real one …" I whimper when his fingers brush my pussy. "I shouldn't have said yes."

"Why did you then?" he muses.

"Because I was afraid I'd lose my job if I didn't."

"I wouldn't fire you," he says. "How could I?" he growls, biting his lip in such a seductive way it has me all riled up. Especially when he starts rubbing my panties. Oh, God.

"So it was just an empty threat?" I ask.

"No, more a move of a desperate man." He nips on my earlobe and sucks on it, making me moan. "You have to believe me. I didn't want it to go the way it did."

I shake my head. "Wait … what?" Coming to my senses, I push him off me.

"I didn't want her to come."

"Yes, but you just admitted that your threat to fire me was vapid. You had me sign a contract knowing it would go your way regardless."

"Yes … well, I like to get my way." A smirk grows on his face. "Nothing wrong with that. At least, I didn't hear you complain when I gave it to you. And trust me, there's much more if you only give it a try."

I wince. I should so slap the shit out of this guy right now, and I'm so very tempted to do exactly that … if it wasn't for the charges that'd be hanging above my head if I did. "I knew it. You used me. It was all a lie." I turn around and open the door before I do something illegal … like smack him over the head with a plant and bury his corpse somewhere no one can find it. Maybe I'm overreacting, but sometimes a bitch just wants to kill someone. "You're disgusting."

"Where are you going? We were just getting started," he says.

"Go fuck some other assistant, since you seem to care so much about fucking and so little about speaking the truth."

"Hey … that's not fair," he says. "I don't just *fuck* anyone."

"Well, you screwed me over all right."

"Wait." He grabs my hand, but I jerk free. "I'm not done yet."

"I am. Bye." And then I waltz out the door as quickly as I came. I won't let that man seduce me. Not again.

CHAPTER TWENTY-TWO

I went straight home after what he did in his office. I can't believe I almost fell for his tricks again. Seducing me like that while he knows perfectly well what he did. I would punch him in the face if I wouldn't end up in jail. He's not worth the trouble.

On my laptop, I type so fast the keyboard might break. This story needs to get out of my heart and on paper as soon as possible. I'm writing as much as I can, looking up information in between, trying to make my stories as slick as possible. They're not just about Leo King now. Oh no, I'm way past that chapter. I'm actually writing some articles so I can sell them to a magazine and hopefully land a new job.

That's right, I'm going to quit and find something else to do. Something meaningful, somewhere far away from that prick.

I'm away from the office, even though it's not allowed, but whatever. What's he going to do? Fire me? Good luck.

I love writing. Heck, this has been my dream from day one—to write articles for a bustling magazine. I adore the idea of finding my own words on paper, especially when they're read by many. Specifically when talking about relationships, traveling, or faraway countries. Yeah, that'd be nice. If I could travel the world and write about all the cultures I visited, and it'd all be at the cost of the magazine, that would be like … ugh, a dream come true.

Sadly, dreams have always just been dreams for me.

I've yet to pursue it. I simply didn't have the funds to visit the classes necessary to write good articles. Heck, I didn't even have money to pay my own rent, which is why I ended up working for Leo King. I kind of just rolled into that job because I needed the money, although the experience looks nice on my resume as well.

Now, not so much.

Which is why I've decided that today is the day I take up my lifelong dream again. Write until you drop dead, right? Yeah … But somehow, every time I come up with a good subject to write about, I can only think about Leo and how much I want to shove the pen I'm holding into his ass. I can't concentrate for shit. Time to call out the big guns.

Distraction.

Good distraction.

FROM: doritoslover@gmail.com
TO: mrawesome@hotmail.com

Hey,

How are you? I could use someone to talk to right now, but if you don't have time, I completely understand.

Xx
S.

FROM: mrawesome@hotmail.com
TO: doritoslover@gmail.com

I'm fine, but I think you want me to ask *you* that question. Reversed psychology.

Anyway, is there anything I can do to lighten up your mood? Let me guess … your boss is an asshole?

A.

FROM: doritoslover@gmail.com
TO: mrawesome@hotmail.com

Gee, how'd you guess? LOL
Really, I want to shove my pen up his ass. And I would if I was near him. Hypothetically, of course. I hope the CIA doesn't read this shit. Don't want to end up in jail. Who knows what his connections are? He's a powerful prick, after all.

Xx
S.

FROM: mrawesome@hotmail.com
TO: doritoslover@gmail.com

How about you spend your time thinking about what I want you to do instead? That should stop your murderous thoughts. At least, from your words, I can detract you'd want to kill him. Hypothetically, of course. If the CIA is reading along, at least they know how much he's hurt you. Don't tell me where you bury his body, though. I don't want to be an accomplice.

A well-meant apology for him, from me, in his place. You deserve better.

A.

FROM: doritoslover@gmail.com
TO: mrawesome@hotmail.com

LOL. You make me laugh. Don't apologize, it's not your fault. I refuse to feel down because of him, so … bring it on! I'm ready to play ;)

... Sir.

Xx
S.

FROM: mrawesome@hotmail.com
TO: doritoslover@gmail.com

All right ... we'll do something else today if you're up for it.
I want you to go shopping. Buy yourself something nice.
Something sexy. Lace. A little bit of black ... or red. I want to see
what you look like in those clothes. We'll play when you get back
home. That way you have something to look forward to.

A.

FROM: doritoslover@gmail.com
TO: mrawesome@hotmail.com

Yes, Sir! I'm on it. Luckily, I still have his credit card so this
should be fun!
Screw the rules. I'm going to make him regret giving this to me.

Xx
S.

FROM: mrawesome@hotmail.com
TO: doritoslover@gmail.com

Hahaha, you cheeky girl. I will have to punish you for that later ...
that's no way to behave. However, I will allow you to use it, only

once. I will make you spank yourself for purposefully doing something bad, though.

I like it when my Princess is bad, but only in a naughty way. Not in a bitchy way.

Now go buy 1 item with that credit card. 1 item. Nothing more.

I expect you to be back in two hours. Talk to me on the app when you are.

A.

FROM: mrawesome@hotmail.com
TO: doritoslover@gmail.com

Yes, Sir. I'm sorry, I should know better … it's just so hard not to be bad.

I'm going shopping now. I'll speak to you later!

Xx
S.

I close down my laptop, grab my purse, and hurry my perky ass out of the door to do some happy shopping.

***

One hour later …

It doesn't take me long to find the perfect outfit for Mr. Awesome with both black and red in the fabric. Just thinking about putting it on and showing it off to him already gets me high from endorphins. God, what a good fuck partner can do to you. Sometimes I wish he was my boyfriend, but I guess that's just wishful thinking.

Plus, it would be kind of weird … what if he was totally not my type? We'd never be able to get it off like we do on the phone if that was the case. Nope, what we have now is pretty good, and I don't want to spoil it.

I'll just have to think about what to do about this situation while enjoying a nice pumpkin spice latte. Nothing like some coffee after a shopping spree.

Right when I sit down at a table in the corner of Starbucks, I hear a couple talking quite loud, which immediately draws my attention.

Holy … shit.

Oh, my God.

It's Leo and that woman, Marilyn.

CHAPTER TWENTY-THREE

"What the ..." I mutter to myself, putting down my coffee.

I listen to the conversation they're having while trying not to be noticed.

"You had to go and ruin it," Leo says.

"I was *trying* to help you," Marilyn says.

"No, you were trying to sabotage me. Like you always do."

"I'm not! I was trying to help you out."

"Tsk, you call that helping? Showing up after telling me you wouldn't?" He frowns. "You told me you didn't want anything to do with me."

She fake smiles. "That's because of your choices, not mine."

He sets his coffee cup down so hard the coffee splashes over the edges. "I didn't choose for you to be the horrible stuck-up bitch you are."

Holy shit. Talk about marital fights. This shit is real.

"Well, excuse me for finally giving you what you deserve."

"Is that what you want? To hurt me?" Leo stands up. "You've done it, all right. You try to ruin my chances with this company. With her. You ruin everything."

My cheeks flush. *With her?* Does he mean me?

He grabs his coffee cup and throws it in the trash. "I'm out of here. Talk to me when you're ready to quit this crap."

"Leo ... we're not done talking yet."

"I am." He grabs his coat and waltzes toward the door, leaving her there. While I wonder what the fuck is going on, Leo suddenly turns his head and looks straight in my direction.

The moment he sees me, his eyes widen and he freezes in place.

Oh, shit.

Oh, fucking shit.

No!

I duck, not wanting to be seen, but of course, it's already too late for that. Ridiculous. Hiding like I'm a kid.

Instead, I grab my cup and make a run for it, out the other exit.

"Sam?" I hear him call, but I'm already well on my way running the other direction.

Oh God, I do not want to talk to him right now. It feels as if I just snooped on a very private conversation, even though it was loud and clear for everyone to hear in Starbucks. I wasn't the only one ogling the fighting couple, but oh boy, the moment Leo saw me, shit has just fallen down on top of me.

Goddammit. Why did he have to come here, out of all places? It's like my favorite place, and now even that is ruined.

"Sam, wait!" he yells.

I can hear his footsteps behind me. I'm not nearly as fast as he is.

I look back to see his concerned face, and all it makes me do is wish I never came here.

But then my feet bump into a pot and my face is slapped by a plant, and I'm almost tumbling over until Leo catches my hand.

"Gotcha."

"Oh, my God," I say, pulling myself away from him as quick as I can.

"I can explain," he says, holding up his hands. "What you saw in there was real."

"Jesus, can we not do this here? Please?" I ask, looking around.

"All right. I don't want to make a scene. Let's go sit on that bench over there and talk things out."

"What guarantee can you give me that I'll feel better afterward?"

He cocks his head. "I promise you will. If not, I'll give you free rein to slap the living shit out of me."

I want to give him a chance. I mean … if he really meant me when he said that she ruined his chance with me, maybe he does care more about me than I thought. "Promise?" I say.

"Promise. She already slapped me on this cheek, so I might as well let you do the other half."

"Leo!" I bark. "Are you kidding me?"

"I wish," he chuckles. "She hits quite hard."

I roll my eyes, laughing a little to myself because I don't want to give him the satisfaction. But when he sees my smile, a smirk appears on his face.

"I like it when you laugh."

"Oh, c'mon. Keep the flattery to yourself. Let's get this over with."

"I meant it, though," he says with a wink. "Your smile is like coffee. Addictive. Rich."

"Bitter," I add.

Now, he laughs. "No, that's just you, and for the right reasons."

"Hmm … tell me about it."

"I will."

We sit down on the bench. I place my plastic bag with the sexy outfit in my corner so he won't snoop, and I lean as far away from him as I can. I don't want my physical attraction for him to cloud my judgment.

"So … did she really hit you? You know that's a criminal offense, right?"

"I called her a bitch, so I guess I deserved it." He laughs. "I don't mind. I'm not going to sue her over it. Sometimes you just get what you deserve." He smirks, looking my way. "Like with you. I definitely got what I deserved from you. And I'm sorry I put you through all that."

I sigh. "All right. I'm going to give you a chance to tell me why you lied to me, but you'd better not lie to me again, mister …" I growl.

He chuckles. "I wouldn't dare."

The way his eyes narrow and his lips tip up into a devious smile tells me that this man enjoys pushing my buttons. I sip from my cup when he notices I'm looking at him smile. Goddammit. I feel caught in the act. Luckily, the steam from my coffee camouflages my red cheeks.

He rubs his hands together and clears his throat. "Okay … here we go."

"This should be interesting …" I murmur.

"Not really, more like embarrassing." He raises his eyebrows. "Basically, I am married to her. Legally."

"So, she *is* your wife?"

"Yes."

"It's not fake or anything?"

"Well ... the thing is, it's kind of against my will."

I frown, looking sideways at him, because I can't believe what I'm hearing. "What?"

"It's complicated."

"That's an understatement," I jest.

"Hmm ..."

When he doesn't speak up again, I say, "Start at the beginning. That way I can get the complete picture."

"Well, Marilyn is one of the oldest relations of the company."

I snort when I hear the word old. I imagine her with wrinkles, and it makes me feel good. Yes, I'm that childish.

"She's worked with us even before I became the CEO."

"The company belonged to your father."

"Yes," he says. "And I used to work closely with her. Until I became CEO."

"Oh ..." Everything starts to click. "Instead of her."

"Exactly. Because of her outstanding work for the company, she expected to get the job, but then I did," he muses. "And that didn't go down well with her. We talked a lot. Yelled a lot. There were plenty of fights in the office, and I totally understood her anger. She felt betrayed. And I didn't want to lose a friend. Neither did she. I mean, we were basically torn apart by this position. I almost didn't want to take it."

Leo glances my way with the most sincere look I've seen in ages.

"I thought I could handle it, and these last few months were going so well, I thought she was over it already. I mean, everything was going well."

He sighs, and I take a sip from my coffee to take it all in for a second.

He shakes his head. "Marilyn has always had this ... thing for me." He smashes his lips together. "I didn't realize it at the time until it was too late."

"Until you were suddenly married?" I laugh. "Sorry, that was a bad joke."

"It's funny because that is actually what really happened."

"What?" I exclaim. "You must be shitting me, right?"

"I wish." He rolls his eyes. "Seriously, if I'd known, I would have never have gone to Vegas with her."

I lean forward. "What really happened when you were there?"

"We were celebrating a deal she'd just made for the company. Of course, I let myself get carried away. I mean, she practically begged me to party with her. I couldn't say no, after all our arguments. I wanted us to be good again."

"And then you got married …"

"While I was drunk, yeah."

"But you got married." I make a face. "I mean, you have to take accountability for it."

"She got me drunk. On purpose."

"What?" I gasp.

"She admitted it to me. On the phone." He takes a deep breath. "She said she wanted to make me feel what I'd made her feel all those years. That's when I knew it was deep."

"Wait … what? She baited you into a marriage?"

"I feel uncomfortable that I have to admit it, but yes."

"Holy shit," I say.

"Tell me about it."

Suddenly, laughter bursts from my mouth. Uncontrollable, loud, stupid laughter. "I'm sorry," I say. "I shouldn't be laughing at this. That's bad."

"No, it's all right. I know, it's pathetic."

I gulp down some coffee to stop myself from laughing.

"I wish that was all there's to it. I mean, I was in shock when I realized that I'd married her."

"I can imagine. With a woman like her …" I shake my head. "Actually, I don't want to imagine." My body shivers from the thought.

He chuckles. "Me either, which is why I was even more horrified when I found out she did it on purpose. Even when I told her I didn't want to get married and that it was all one huge mistake, she didn't want to quit."

"What? You mean she's stringing you on, on purpose?"

"She won't let go of me as her husband until she gets a large bonus. She says it's only fair because I stole her job, so this is the payment."

My jaw drops. "Are you kidding me?"

"I wish I was, but she really believes she has a right to the company, and now that she's found a way in, there's no way she's letting it go."

"Oh, my God. Some people ..." I'm at a loss for words.

"It gets worse because when my parents found out they believed it was real. They wanted to meet her. Then news started spreading about my marriage to her, next thing I know even business partners wanted to meet her. They'd heard she was behind a lot of deals for the company, which is true."

I nod along, listening to his longwinded story.

"Except, she wasn't at all willing to pretend to actually be my wife until everything had calmed down, so we could organize an annulment and arrange something for the family to believe. I mean, she blatantly said no to every idea I had. She just would not give up on trying to get the annulment through as quickly as possible, sucking me dry of my money."

"Jesus," I mutter.

"Basically, she just said screw you. She wanted me to suffer. She was waiting for a chance to see me fail, like, with my family and having to tell them it was all one big fucking joke ... She wants me to make a fool out of myself."

"But why did she show up at the hotel then?" I ask.

He frowns. "I don't know, really. Maybe she changed her mind. Or maybe she realized what I was doing and made an attempt to sabotage it." He looks at me with a sarcastic smile on his face. "She enjoys ruining me."

I shake my head, unable to comprehend or understand the vicious jealousy of this woman. "I can't believe it ...You're not in the process of divorcing her yet?"

"I am, but she isn't. She has yet to sign the annulment. I don't think she ever will do it, at least not willingly."

"Well, can't we make her do it then?"

"We?" He narrows his eyes at me, smiling like the smug bastard he is. "Hmm ... you sure do want to get me out of that marriage quickly. I'd almost be inclined to say you want me for yourself."

I shove him. "You know what I mean. I want to help."

"Your help is much appreciated, although I don't think it will make her sign the contract. Plus, I don't want to bother you with any more of my shit than I already have."

"Well, isn't there anything we can do?"

"I'm trying. I'm speaking with my lawyer soon, and then we'll see what can be done. But she is persistent in getting as much out of this as possible. It seems to have been her plan all along. She didn't get the CEO position, so now that she's married to me, who did, she'll suck me dry."

I frown. "What a bitch."

"Now, now … that's no way to act, Sam," he muses, gazing at me from under his eyelashes. "Even though you're right."

"Tsk, you called her a bitch yourself. No way in hell you're teaching me how to behave now." I drink the last few drops of my coffee and feel rejuvenated already. God, the truth does some good.

"True. You're always so onto me. Like a cat. Meow." He makes raking motions with his fingernails, which makes me chuckle.

"Sorry, but when I hear stories like that, I just want to cut a bitch, if you know what I mean."

"I know what you mean, and trust me, I've thought of strangling her with that fur coat she has because of the viciousness of her plans." He winks at me. "We are like-minded, you and I. I love that feistiness in you."

"Yeah, you say that a lot." I smile, looking down at the tiles on the floor.

"That's because it's true," he says.

I look up to see his gentlemanly smile, and it makes my heart flutter in a way it shouldn't. Why do I feel something for a guy who kept all of this information from me? Like, he can't be trusted, so why do I let myself feel this way?

"Why didn't you just tell me all of this, Leo? It would've made things so much easier."

"I've wanted to. Believe me, I thought about it every day. But I felt so … stupid for falling for her tricks. I didn't want you to think I was a … loser."

I sputter out my laughter when I hear that word. "Loser?"

"Yeah …" He frowns. "It's kind of dumb. I should've realized she'd do this shit. And really, who the fuck gets married while drunk? And then gets fucking extorted with it? I mean, it's like stupidity, in a nutshell."

"I don't think you're stupid. You just made stupid decisions."

"That's the same thing," he jokes.

"No. You're smart, but only when it comes to business deals. Not when it comes to how to deal with ladies."

"Are you saying I'm not a ladies' man? That's hurtful, Sam," he says with a stark voice, but I can tell he's being sarcastic, especially when he scoots closer. "If you really think that, give me a chance to show you how much of a gentleman I can be."

I lean back. "Wow, down boy, down."

He laughs. "You are so asking for it."

"For what?" I ask when he leans back against the bench, his arms draped over the back, legs spread as if he's the alpha. I kind of like the pose. It's so … manly. Dammit.

"You know what I mean," he says with a gruff voice that gets me all fired up.

"As if I would let that happen."

"But you thought about it," he says, smirking.

"Wipe that smirk off your face, Mr. King, before I do it myself." I throw my cup into the bin next to the bench.

"Oh, so we're back to last names now?"

"If I remember correctly, you were the one who started that," I retort.

"I can undo it again if you want." He leans in again. "I can undo many things."

"With your eyes, I bet." I laugh. "Keep your hands to yourself."

"Aw, but it was just getting fun again."

Fun, there he goes again. I knew it. All these sexual innuendos only lead to one thing, and that's never a great relationship. I'm looking for more than just sex.

"I need more than just *fun*. I can get that anywhere. Heck, I'm getting that plenty of times," I muse, just to get under his skin.

Suddenly, I realize I was having that kind of *fun* only an hour ago, and it's almost past the time I was given to get back. Shit!

"Argh, I have to go," I say.

"Wait, what? Why?" he asks. "We were having a nice conversation, and now you're bailing on me?"

"I'm not, but I just have this … thing I need to do."

"Does this *thing* involve running away from me? Because it sure as hell looks like that's what you're doing."

"No, I—"

"Hey, if you're not interested, all you had to do was say it," he says, smiling like an idiot.

"No, that's not what I was saying." I check my phone and notice the time. Only a few minutes left to get home. Crap!

"Then you are interested?"

"What? No, I didn't say that, either."

"Then what?" He laughs. "You're just going to leave me hanging."

"It's complicated, all right!"

"I know it is, and I'll take the blame for that. So, what's in that bag you're holding so tightly?" He points at my lingerie.

I blush, hiding the bag behind my back. "Nothing."

"Of course, there is," he chuckles.

"It doesn't concern you." I frown. "Stop being so curious. It might kill you one day."

He laughs. "It probably will. Or you will. Either way, I'm screwed."

"You bet."

"I'm trouble, I know," he jests, eyeing me from top to bottom, making me feel all self-conscious again.

I roll my eyes. "Yes, which is why I'm not going to say yes to anything you say right now. Especially not with you trying to seduce me and all."

"Oh, I wasn't trying to do anything, Miss Webber ..."

I sigh. "Oh, here we go again. You're using your charms to persuade me to forgive you."

"I thought you already had."

"Nu-uh. It takes more than just explaining what happened to forgive you for what you did. You lying ... fine piece of man ass ..."

He chuckles and gets up from the bench, too. "But you want this ass as much as I want yours."

"Not on your terms, though."

"What are your terms then?"

"I don't have time for this, Leo. I have to go, like ... right now. So, excuse me and maybe I'll see you later."

Right when I'm walking away, Leo yells, "You'd better show up for work, though."

Fucker. Even after telling me everything, admitting to me that he lied and acting like an oversexed pig, he still demands that I come work for him.

I stick up my middle finger while running away.

The saddest thing is that underneath all the hatred and loathing for his attitude, I actually still have the hots for him. It's like chocolate fudge cake; it's bad for you in so many ways, but you just can't stop eating that motherfucking delicious cake.

Ever.

CHAPTER TWENTY-FOUR

When I get home, it's already past the time Mr. Awesome and I had agreed upon. It might seem stupid that we'd adhere to rules this strongly, but that's how it works in these kinds of relationships. I have to do what he says. Otherwise, it's no fun. That's why I know I'm going to get punished for being late now.

I only hope it won't make my toes curl. It's probably going to be something insanely cruel.

As I open my phone and sit down on the couch, I quickly unpack my lingerie and struggle to put it on, almost falling nose-first into Doritos salsa that I left on the table before leaving the house. It smells so good that I take another bite before opening up the app.

S: I'm back!

It doesn't take him long to reply.

Mr. Awesome: You're late. Punishment is due.
S: I'm sorry, Sir. It won't happen again!
Mr. Awesome: I accept your apology, but you will still be punished. One strike for each minute. Grab a soft brush and hit that ass. Send me pictures as proof. I want it red and swollen.
S: Yes, Sir.

Sighing, I close the app. I shouldn't be upset because hey, I love spankings, even though I have to do it myself. I'm just disappointed that I couldn't make it in time, and … you know, please him. I'm sorry, that's just what I like … no, wait, I'm not sorry for being who I am. I love pleasing Mr. Awesome because he gives me pleasure in return. It's a mutual relationship of give and take, nothing to be ashamed about.

Too bad I can only share it with him on the phone and not in real life.

I grab my brush and position myself over the couch in a way that I can spank myself. It hits quite hard and firm but nice. It isn't supposed to be nice, I'm trying to remind myself. This is for not paying attention to the time, which I'm doing right now. One strike for each minute passed, which is fifteen. It's not hard, but by the time I'm done, my ass is sore and sizzles when I try to sit down.

S: I've completed the task, Sir.
Mr. Awesome: Pictures.

I lean back and take a few photos of my ass in the new lingerie, hoping it's visible that I got quite a few good hits. When I look at the pictures, one of them clearly shows a red, plump ass and an exact mark of where the brush landed. It looks like it would hurt a lot, but the excitement is bigger than the pain I feel.

I send him the picture.

Mr. Awesome: Well done, Princess. Did it hurt?
S: Yes, but I quite liked it, actually.
Mr. Awesome: You know that's not the goal.
S: Yes, Sir. I can't help myself. This just adds to the teasing.
Mr. Awesome: All right, I will extend your punishment then.

I frown. What is he doing?

S: Why?
Mr. Awesome: Tsk, no back talking. Behave, Princess.
S: Sorry, Sir. I just don't understand.
Mr. Awesome: I know I said we would have playtime, but I feel like your punishment should last a little longer. I don't

want you to enjoy it. I want it to be aggravating, so you learn not to do it again.

S: What do you propose then?

Mr. Awesome: I want you to go out tonight. Take a friend with you. Have a couple of drinks. You can't return until it's past twelve. Only then will we continue, and not a moment sooner. You want to please yourself? Not now. It will have to wait.

S: You're leaving me hanging?

Mr. Awesome: This is playtime, and during playtime I make the rules. The rules you obey. The rules you must follow or otherwise be punished. Did you not agree to these terms?

Wow. He sure is strict today.

S: Yes, Sir.

Mr. Awesome: Then don't question me again. Now, you will also wear the lingerie underneath your outfit when you go out. I want you to be dressed up the entire time and feel it while you walk the streets and sit down somewhere to drink. Think about the fact that these clothes mean that our playtime is still going on and that you must obey my rules. You are dressed that way for me and only for me. You will think about what I will do once you come back home, but no sooner than midnight. Yearn for it, Princess. You'll learn to appreciate being on time.

S: Yes, Sir. I will.

I close my phone and sigh, feeling the frustration build up over the fact that I'm not getting any right now. I can choose to just ignore everything and pleasure myself anyway, but that would take all the fun out of it. I guess I'll just have to listen to him and do what he wants. In the end, I know it'll be worth it. But Jesus, he's making me wear this all night, knowing what awaits me when I get home. It's like dangling a cookie in front of my eyes but never giving it to me.

Well, no point in wasting time. Better go cook and invite Stephanie to come and join me for a few drinks. I'm making spaghetti carbonara the way my grandma taught me with fresh ingredients. While dicing the onions, I text Stephanie.

Samantha: Hey girl, u up for a night out in town? We should catch up.

It takes her a while to respond.

Steph: Hey!! Sry, but I'm with a guy right now.
Samantha: OMG, rly? Don't fk with me.
Steph: No joke. 10+ on the looks.
Samantha: U have to send me a pic later, kk?
Steph: Yeah, first thing tomoz, but first gonna enjoy a wild night.
Samantha: Big one?
Steph: HUGE! Mouth = on floor. *lick*
Samantha: Nice! Gimme some of that.
Steph: He knows exactly what to do with his fingers... so I'm good!
Samantha: *Jelly*
Steph: I'll clone him for you.
Samantha: LOL, yes please. Could use a real man right now.
Steph: Sry honey. I wanna come join u, but I can't pass on this guy. Rain check?
Samantha: Ofc. Dw. Have fun!
Steph: Thanks!

Moments after I put down my phone, I get another text. Surprisingly, it isn't from Stephanie.

Leo: Can we talk?
Samantha: That depends on what you have in mind.
Leo: Oh, nothing special. Just a continuation of this afternoon.
Samantha: Only if you behave.
Leo: Swear on my life.
Samantha: Why do I not believe you?
Leo: *crosses fingers*
Samantha: I knew it. It's impossible.

What an asshole, but he makes me chuckle, nonetheless.

Leo: You just have to accept that our attraction is undeniable.

Samantha: My fist in your face… that's undeniable.

Leo: I'll take that. I'll take anything if it comes from you.

Samantha: Is that supposed to be flattering? Or just plain-old stalkerish?

Leo: I'll go with the latter. Never refuse a refreshing outlook on life.

Why is it that this man always brings a smile to my face? It's like my brain is sending two totally different signals. Stop it, brain.

Samantha: You're crazy.

Leo: Crazy for wanting to hang out with you, but I do.

That just made me want to barf. He's really trying to charm his way back. That, or he's despicable for insulting me.

Samantha: Keep going and I'll leave you hanging.

Leo: You won't …

Samantha: Who knows?

Leo: I do because you need to know what I meant when I told Marilyn she was the reason I lost my chances with you.

Shocked, I gasp at my phone, almost dropping it in the trash, where I was just throwing the eggshells in. How does he know?

Leo: Oh, yes, I know you heard everything. Surprised?

It takes me a few seconds to come up with a witty response.

Samantha: Hardly. Everyone could hear your fight.

Leo: Oh, so that's why it took you so long to reply.

Samantha: I was busy cracking eggs, and then had to contemplate whether to throw them away or bring them with me so I could throw them at your face.

Leo: HA! So we have a date.

Samantha: A date? No. Hell no.

Leo: But you're coming to see me, so I'd call that a date.

Samantha: Call it whatever you want. I just need a drink.

Leo: That can be arranged. As long as you come meet me.

Samantha: Just a drink and talk. Nothing more.

Leo: I can't promise anything except the drinks.

I roll my eyes.

Samantha: Fine. Dive Bar around nine-ish.

Leo: I don't do 'ish'. I'll be there at nine. If you aren't, I'll wait.

Samantha: Oh, such a gallant knight.

Leo: I can be anything you want, Sam. You just need to imagine it.

Samantha: I imagine a lot of things, but they never come true. Only the bad stuff. Especially when it concerns you.

Leo: But you do imagine things with me. That's a start. A good start. Imagine me doing a whole lot more.

Samantha: Oh, here we go again.

Leo: Don't blame me for trying.

Samantha: I don't know why you bother.

Leo: I don't know why you think I wouldn't. See you around nine.

I mull over those last words as I'm really trying to make sense of it all. Is he really that interested in me? Or is it just a game to him? A way to get me in bed? Again, I might add. I shouldn't fall for it and not be so stupid as to go out with him, but I really need the distraction, and Mr. Awesome has ordered me to go and have a fun time, so basically … I'm screwed.

CHAPTER TWENTY-FIVE

I make my way to the local pub, the Dive Bar, where I find Leo sitting at a table already.

"Sam ... how lovely of you to actually come and join me," he says, smiling widely. He gets up from his chair and holds out his hands. "Let me take your coat."

"Acting all chivalrous now, huh?"

"It's not an act," he muses, winking at me when he comes closer.

He stands behind me as I slip off my coat, his fingers gently stroking my arms, creating goosebumps everywhere. The scent of his aftershave is quite strong today. That, or I'm seriously addicted to his smell. Damn.

We sit down at the table, which surprisingly also has a couch to the side, and he orders beer for the both of us.

"I'm surprised you actually said yes," he says.

"To what?"

"Coming here."

"Oh, I thought you meant the fake wife thing," I say, breathing out a sigh of relief.

"That, too." He chuckles. "I didn't expect any of it to go the way it did, to be honest. And I don't mean you. You ... you were perfect." He gives me a cute smile that makes it hard for me to retort.

"I'm surprised I went along with it all. Well, you did threaten to fire me," I say as the waitress puts down our drinks.

"I shouldn't have, and I'm sorry. It was a stupid decision by a cornered, desperate man."

"For once we agree."

He laughs. "Well, to be fair, it was a great temporary solution to my problem."

"How? I mean, honestly, how long did you think we could keep up this charade?"

"Honestly? A while. We were convincing. My parents believed it."

"Yeah, but for how long? And what would it have mattered if you had to tell them the truth anyway?"

He sucks in some air. "I wasn't actually planning on telling them to begin with."

"What?" I exclaim.

"I just wanted them to believe it was real so I could fake-divorce you and then have it all be over with."

"So you were planning on keeping this real all along?"

"Yeah, but it was going fine."

"Fine? Are you kidding me?" I want to throw my beer at him, but that would be a waste ... of the freaking beer.

"Yeah, it was. I mean, you were definitely believable as my wife."

I take a gulp when I hear that word. He says it in a way that makes me think he's completely enamored with the idea.

"Until she showed up," he adds. "She ruined everything."

"How did she know where to go anyway?"

"Oh, I always stay at that hotel when I visit my parents. When I got that text back in our room the morning after the dinner, I knew she was up to no good."

"Ah, no wonder you were so hasty and practically dragged me out of bed."

He scratches his head. "Yeah, that was rude, I admit. I just wanted to get out of there as fast as possible."

"Before we met."

He raises his eyebrows. "Something like that." A cute smile appears on his face.

"So, she's your real wife ... How did that actually happen?"

"Well, like I said, we were celebrating a deal, she got me drunk, and then married me on purpose."

I chuckle a little. "That's it? I thought there was more to it that you just didn't want to tell me. But that's all there's to it?"

"Yeah?" he asks as if he isn't sure. "What else should there be?"

"I don't know. I actually expected you guys to … you know …" I shrug.

"You think we had sex?" he asks, his lips still parted as he waits for my answer.

"Well, no. I mean, maybe. I don't know. Did you?" I'm stumbling through the words causing my cheeks to turn red.

His left lip curls up into a smile. "If I said yes, would that make you jealous?"

"Oh, my God!" I punch his arm. "You asshole."

"It was worth a try."

"No, just no."

"Well, if it makes you feel any better, no, we did not have sex. Although, I did think about it …"

"I bet you did, you manwhore," I muse.

Now he punches me, but softly, like he's worried I might break. "She practically threw herself at me. It was hard to resist."

"Then why did you? Why not give her what she wanted?"

"It wasn't what she wanted. She was just using my lust against me so she could gain control over the company."

"Ah-ha …"

"Besides, my mind was somewhere else." He winks at me, which makes me flush even more.

"About that … you said something about chances … with me? Or something." I twirl my hair.

"You heard what I said in Starbucks." He crosses his arms and looks intently at me from across the table. "I meant every word of it."

I swallow away the lump in my throat, suddenly getting all heated up.

He leans forward and looks straight at me with those sultry eyes of his. "I wasn't lying when I said I've imagined you doing things to me while under my desk. Or when I said that you should've dressed like that long ago." He licks his lips, which makes me bite mine. Good Lord.

"There are a lot of things I think about on a daily basis and most of them involve you."

Holy crap.

I grab my bottle of beer and chug down a whole lot until I almost choke on it. I can't handle this confession. It's too much. Why? Because I have no fucking clue what to do with it. Like, he's Leo fucking King for crying out loud. The CEO of the company I work for. And he wants me … How in the world is this ever okay?

"I can't do this, Leo," I say, already tipsy drinking my second bottle. "I want more …" I sigh.

"You want what? I can give it to you. Anything you want." He gets up from his chair and scoots to the couch next to us. Then he grabs my hand and drags me there, too. I let him … I don't know why. I'm just too tempted. Or too tipsy.

"Stop questioning everything, Sam."

"But I don't believe you. After all those lies … how can I ever believe you want me?"

He places his hand on my lap and squeezes my thigh, sending all kinds of signals that make my senses go haywire. "Believe me when I say I want you."

"But you're my boss," I mutter, when his fingers start moving up and down my leg.

He leans in to whisper in my ear. "I don't care." His hot breath lingers on my skin, making me delirious with need. Oh, why did it have to be tonight that I didn't get laid? Now I'm practically panting from just his touch.

I quickly grab the next drink and take a sip, trying to ignore my feelings, or rather my bodily fluids … my pussy is definitely tingling all right. It's becoming increasingly hard to ignore the way my body yearns for him, especially considering the lingerie I'm wearing underneath my regular clothes. I almost feel like a drunk stripper, and at this rate, I might actually turn into one.

"One taste …" he murmurs in my ear, kissing me softly on my neck. "One kiss." His lips move to my earlobe and suckle on it. "One lick." A soft moan escapes my mouth, and when he stops I wish he'd continue. And then he whispers, "It's not enough."

CHAPTER TWENTY-SIX

I shudder as he retreats and leans back to look at me from top to bottom, eyeing my reaction. Just his eyes are enough to make my heart flutter. He's hunting for me like some animal. How in the world am I ever going to get through tonight? I made a promise to Mr. Awesome, but it's so damn hard to keep it together right now. I just have to keep in mind what kind of an asshole he is and that he only cares about fucking.

"Waiter! Tequila, please," I say, taking a deep breath.

Leo chuckles. "Sam, don't you think that's too much?"

"No, not with you around." I clear my throat. "Besides, I can make my own decisions perfectly fine. I don't need you to watch over me."

"I'm just worried that you're overdoing it because of me."

"Because of you?" I gasp. "Nonsense." He's right, but I won't give him more reasons to pat himself on the back.

He smiles and muffles a laugh. "Fine. One for me too, please," he says to the waiter when he brings me my drink.

"What are you doing?" I ask.

"Well, if you're getting smashed then so am I."

"Why?"

"I don't know. You tell me," he muses, narrowing his eyes.

I roll my eyes. "There's more to life than screwing with everybody you meet."

"Like drinking?"

"No, that's just a side effect of hanging out with people like you," I retort.

He laughs. "Except, I don't screw with everyone."

"Oh, I feel so special now." I take a sip of my tequila as his drink arrives.

"You should because you are."

"Oh, stop with the flattery," I say. "It won't get you anywhere."

"Then what do you want to hear? I already said I'm sorry. I already showed you how much I want you. I want to make up."

"Start by talking then," I say.

He frowns, confused. "About what?"

"Things …"

"Things?" he repeats, chuckling.

"You know, a conversation … like regular people." I smile. "Like, how was your day?"

"Good, although a bit busy and a tad difficult."

I shake my head laughing. "Oh, this is going to be a long night."

"Why? Am I that annoying?" He wriggles his eyebrows, making me laugh.

"I know you're doing it on purpose."

"Who cares." He scoots closer again and then slowly folds his arm over my shoulder. "I just want to have a good time."

I look at the clock. "Well, I have until twelve so that's how much time you get to convince me that you're not a complete asshole."

"Why twelve? Are you running away and leaving your glass slipper at the door then? Because if I have to cross the country to fit the shoe onto your foot, I will."

I giggle, and somehow, I realize that I actually quite like being in his presence.

**

After almost ten drinks, a lot of laughter, and stupid comments, I'm about as smashed as can be, and so is he. When I check the clock, three hours have passed.

"Oh, my God! It's so late," I say.

"What?" he asks, almost tipping over.

I laugh, shoving him back so he doesn't fall onto my lap.

He chuckles. "Aw, can't I just lean on you a little?"

"No, I have to go, Leo!"

"Why?"

"It's twelve 'o clock. I have to get home."

"You sound so much like Cinderella." He smirks. "You remind me of her, too."

I roll my eyes, trying to get up, but I almost fall down because I can't walk for shit after so many drinks. He grabs me and barely manages to hold onto my dress while I'm bent over, my ass sticking straight up in his face.

"Whoa."

"Nice outfit."

"What?" I say, straightening my back and patting down my dress.

He gets up from the couch just as drunk. "I see what you're hiding under there. BOO!" He laughs like a half-assed idiot.

I shove him down when he tries to get up. "Hey! Don't look under my dress, you ass."

"I can't help that you were shoving your butt up in my face."

"You caught me!" I say, stumbling across the floor.

"Yeah, you would've hit the ground if not for me."

"Well, thanks!"

"Don't mention it!"

We both walk out the door, completely wasted.

"So, what now?" he says.

"We go home."

When I start walking, he says, "Wait. Let me call my chauffeur."

"Your chauffeur? You mean a limo?"

"Yeah."

I gasp. "Are you sure?"

"Why not?" he muses as if it's the most normal thing in the world.

"Okay ..." I say, perplexed that it comes so easy to him.

I feel a little embarrassed stepping into a car this way. However, it's not like I'm going to get far in this outfit, on these heels, this intoxicated.

When the limo arrives, Leo steps forward and holds open the door for me. "After you."

"Such a knight," I jest.

"My name isn't King just for show." He winks, and we both laugh like idiots as we sit down in the backseat.

Leo tells the driver to go to my place, and then the blinds close, giving us more privacy. I search through my bag for my phone, but when I have it, Leo snatches it away.

"Hey! Give that back," I say.

"No." He tucks it into his pocket. "You have plenty of time to look at that when you're home. I want as much personal time as I can get with you."

"Tsk, you had your chance, Leo."

"Not a good one, though, considering all the shit I put you through."

"True. You did make me do a lot of stuff."

He cocks his head. "Tell me the truth. Wasn't it even just a little bit fun? Some parts?"

I roll my eyes then press my thumb and index finger together. "A tiny, tiny bit."

"Well, at least it's a start." He laughs. "I should really make up for that."

"You can start by giving me the money you promised," I say, eyeing him from the side.

"Are you afraid that I won't give it to you?"

"Maybe."

"Christ, I'm not that kind of an ass," he says, shaking his head. "Of course, I'll pay you for all the trouble I put you through. As a matter of fact, I'll double it."

I laugh. "Now you're shitting me. That's the alcohol talking, right?"

"Nope," he says with a huge grin on his face. "I just want to give back what I took from you, and since I can't give you back time, I figured money might help." He scoots closer and places a hand on my leg. "I want us to be on good terms again."

I swallow away the lump in my throat. "As friends, you mean."

He looks at me with those half-mast chocolatey eyes of his, mesmerizing me as he parts his lips. "Oh, no ... definitely not as friends."

There's an unmistakable hint of naughtiness in his eyes that I simply can't turn away from. He leans in closer and closer until his lips are so close to my skin that I can feel his hot breath tingling. Oh, dear Lord. I can't keep my resolve intact.

"Leo ..." I mumble when his fingers slide up my leg.

"I love it when you say my name like that …" he whispers in my ear. "I'll hear you scream my name tonight."

"We can't …" I mutter as he starts nibbling my earlobe. My breath comes out in short gasps because I'm unable to think straight from his nibbles and kisses. That, or it's because I'm totally smashed.

"Why not? You and I both know you want to," he murmurs, kissing my neck gently. "I want you, Sam. Come home with me. Stay the night. Let me suck your nipples, lick your pussy, and fill you with my cock until you scream my name. Say you'll let me, or by God, I will take you right here, right now."

"Do I even have a choice?" I ask, whimpering as he gets closer with each second.

"Yes, but you won't say no. I know you too well. So, one way or another, I'll have you tonight. Whether it's in this car, on my table, or in my bed. I *will* fuck you."

Oh, I give up. My body is ready.

CHAPTER TWENTY-SEVEN

His sultry voice is too much to take. Screw the promises to Mr. Awesome. To hell with getting my phone back. Fuck the time. Better yet, fuck Leo, literally. I'm going for it.

I turn around and smash my lips into his. His eager mouth returns my kisses with fervor, sucking on my lips like he's never tasted them before. Our mouths are drunk on love … and liquor, and I don't think I care even the slightest bit. Just as long as I can have him, just this night. As long as he loves me, just this night. God, I've needed this for ages.

His hand slips up my thigh, brushing along my pussy. My moan is silenced by his kiss, his tongue dipping into lick the roof of my mouth. Our tongues engage in a furious battle of lust, pure need emanating from our pores. All I can think of is his lips on my mouth, his hands on my body, and his cock deep inside me.

"Fuck, I want you so fucking much," he murmurs against my lips.

"I hate you …" I murmur.

He chuckles against my mouth. "I know you do. You hate that you want me so much, even though I'm a fucking bastard." His lips linger on mine. "Nothing's going to stop me from loving you, though. I want you too much."

"Me, too …" I can't even pronounce words properly.

I'm consumed by his tantalizing mouth, wanting it all over my body. It's never enough. His filthy mouth, dirty mind, and sexual appetite are just the kind I'm looking for. As rough, hotheaded, and dominating as Leo King is, he's exactly what I need.

"God, you taste so good, Sam," he murmurs. "I should've done this ages ago."

His words are like chocolate to me—sweet, delicious, and addicting.

For a moment, he takes his lips off me, and then he presses the intercom button. "Take us to my place."

I don't even bat my eyes as he moves in for the kill again.

I can ignore my needs all I want, but that's the truth. I want him so badly that he intoxicates me. Especially when he pushes me to the window with his body, cornering me. My breathing falters as his kisses grow deeper, leaving my lips to occasionally peck my chin and neck. One of his hands is on my waist, the other cups my face while he kisses me senseless. My fingers are entangled in his hair, pulling him closer with each kiss. It's getting so hot in here that the windows are fogging up. I don't even notice when the limo comes to a stop.

"We're here," he murmurs against my raw lips.

When he slides off me, I wish he didn't. I'm having a hard time keeping my eyes off him as he opens the door and steps out flaunting a huge hard-on. It doesn't take long before he opens my door and lifts me up in his arms. The car drives off to who knows where, but I'm stuck watching Leo's mesmerizing eyes as he walks with me up to his door and into his home. Despite me working closely with him, I've never actually been inside, and oh boy, it does not disappoint.

"Oh my," I say, staring at the high ceilings and luxurious-looking furniture, the big living room, dining room, and kitchen all connected in one. There's a huge staircase in the middle of the hallway and a chandelier illuminates the entire thing.

"Like it?" Leo asks, draping off my coat and hanging it on the hanger.

"Yeah ..." I mutter, walking into the living room. I spot a bag of Doritos lying on the table that I simply can't ignore. Liquor always makes me hungry as shit, so I grab it and take a few out. The taste is delicious, Cool Ranch, one of my favorites.

"Help yourself." Leo chuckles.

"Sorry, I just love these. It's like you knew I was coming." I laugh, eating a few more.

I sit down or rather sink into his couch. God, if I had a couch this comfy, I'd never get off my fat ass. Ever.

He walks into the room, too. "I had a bit earlier. I like the flavors."

"It's just too good," I add.

"I feel the same about you." The left side of his lip inches up into a cheeky grin, which is just too damn sexy. "Which is exactly my problem."

"Oh, I'm *your* problem now?" I scoff.

"*We've* got a problem, Miss Webber." He sits down beside me.

My jaw drops, but I have no clue what to say. "First you say you want me, now you've got a problem. I think you're the one with problems here, not me."

He cocks his head. "I didn't mean this." His finger goes from me to him and back to me. "I'm talking about the fact that you have been doing something very ... bad." The way he says it makes chills run all over my back.

"What do you mean?" I frown.

He scoots closer, folding his arm over the back of the couch so he can come near me. "You can pretend you're innocent all you want."

His free hand runs over my thigh, tickling my senses. I'm still hot and bothered from what happened in the car, and with him being this close, it's hard not to throw myself into his arms. However, I want to know what he has to say.

"But you and I both know that's not the truth," he whispers into my ear. His tongue quickly darts out for a taste.

"Hmmm ... go on," I say, curious where this game is leading.

His hands are all over the place, rubbing me in oh, such a good way, reaching and grabbing for my thighs, ass, and then up to squeeze my boob. He groans in my ear, which makes me moan as well, especially when he presses his lips to my skin again.

"You've been a bad girl," he says.

His hand slips into my pocket, and before I know it, he's taken out my wallet.

"What are you doing?" I ask.

He takes out a certain card. A credit card. The one that he sent me.

I gulp when he holds it up. "The online statements I saw this afternoon from the credit card company don't lie. You've been using this without my permission. Multiple times."

"Sorry," I blurt out. "I shouldn't have done it."

"You shouldn't have. Was it to punish me?" He raises an eyebrow.

My cheeks turn red because I'm ashamed to admit that it's true. "Sort of. I was in a very … very bad mood."

"Hmm …" He smirks, placing the credit card and my wallet on the table. "I understand your reasoning. After what I did, I expected a little payback. However, my curiosity is piqued now … tell me, what did you buy with it?"

My eyes widen and immediately I'm aware of the outfit I'm wearing underneath these clothes. I suddenly feel the urge to cover up. Oh God, what will he think of me if he sees this?

"Uh … nothing important," I say, smiling awkwardly.

His index finger tiptoes from my leg up to my thigh, toying with my senses as he expertly avoids the one spot that I want him to touch the most. "Hmm … I guess you'll tell me soon. I'll get it out of you, one way or another."

"It's kind of embarrassing, and in hindsight, kind of stupid," I say.

He chuckles. "I know, Miss Webber, which is exactly why I want to know." He leans in further, so close that our noses would touch if he'd come one inch closer. "I want to know everything there is to know about you." His hand slides between my thighs, parting my legs. "There are only some things I know."

"Like what?" My breathing comes out in short puffs when he leans in to press a kiss on the corner of my mouth.

"Like that you enjoy a dominant hand."

His hand nudges aside my legs, parting them even further, and I let him. I'm letting him do whatever he wants. It's what I love the most, and he knows it. He knows I love to give up control.

"And you know I love to tell people what to do," he murmurs against my lips, almost kissing me. Almost. I'm inching forward to feel his lips, but he won't let me. He keeps moving back, withholding me from pleasure. It's like he enjoys torturing me.

"I know what you want, Miss Webber, but you won't get it so easily."

"You just said that you want me," I say.

"I do." His hand now cups my pussy, causing me to gasp. "I want to feel your wet pussy all over my hard cock." He groans. "But you've been very bad, Miss Webber, and I can't let that go unpunished."

"Huh?" I mutter, unable to control the moans that come out as he starts rubbing my pussy.

"You know what I mean. You know what I want. You know what you want ..." he growls.

Punishment ... I know what he said, and I know what he means. I just can't believe it—it's almost too good to be true.

His fingers slide underneath the fabric of my dress and creep up until my panties are exposed. "Lie down on my lap," he says.

Biting my lip, I'm unsure of what to do, but when he spreads his legs and nods down, I move up from the couch.

"The safe word is pear. Do you understand?"

"Yes," I answer.

"Repeat what I said."

"The safe word is pear."

"All right. Your head that way." He points to his right side.

I move on top of him but then he twists me around. "Ass up." I'm taken by surprise as he rips up my dress until my lingerie is exposed.

"Hmm ... very nice," he muses. "Is this what you bought?"

"Uhm ..." Saying yes is like admitting to being a criminal ... and a sex addict.

Suddenly, he slaps my ass. I jolt up from the pain, a moan coming from my mouth.

"Speak up," he says gruffly.

"Yes, Mr. King."

"Hmm ... you have quite exquisite taste, Miss Webber. I like this. You must've known this was going to happen ... otherwise, you would never have put it on."

I don't want to tell him the truth because it's even more ridiculous than his theory. So, I just go along with it. "I'm glad you like it."

"You should wear this kind of lingerie every day," he muses. "Every day a new one. Every day something new to enjoy." I look up at him and watch him bite his lip, hissing. His cock bounces up and down in his pants, pushing into my belly.

"Turn around," he says.

When I face away, his hand circles over my bare ass. And then his hand comes down again, causing me to shoot up momentarily. He places his free hand on my back, and he says, "Try to relax."

"I've never had this before ..." I mutter.

"You've never been spanked for being a bad girl?"

"No … I haven't."

A sound comes from his mouth that I can only describe as a mixture between a naughty chuckle and an aroused growl. "There's always a first   for   everything."

CHAPTER TWENTY-EIGHT

He hits me again, and it sizzles on my ass so badly that it hurts. "This is punishment for not giving me back my credit card and for using it without my permission."

He slaps my other cheek, and I can feel the waves tingle through my entire body. It's not so much painful as it is arousing, especially with his cock prodding me. I feel so exposed … and oh, so bad. I'm lying here, taking a spanking from my boss, Leo fucking King. Oh dear Lord, this is hot.

"How does it feel, Samantha?" he suddenly asks after spanking me ten times on each cheek.

"Good," I murmur. "Very good." It's quiet for some time, so I ask, "Is that bad?"

"That depends on how you look at it. You've been bad, and you should feel bad, but you can enjoy a good spanking just as much. Especially when it leads to more. Admitting that you did something wrong can sometimes lead to great rewards."

His hands rest on my ass, which feels quite sensitive. "So plump and pink," he murmurs, sliding his hand all over my bum. "Don't give me more excuses to do this, Miss Webber, because I *will* take the opportunity and use it thoroughly."

"I can't promise you anything, Mr. King," I muse, smiling to myself.

He smacks me again, and my body bucks in response. The sizzle shoots through my veins like lightning, lighting up my body.

"I know you're a bad girl. I've known for quite some time. That's why I can't resist having you."

His hand slips down between my thighs and toward my pussy, cupping it, gently massaging my sensitive skin. Everything feels so good—his touch, his taste, and the way he's rough and gentle at the same time.

With his fingers, he parts my inner lips and starts toying with my clit, flicking it back and forth, teasing me senseless. His other hand presses me down on his lap, holding me in place. It's as if he enjoys keeping me down, facing me away, making me witness the power he holds over my body. Because even though he forces me in place, I could still say no. I could still put a stop to this. But I don't. I don't want to. I want more, so much more.

His fingers circle my pussy, slathering my wetness all over.

"So wet, so willing," he murmurs. "Have you ever come this way?"

"After a spanking?"

"That too, but I'm talking about lying on someone's lap. *My* lap."

"No, but what you did feels good …"

He leans forward close to my face. "Let me make you feel even better then," he whispers.

He pulls aside the string of my panties. "Let me satisfy this eager pussy."

He dips his finger in, making me moan as he slowly starts thrusting in and out, increasing his speed with each stroke. First one finger, then two. With his thumb, he plays with my clit while his index finger and middle finger work my pussy. I'm writhing in his lap, desperate for more. His cock poking my side makes me aware of the fact that he enjoys this just as much, if not more. It feels as though it's urging me to pleasure it, and I can imagine myself coming all over him. My brain has already gone into fuck mode, and all I can think of is pleasuring him because he makes me feel so good.

The way he circles around inside me pushes me to my limits.

"Oh, God …" I mutter.

"Are you gonna come for me?" he asks softly. "Are you gonna come all over my fingers, Miss Webber?"

"Yes," I whisper, barely holding it together.

"Do it. Come for me, Miss Webber."

The explosions follow quickly, making me writhe in his lap. He holds me down while still playing with my pussy, prolonging the intense orgasm. When it has subsided, I lie motionless in his lap, breathless.

"Hmm … You came so quickly. Was it because of my voice? Was it because I told you to do so?"

"I think so, yes," I murmur. Something about the way he speaks my last name, with authority, that controls my every thought.

He smiles when I look up. "Perfect."

I still feel his cock prodding my belly, now even harder than before, and I can't help but think about how I can please him.

Suddenly, I feel him pull my zipper down. "Stand up, Miss Webber. Take off your dress."

I slide off his lap, feeling his eyes bore into my skin before I even see them. Those dark, sparkling eyes have something in them that command me to act. It's like he holds control over me with just a look.

"Let me see what's underneath," he says with a gruff voice that makes me shiver.

He's biting his lip when the dress slides off my shoulders. Tension rises, and when it drops to the floor, a glint is in his eyes. I suck in a breath, watching him revel in the sight of my lingerie.

"Beautiful."

I almost grin but bite my bottom lip instead.

"Come here," he says, holding out his hands. He grabs me by the waist and pulls me on top of his lap. His hand slides from my belly to my breasts, cupping them, reawakening the lust inside me. I hiss when he pinches my nipples through the lace. Then his hand slides up along my neck to my chin, pulling me forward. He presses his lips onto mine, kissing me deeply. His tongue darts out to lick mine while his hand cups my face and pulls me closer. I can feel his cock bounce in his pants, arousing me even more. His tongue swipes eagerly over the rim of my mouth.

"Reach into my pocket," he murmurs against my lips.

With my free hand, I fumble in his pocket while my mouth refuses to unlatch from his. I fish out a condom and look at him, our mouths unhooking momentarily.

"Open it. Take my cock out and put it on," he commands.

I do as he says, zipping open his pants and slipping his cock out of his boxers. His length still catches me by surprise, and it never fails to make my mouth water. I take the condom from the package and roll it over his hard-on. He groans when I'm at the base.

"Come here," he growls.

His seductive eyes are half-mast, and he pulls me in for a kiss when I'm done. He sucks on my bottom lip and licks the roof of my mouth. His kisses become more voracious as I slide up and down his lap, teasing his cock.

"You naughty girl," he whispers against my lips. "Teasing me like that."

"I can't help myself," I say. "I just love to torment you."

"I know, which is why I'm gonna give it to you right now."

He grabs a hold of my waist and shoves me over his cock, pushing the tip inside. One hard thrust makes me moan out loud as he buries himself deep inside me.

"Feel that? That's how much I want you," he growls.

And I do. I feel his cock pulsate inside me with each stroke. We move in rhythm as he lowers me over his shaft and deepens the thrust. My hands rest on his shoulders, his eyes boring into mine as we move in sync, pleasuring each other.

"Keep your eyes on me, Miss Webber. Don't look away," he says with a husky voice.

He takes my hands off his shoulders and folds them behind my back, holding them in place by my wrists. "Keep your hands behind your back and fuck me, Miss Webber. Let your pussy do all the work."

His dirty words have me in delirium, almost ready to come again as his thrusting is just too delicious. He bites his lip and hisses with each stroke, and I watch him come close to the edge. I bet he sees the same in me, which is only more arousing.

"Fuck, you're so tight," he growls.

He leans forward to bury his face in my breasts. With his fingers, he pulls aside the tiny bra, exposing my breasts. A moan slips from my lips when his mouth covers my nipple and he starts sucking. With his tongue, he circles the tip, and then he gently bites down.

I gasp, feeling the heat rise between my legs.

"Oh, Leo," I murmur.

"Scream my name, Sam," he whispers.

The sudden switch to my first name has me undulating on his lap, ready to come again.

"Leo, I'm coming!"

"Yes." He tugs on my sensitive nipples with his teeth. "Come all over my cock."

The waves come before I realize it. "Oh, Leo! Holy shit," I moan.

He sucks hard, so hard it makes me come. I fall apart on his lap, the orgasm rippling through my body like a storm. His cock still pounds into me as he lifts and lowers me all by himself. He groans out loud, his muscles tensing around me, and then I can feel the warmth fill my pussy. A loud roar bursts from him, followed by a tug on my chin and a deep kiss on the mouth. I can feel him come apart inside me, underneath me, inside my mouth, in my pores, everywhere. It's unlike anything I've ever experienced.

We're both panting, desperately clinging onto each other, wanting more, but our bodies are spent. His cock deflates and I lift myself off him. I have the incredible desire to pleasure him, just as he did me. I want to feel him, taste him, have him everywhere.

So I slide down between his legs, knees on the floor, peel off his condom, and lean forward to lick his base.

He groans, sucking on his lip. "Oh, Miss Webber. You spoil me."

I kiss his flaccid dick, which still thumps as I suck up all his cum. I never thought I would do this, but it feels so natural. Like I'm supposed to pleasure him and enjoy every part of him, even the dirtiest bits. It's like I've wanted to do this all along.

That, or I'm so fucking drunk that I don't even know what I'm doing.

"You're such a naughty girl," he muses as he watches me lick up all his juices. "Do you enjoy the taste of my cum on your tongue?"

"Yes," I purr, licking his shaft from the bottom to the top. I can see the goosebumps spreading on his skin. "I love your taste."

"Hmm ... that's right, suck it all up." He leans back to enjoy the view, which strangely makes me feel empowered.

When there's no more cum, I lick my lips and swallow. "Hmm ..."

He smiles. "I love how you offered yourself. I didn't even have to ask. You naturally sink into the submissive role," he says. He leans forward to caress my cheek with his thumb. "Gorgeous and mine for tonight."

With his index finger and thumb cupping my chin, he lifts me up into standing position with him. Suddenly, he picks up me up from the floor.

I squeal. "What are you doing?"

"Carrying you to my cave where I plan to spend the rest of the night fucking you senseless."

I giggle because he's such a caveman sometimes, which makes this reference all the more funny.

"You find it funny, Miss Webber? Do you have any objections against me spoiling you?"

"Oh, no, not at all."

"Good." He smirks. "Because you won't be getting out of my bed until daylight. I have plenty of rope to tie you up, and I'm not afraid to use it."

"Threatening me now, are we?"

A devilish grin spreads on his face. "You and I both know you want me to chain you to the bed and fuck you over and over again."

I bite the side of my lip. "Does that involve more cum?"

"You really do like my taste, don't you?"

"Yes, actually," I say, laughing a bit. "I'm weird." I don't know whether that's me or the liquor talking.

"No, you're not weird. It just means more fun for me because I get to come in your mouth and you'll eat it all up."

"Hmm … I like your dirty mind, Mr. King. I'd take your cock any time of day."

"That's what I like to hear!" He slams open the door with his foot.

"It's just that good," I muse. I know I'm boosting his ego, but I think he deserves it after tonight.

He carries me into his bedroom, and I gasp at all the toys standing on the cabinet in the corner. I bet loads more are hidden inside. Oh, my Lord. This is going to be so much fun. I feel like a kid in an amusement park, waiting to try out all the new thrills.

When he sees the surprised yet excited look on my face, he asks, "Better than Doritos?"

I grin. "Way better."

CHAPTER TWENTY-NINE

When the light enters the curtains, I sit up straight in bed.

Holy shit.

This isn't my house.

I look around, discovering yet again that this cabinet, this wallpaper, these giant windows, and this bed certainly do not belong to me. This is Leo King's house.

What am I doing in Leo King's house? What the fuck have I done?

I look to my side and find Leo snoring beside me, his arms above his head, his legs spread wide, partially covering mine. My eyes widen. He's naked. I'm naked. We're naked!

Oh, my fucking God.

Oh, Jesus.

I had sex with him.

Again.

Oh, fucking hell.

I said I wouldn't do it, that I wouldn't fall into the trap, but here I am, lying in his bed, naked with him.

I don't even remember half of it, but all those toys tell me that we didn't just do it once or without restraints. All I remember is sitting in a bar, drinking, laughing, kissing … and then some sex. And oh, God, I licked his cock.

I scramble off the bed, kicking the blanket and Leo off me, almost tumbling to the floor. I managed to catch myself in time, but then I notice the mirror, which shows my naked ass. I have a roaring headache, and the damage from last night is clearly visible. My clothes and lingerie are spread out all over the room, and I jump across all the toys and his clothes to find them and put them on. I find my dress draped over the couch, and once I have it on, some creaks are audible behind me.

"Good morning."

Shit. I turn around, and there's Leo, staring at me … butt naked.

My eyes widen as I look down at his junk, which is still quite huge. When he notices my eyes, he looks down too, and then back at me, smiling like a fool. "Ha, I guess we had fun last night."

"Fun? I barely remember it," I say, looking under the couch for my shoes.

"Yeah, I thought it was. Are you regretting it or something?"

"Don't you? I mean, God, we were wasted," I say, putting on my shoe while holding onto the couch so I don't fall over.

"Who cares? We were both drunk, but we're responsible adults. We know what we're doing."

"I don't," I say, shaking my head.

He frowns. "What are you doing?"

"Trying to find my other shoe," I say, looking under the table.

"You threw it out the window."

"What?" I gasp. Oh, fuck no. "Seriously?"

"Yeah, along with some other things, like your bra." He grins.

No wonder I couldn't find it. Oh God, what if someone else did? "I have to go."

"What? Why? You haven't even had breakfast yet. Let me make you some coffee first."

"No, no, I have to go now," I say, grabbing my bag.

"Why are you in such a hurry? It's like you're terrified of me. Are you mad at me or something?"

"No, I think…" I don't know what to feel right now. I'm not even sure I know what I'm doing, but I made a mistake. Big time.

"Then what? We had sex. Nothing wrong with that."

I stop in my tracks, turn around and say, "Leo. I licked your cum." I point at my mouth. "I had you in my mouth."

He chuckles like he just got handed an extra bonus payment. "Yeah, that was fun, too."

"Without a condom!" I yell.

"What, are you afraid you might contract something from me? No, oh no. I'm clean."

"How do you know?" I scream. "For all we know, I might be carrying some STD now. Oh God, what did I do?" I slap myself on the forehead. "I licked your fucking cock. How could I be so stupid?"

"Believe me, I'm clean." He walks to his cabinet and takes out a paper. "And if you don't believe me, here's the proof."

He hands me the paper, which I snatch from his hand so he doesn't have more excuses to come closer. Naked Leo is not in my scope right now.

"You didn't make a mistake," he reiterates. "I don't have anything, and I assume you don't either. We just had sex. It's no big deal."

"No big deal?" I frown, looking at him. The paper does say he's clean, but it still doesn't make any of it okay. I push it back into his hand. "I have to go."

I turn around and walk toward the door.

"Hold up."

"I can't do this, Leo. I can't keep doing this. Whatever it is."

"What?" He frowns.

"I didn't want *just* sex."

"What do you mean? I thought you wanted this."

"No, I do, but not like this. Not … coming out of a bar, completely smashed, just for the fun of it."

"It wasn't fun for you?"

"It was, but I don't just fuck people, Leo. I don't fuck," I exclaim.

"And you think *I* do?" he says, making a face. "You think I just fuck every girl I meet?"

"No, I'm not saying that. Ugh, it's all coming out so wrong. I just … I let myself be seduced, again. I can't, I just can't … ugh." I open the door.

"Wait, Sam. Stop. Don't go," he says.

Too late, I've already stepped outside and closed the door.

CHAPTER THIRTY

I quickly gathered my things from the pavement before I went home. I was lucky my bra and shoe were still there, although it makes me cringe thinking about how many people saw it. I can't imagine what they must've thought. Not that it mattered because I was far too busy calling a cab and hurrying my ass inside. Right when it drove off, Leo stood outside, calling my name.

I'm not sure I want to know what he has to say.

Part of me wants to get past this, wants to move forward. Like, knowing what he really thinks about me is helpful, as it'll help me move on to another guy. But I shouldn't be having this problem in the first place. If only I didn't have sex with him … twice … there wouldn't be anything to get over.

The real problem here is my heart. I'm fleeing the scene because I know I can't handle the rejection. Classy, I know, but I acted in the moment. It's stupid, but I fear the answer he'll give me. I mean, he's Leo King. He fucks girls. He takes them and tosses them out. He's a ladies' man. Like I'd ever be enough for him. Besides, he wouldn't want someone like me as his *real* girlfriend, let alone his wife.

And I *want* a man, a boyfriend, a husband. I'm looking for something more than just a casual fling. And that's the sad truth, which I'm too afraid to face.

I sit down at my computer with a cup of steaming hot coffee and open my email. There are a ton but most notably one from

Stephanie.

FROM: Stephster@gmail.com
TO: doritoslover@gmail.com

Hey, girl!!
Why aren't you answering your phone? Did Leo abduct you? I swear, if I have to punch his face, I will. Just tell me you're okay. I can swing by if you want me to. Just talk to me! I'm depraved!
LOL

Xoxo
Steph

Oh dear fucking God.
I reach for my purse and throw out everything then come to the realization that I don't have my phone. I don't have my fucking phone. It's gone.
I want to scream because I know Leo has it. Oh God, what if he sees all the text messages between me and Mr. Awesome? Or our emails? All the accounts are connected, you don't need a password to login, it's all there, and I didn't have the time to put a lock on my phone yet because it's brand new.
Oh, holy fucking shit.
I'm doomed.

FROM: Stephster@gmail.com
TO: doritoslover@gmail.com

Hey!! :)
Well, to be honest, yes, I was abducted. They took my brains out. I'm back on Earth now with a head full of Doritos. Now I can eat straight out of a bowl without having to grab something in the

kitchen! Cool right? :P

And yes to the face punching, please! Goddammit. Well, might as well punch me too, while you're at it. Seriously, I'm too afraid to admit it, so don't you fucking laugh when you read this (or I will kill you – I swear, I will), but ... Leo and I slept together again.

Goddammit.

I know what you're thinking right now, like 'Sam, what the hell were you thinking!?', which is exactly what I'm thinking right now. To be honest, I don't even fucking know. We got drunk. We kissed. We went to his house. Next thing I know, I wake up in his bed and we're both nekkid. I'm sorry, I don't want to give you any pictures, but you get the picture LOL

I'm trying not to freak out right now. My vagina did it again. It wasn't me, I swear.

Okay, I'm a big fat liar, I know, but I couldn't help myself.

I need help.

Send help. Before it's too late.

Too late, the Martians are coming to beam me up again.

P.S.: Tell me how your date went. I'm dying for some good news.
PPS: My phone was abducted too, so don't text. Email back.

Xx
Sam

I need to figure out how to get my phone back from Leo without making a scene. I hadn't planned to go to work today either, but now that he still has my phone, I feel like I have no other choice. I mean, he isn't going to stay home, right? He's the CEO. He can't stay at home.

Suddenly, a new email blinks onto my screen. It's from Mr. Awesome. Crap, I totally forgot I had an agreement, and I ditched it last night. He must be pissed.

I open the email, expecting the worst.

FROM: mrawesome@hotmail.com
TO: doritoslover@gmail.com

We need to talk.

A.

It's really bad, and worst of all, I don't know how to respond. I agree, we should talk, but not for the reasons he thinks. This thing we're doing, it's toxic. Just like Leo. These men can pleasure me, yes, but I'm looking for so much more, and neither of them is able to give it to me. I can't keep doing this, I can't keep my heart at bay when it involves sex. I thought I could, but ultimately, that was just a lie that I told myself so I could experiment and have fun. Sometimes experiments end up badly.

FROM: doritoslover@gmail.com
TO: mrawesome@hotmail.com

I agree.

I'm sorry that I have to tell you this, but I cannot continue doing this. I need someone in my life who can be there for me, physically, emotionally, and well … you won't. I can't ignore my heart.

Please don't take it personal. I enjoyed every second of what we did. However, it's time for me to move on and find someone with whom to spend my life. It's not my intention to hurt you, and I'm sorry if you feel bad. It's just for the best.

Xx
S.

After twiddling my thumbs and sighing a lot, I finally gather the courage to press the send button. The moment I send enter, I already feel a huge weight falling off my shoulders. This is something I should've done sooner but was too afraid to do because I didn't want to lose what we had.

However, what we had was a thin thread, and I'm looking for a solid rope, someone to hold on to. He won't be that man for me. He said so himself, no personal details. I doubt he'd ever stray from that path.

My computer beeps again, and an email pops into my screen. Wow, that was fast.

FROM: mrawesome@hotmail.com
TO: doritoslover@gmail.com

I understand. Is there someone else in your life? I hope you will give him a chance. You deserve to be loved. The only regret I have is that I didn't try harder to please you.

I have one final gift for you, though. Please accept it.

Open your door.

A.

My heart just skipped a beat. Immediately, I scoot my chair back, far away from the computer. The further I get, the more I can pretend the words on the screen don't exist. I think I might pass out. Did he just say 'open your door?' How in the world ... does he know where I live?

A knock on my door has me jolting up with a scream.

"Who is it?"

Nobody answers, not even after a few minutes pass. Sweat drips down my back as I stare at the door. Another knock follows. My legs tremble as I walk toward the door, terrified of who I might find. Did Mr. Awesome really find out where I live? Do I finally get to meet him? Oh God, all kinds of images float through my mind, like what he would look like and how he would talk ... what he'd say to me.

Does he have a cute face or will I be shocked at how different he looks from what I imagined?

Maybe wanting to meet him wasn't such a good thing, after all. Anonymity does have its charm.

However, I can't ignore the stranger knocking on my door.

I take a deep breath and straighten my dress, trying to look as natural as possible, despite the fact that I'm still completely wasted from last night.

When I open the door, I'm in for a shock.

Like, complete, heart-stopping, jaw-dropping shock.

Leo King is at my doorstep.

"Wha ..."

"I know what this must look like but hear me out."

"What in the fucking world ..." I mutter, frowning, my body still frozen from the shock.

His eyes slide from left to right, and then he fishes something from his pocket. My phone. He holds it up. "I wanted to give this back to you."

I take it from his hands without saying a word. I have no clue what to say. All I can think of is that I must be in some kind of TV show because this shit just got surreal.

"Sam, I ... I'm sorry. I didn't want you to freak out."

"No ..." I mutter. If this is true ... no, it can't be because that means he's been lying to me all this time ... and I'm a complete idiot.

I try to slam the door shut, but his foot blocks the way. "Wait," he says.

"Oh, my God, what the hell, Leo," I say.

"Please, just listen. I didn't just want to have sex with you. That was not my goal. Yes, I loved it, and yes, I want to do it again. But that doesn't mean I don't want more. I'm not what you think I am, Sam. I'm not some manwhore who randomly fucks every lady he desires." He places his hand on the wooden door and leans in. "I don't want this to end. I don't want a one-night stand. I want you," he says.

My heart is melting in my hands.

"But you ..."

"I let myself get carried away back at the bar and last night. I'm sorry, it's just ... hard to resist you. I can't control my urges around you, it's like ... I feel like an animal when I'm near you, and all I can think of is having you in whatever way possible."

I swallow away the lump in my throat as I listen to his words, not knowing how to reply.

The look on his face is sincere, and even though I hate him for all the lies, I can't help but feel for him right now.

"I need you, Sam. Not just as an assistant. I need you … in my life as more than just friends. Do you think that's possible?"

"I don't know …" I murmur.

"I know I can be an asshole, and I sometimes forget about the consequences of my actions, and I make rash decisions based on impulse rather than well-thought-out plans. But that is why you're perfect for me in every way. You make up for all those mistakes."

It feels like my heart is glowing and dropping to the floor like a puddle, much like me. Yep, I've been reduced to a puddle of warmth. But how can these words fix the lies? How can they make up for the broken trust? How can he ever be the right man for me when he has treated me like shit these past couple of weeks? It makes no sense. Why would he care about me when all he's done and proven is that he cares about himself above all else?

"Why should I believe you?" I ask.

"Because it's me, Sam," he says. "This is the real me." He places his hand on his chest. "I'm not lying when I say I want to make you happy. I can make that happen, in more ways than one. I know how to do it in bed, and I can learn how to do it in other areas, too."

"How do you know what I like in bed? We barely know each other. We just had a one-night stand … well, two one-night stands. But that doesn't mean you know what I like."

His chest expands to take in the oxygen. "I have to show you something. Promise me you won't freak out."

"Okay …" I mutter.

He takes out his cell phone, and for a second I think he's going to show me a picture, but then he keeps on typing. And then my phone buzzes. I look at it, thinking it's just another fancy way of him trying to say sorry.

Except it isn't Leo texting me. It's Mr. Awesome.

My hands begin to tremble. My breathing falters. The phone drops to the floor.

"It's me," he says.

"No …" I mutter. I can't believe it. The implications are too difficult to handle.

He holds up his phone and shows me his gallery. One of the latest downloaded pictures is the one of my boobs I sent to Mr. Awesome.

Oh, holy fucking shit.

I take a step back, and he takes a step in.

"You're Mr. Awesome?" I say, barely able to speak coherently.

"I wish I could say no so you wouldn't have more reasons to be pissed at me, but then I'd be lying."

"No … you're lying right now. You got that off my phone, right?"

"Remember those dick pics I sent you? Ever spotted that mole on the edge of my V-line?"

I shake my head.

"Go look," he says, looking down at my phone.

I immediately pick up my phone and scroll through the images until I find it. There is indeed a mole, but I never focused on it before. Except, when Leo lowers his pants to expose that exact same mole on the exact same place on his V-line, it suddenly makes sense.

I think I'm about to faint. "You're really him? Mr. Awesome? You're the one I've been talking to all this time?"

He closes the door behind him. "It's me, Princess. The one and only."

CHAPTER THIRTY-ONE

"You're Mr. Awesome?" I repeat.

I just can't believe what I'm hearing. Thoughts race through my mind, the consequences of this truth. It means that he knows everything—all that I've said *about him* to Mr. Awesome, all the horrible stuff. And more ... so much more.

"Yes," he says. "It's me. It's always been me. There's no one else behind that account and those emails. Just me."

I shake my head. "Why?"

He takes a step forward in an attempt to defuse the situation. It's not working, though. "You want to know why I signed on to that app and started texting you, or you want to know why I didn't tell you?"

"Why are you telling me this now?" I ask, my lips trembling from anger.

"Because you were angry at me, and then you wanted to say goodbye to Mr. Awesome. I couldn't just let you go. I had to tell you the truth before you'd call quits on ... well, both of us."

"So, Mr. Awesome is just a fake persona to you. Just like all your other fake shit." I fold my arms.

"No, it's not fake. It's really me," he says. "I like what we have, Sam."

"*Had*," I interject.

He purses his lips. "I don't want this to be over."

"Yeah, well you should have thought about that before you lied to my face."

"I didn't lie to you, Sam. I just didn't tell you."

"Why?" My voice is getting louder and louder. I'm so pissed off right now. How could he lie to me like that?

"Because I was afraid of what you'd think of me if you found out. Like now. But I knew that one day I'd have to tell you. I just didn't think it'd go this far."

"You didn't think I'd actually want more than just a stranger on the internet? Or a one-time fling with Mister King himself?"

"No, that's not what I mean ..." He scratches his head and sighs. "Goddammit."

"So this was all just some innocent experiment to you. All fun and games."

"It was, yes, but now it's so much more than that." He steps closer again, which makes me back away. "Please, don't be afraid. You're backing away from me. I'm not going to hurt you."

"I don't want you to touch me."

"Why? I'm still me. I'm no different than before."

"Yes, you are! It's like ... two people just merged into one, and I can't cope with it, all right. I just can't."

"Okay." He holds up his hands. "I'm just trying to explain."

"Explaining won't erase what I'm feeling now. How betrayed I feel."

"But it will help you understand," he says, frowning.

"You used me, Leo. First, for your wife problems, and now, for your sexual pleasures."

"Oh, c'mon, it's not like you didn't enjoy it."

I frown. "I did, but that doesn't take away from the fact that you put your own needs first."

"I know, and I'm sorry for that. That's why I'm trying to come clean and make it all up to you again." He smiles gently. "I care about you, Sam. I don't want to see you hurt. Especially not from my doing."

It's quiet for a second.

"You ... you're the one I've been talking to all this time," I murmur, gazing off into nowhere. "I told Mr. Awesome, you, *everything* about my boss."

Leo muffles a laugh. "Yeah, that was quite the experience. Funny, too."

My cheeks turn red instantly. "Oh, shit."

"What? Don't worry about it."

"How can you say that? I called you a fucking asshole, and I told Mr. Awesome that I hated you!"

"Yeah, that was kind of bad, but I had it coming," he muses. "It was interesting to read what you really think of me. It put things into a whole new perspective."

"That was personal stuff, Leo. You weren't supposed to see that." I sigh and slam my hand into my face. "Ugh, why was I so stupid to tell a 'stranger' all that stuff?"

"You aren't stupid. Don't hit yourself over it." He takes my hand off my face, which makes me lean back. "It's normal to hate your boss, especially if his name is Leo King." He leans forward to look into my eyes. "I don't care. It only makes me like you more."

"But you … oh, God, all those conversations. And the … things."

"Things … Oh …." He nods slowly, his lips curling up into a smile. "You mean that thing you did in the bathroom, as well as on the airplane … and in your room." The more he says, the bigger his smirk, and the redder my face. "I know everything. I've seen it all."

"Oh, my God …" I mutter, swallowing.

"I made you do all those things, Sam. You liked it. I liked it. We both had fun."

"But you saw my ass, and my vagina, and my boobs on that freaking app!"

"And in the hotel, don't forget that one," he muses.

"Is this all one big joke to you or something?" I sneer. "Stop being so cheerful."

"I can't, I'm sorry. I just feel so relieved now that you know. It's like I finally get to share all my dirty thoughts with you. Only, I already did and fuck, it was hot." A huge grin spreads on his face.

I punch his shoulder. "Stop it. Stop enjoying this so much. I'm feeling horrible over here."

"Sorry," he says again. "But you gotta admit it is a bonus to know it's me instead of some random dude you don't even know."

"I could say goodbye to that random dude and never hear from or see him again! You? Not so much."

"Why would you want to do that? Are you ashamed of what we did? There's nothing to feel ashamed about, Sam. We're two consenting adults, enjoying life."

I frown. "I don't know. This just … it feels wrong." I mull on it. "I just can't put one and two together."

"Would it help if I started calling you Princess from now on?" he jokes.

I roll my eyes. "Not helping."

"You just don't want to admit that you liked what we were doing and now you feel caught in the act."

"No, I'm not!"

He points at his face, circling around his cheeks. "I can see you getting red, you know." He laughs. "It's okay. It happens."

I growl. "Stop. Just stop, okay."

"Is it that hard to see me as Mr. Awesome?" he asks.

"Yes! I can hardly believe it, let alone digest the fact that I told you all my secrets."

"Don't worry about that. I don't care if you said something bad about me. I'm not mad at you. I won't use it against you. And I certainly won't share the pictures. Your secrets are safe with me," he says.

I frown, biting my lip. "Look, I wanna believe you, I really do, but it's too hard for me to trust you right now. Not after I find out the guy who was the only escape I had turns out to be my boss. That, and the fact that you lied to me about your wife, makes it impossible for me. I'm sorry."

He sighs, looking down at the ground. "I understand. Do you want me to leave?"

"No, I just … I have to think about this." I grab my phone and my bag.

"Where are you going?" he asks, when I walk toward the door.

"To my best friend. You can stay here if you want. I don't mind. It's not like you don't already know everything there is to know about me. I might not trust your words, but I know you aren't a burglar out to steal my shit. Not that there's much to steal, so go ahead."

He chuckles. "If you count taking panties as stealing, then I am the dirtiest mugger you'll ever see."

I roll my eyes. "Sniff away. As long as you put them all back again."

"I can't make any guarantees."

"You do realize that this conversation makes me want to kick you out anyway, right?" I say, opening the door.

"I know."

"You want to be kicked out?"

"It wouldn't be wise for me to stick around when you're not here ..." He winks. "You wouldn't be able to resist my charm when you come back."

"Oh please, as if," I say.

He walks toward the door and stops to look me in the eye. "You know me. Once I want something, I won't stop trying to get it."

A devilish smirk appears on his face. "Even if I have to grovel through the earth to get it and jump through fiery hoops to be forgiven."

I muffle a laugh. "We'll see about that, Mister." I make a gesture so that he can walk out. "Let's go."

"I like it when you call me Mister ... it reminds me of a few app conversations I had with a lady who just loves Doritos." He licks his lips. "Although I prefer Sir even more."

I frown, blushing, and then I push him out the door. "Okay, time to go before I smack you on the head."

"Oh, kinky!" he says, grinning as I push him out to the pavement. "I've not been on the receiving end of ass whooping before, but this should be fun."

I push him forward and growl. "You just love to get a rise out of me, don't you?"

He turns around while walking. "Just as much as you do out of me," he says, tilting his head.

"Don't you have to get to work or something?" I taunt. "You're the CEO, after all."

"Business will run just fine without me, Sam. I can come and go whenever I please. I don't need to be there every second of the day, especially not when I have something far more important to do. Like you." He playfully raises his brows.

"Well, I guess the company will go down quickly then," I jest.

"The only thing going down quickly is you. I'll make sure of that later," he says. Then he salutes me. "I'll see you later, Miss Webber."

He winks. "Or should I say Princess?"

"Not in public!" I hiss, making fists.

"Next time in your bedroom then," he says. "No apps. No emails. Just you and me, Princess."

"My name is Sam!" I yell after him as he walks away.

I can still see him laugh, which pisses me off. And then he yells, "I'll make sure to bring the Doritos!"

CHAPTER THIRTY-TWO

When I show up at Stephanie's door, she squeals, slams her hand in front of her mouth, and then drags me in, closing the door behind me.

"Oh, my God! Sam, you have to tell me everything." I throw off my coat as she pulls me into the hallway. "Did you get your phone back?" she asks.

"Yes. He came to my house with the phone. And then he told me that he was Mr. Awesome."

She stops in her tracks, turns around, and stares at me, her jaw dropping. "No …"

"Yes."

"No …"

I muffle a laugh. "Stop saying no."

"Your boss is that dude from the app you were secretly texting?"

"Yes," I say, slamming my mouth shut, feeling embarrassed already.

"I can't believe it!" she yells, shaking her head. "This is too good to be true."

"Good? Oh, no, definitely not," I say as we move into the kitchen. She starts making hot water. "Sit, sit," she says.

I sit down in the chair next to the window and stare outside. I feel totally numbed by what happened today and yesterday. It's like I'm dreaming … only, I can't decide whether it's a good dream or a nightmare.

Stephanie comes back with tea and cookies, which I munch up quickly. "Spill it!" she says.

"Which part?" I ask with a mouthful.

"Everything of course!"

"Well ... most of it is just cringe worthy, to be honest. I mean, first I sleep with him. Twice. And then he tells me he's that dude I had casual fucking sex with."

"What? Casual sex?" Her jaw drops again.

"Oh, yeah ... I forgot to tell you that part."

"Oh, my God, you ho-bag!" she jests, punching me in the shoulder. "I love you."

"For sexting with a stranger? I'm so dirty," I say, taking a sip of my tea.

"No; for just doing whatever the fuck you want." She laughs. "You gotta enjoy life. Who cares if you sext or exchanged naked pictures with a random stranger?"

"He wasn't so random, after all ..." I muse.

"That only makes it better!" she says, smiling. "It's like being handed a winning lottery ticket."

"It's confusing, really. I mean, Leo is one man, and Mr. Awesome was another. And now the two just suddenly merge. It just doesn't make any sense to me. It's weird, you know. To see them both as the same man."

"But it's perfect! He likes you, you like him. You've been chatting with a guy for sex. Now you get to have both."

"Who said I like him?" I look up from my tea.

"Oh, please, it's written all over your face," she muses. "You can't hide shit from me, girl. Don't even try to pretend."

I laugh, sipping up some more of this strawberry tea. My favorite. "Well, maybe. Maybe I like him. Just a teeny, tiny bit." I make a small gap with my index finger and thumb.

"Bullshit. You like him a lot. Otherwise, it wouldn't bother you the way it does. You'd just not want anything to do with him anymore, say goodbye, and find a new job." She reaches for my arm. "Instead, you're here, talking to me about how confused you are. You're not confused. You just can't deal with the truth. You hate yourself for liking him."

"Hmm ..."

"You just like dicks."

I gasp. "Steph!"

"Not in that way, although … yes, definitely in that way, too!"

I throw a cookie at her. "You did not just say that."

"I meant the dick bit more as douchebaggery, but this works, too."

"Ugh, you're not helping."

"I know, that's what friends are for, honey. To smack you in the face with the cold, hard truth." She throws a cookie back at me. "Now eat the damn cookie. You need some cheering up."

I chuckle. "Thanks."

"So, you've been sexting with him … no wonder he suddenly got all interested in you."

"Yeah, it does explain a few things. But I didn't just sext with the guy. I actually told him how shitty I felt about my boss. Imagine Leo reading that crap I said about him … to his face. Oh, God." I bury my face in my hands. "What have I done? I should've never gone to that app."

"Stop! Seriously, stop." She rips my hands from underneath my head, causing my head to bump into the table.

"Ouch," I say.

"That's what you get for slamming your head into my table, idiot."

"Well, you pulled my arms away."

"Because you're talking shit about yourself, and I won't allow it. You had fun on that app. You needed it." She points another cookie at me. "And if you don't stop denying the fact that you enjoyed doing it and don't stop acting all embarrassed for being a woman with needs, I will fucking throw another cookie at you. Just like Iago and that Sultan. I'ma put you in a cage and force you to eat cookies, woman. Don't make me do it." She threatens me with the cookie, almost making me snort out my tea.

"I get it, I get it. No more cookies, please. I beg you," I say, laughing.

"No more shame for random sex. No more," she reiterates.

"Yes, yes, I know," I say. "It's just the fact that he's my freaking boss which makes it so uncomfortable. If it were any other guy, I'd be okay with it … I think."

"Don't think. Stop thinking. Just listen to your bloody heart for once. What's it saying?" she asks, eating the cookie she just threatened me with.

"All kinds of different things, none of them are clear."

"Like what?"

"That I hate him for lying to my face. For not giving a shit all this time and then liking me all of the sudden. For using me. For seducing me into bed."

"You wanted him to seduce your heart first," she says.

"Exactly." I warm my hands on the cup of tea. They suddenly feel so cold.

"Well, sometimes things start reversed. That doesn't mean they're bad or not real."

"But he was never interested in me before! Not before that whole fake wife thing."

"Maybe he was, but he just didn't show you."

"Why? Why would he do that?" I ask, my voice fluctuating in tone.

"Wait." She holds up her hand. "First, another cookie." She holds it out to me. "Eat it. You know you want to. Keep it together, woman. No falling apart on my table."

I snatch it from her hand and take a bite. "Good girl," she says, and we both laugh, crumbles falling from my mouth.

"Maybe he was afraid. Maybe he didn't want you to get hurt. Who knows? Only he does, really. You should ask him."

"But then I come across as the whiny bitch."

"If he thinks that, ditch him right away. We talked about this already," she says, frowning.

I roll my eyes. "Steph …"

"Yeah, I know, you aren't able to actually ditch him because he's your boss. Oh, and you like him too much."

I sigh. "Oh, here we go again."

"Stop denying it. You like him, and he hurt you. That's why you're so mad. Not because of all that shit he did. You know he's genuine. He likes you. Why else would he go through all that trouble to hook up with you?"

"For sex," I say.

"A guy like him can get sex anywhere, honey. He wanted it from you and only you. That says something." She takes a drink from her tea.

"Hmm … maybe you're right. I should just ask him upfront. I'm just being a chicken shit."

"Exactly."

"That's why I came to your house right away. He was at my house, telling me about this Mr. Awesome thing."

"You came to the right place to spout your feelings. Now that we're on that topic, what's the current stance on him and his wife? Is it real?"

"Yes. He explained that he's trying to divorce her, but she won't allow it. She wants his money now. Bitch got hurt, now she wants to suck him dry."

"Holy shit, well that at least puts him in the clear."

"Not really. He got drunk and married her, and then when she didn't want to help him keep up the façade in front of his parents, he got me to help him instead. I mean, it's still pretty bad." I make a face.

"Tell me about it ..." she says, sighing. "Well, at least you know now. He's not as bad as he looks. He's just desperate to keep up a certain image ... and to keep you." She winks.

"Maybe. I really need to talk with him."

"Yes, you do. And if you don't want a relationship with him, at least make sure you get the money he promised you before you quit your job."

I laugh. "Wow, you got this all figured out, don't you?"

"I got you covered, girl." She cracks her knuckles. "You know that."

"Always." I smile. "Thanks for listening. I really appreciate it. We haven't done this often enough lately."

"Tell me about it, sheesh. If my life were only half as interesting as yours was, I'd be jumping through the roof. Instead, I get a date with a smug asshole who only wants to fuck."

"Oh, God, is that the guy from ..."

She nods, which tells me enough. "I'm sorry, Steph."

"Don't be. At least I got great sex. That's already a huge plus. Now all I need is to find a real man. Hey, I heard about this app that can produce wonderful men who love pleasing women and aren't too shy to show their true colors. Think you could hook me up?" she jokes.

I pick up a few crumbs from the table and throw them at her face. "Ha-ha. If only it was as easy as you make it sound. This isn't some kind of perfect fairy tale."

"Life isn't perfect. You just gotta roll with the dice you're given!"

"Oh, such wisdom, Yoda. Write a book about it, must you."

"I wish," she says. "But my writing sucks. I'll leave that part up to you."

"Geez, thanks."

"You're welcome."

We drink our tea, and it's quiet for a second, but then she opens her mouth again.

"You know, I think you should go talk to him."

I chuckle. "No shit, Sherlock."

"Why are you still sitting at my table then?" she retorts.

"Cookies. Why else? Not because of you," I jest, laughing.

She throws another cookie at my face. "Here's your fucking cookie."

"Thanks, I needed that."

"You can ask him to throw cookies at your face the whole day. Better yet, go ask him now." She throws another one.

"Okay, okay, I get it." I hold up my arms to protect myself.

"You obviously care about him or whatever. You have a problem, go solve it."

"But what do I ask? I'm not even sure I want to know the answer."

"Knowing is better than not knowing. Besides, it's not like it can get any worse, right?"

"Gee, thanks, bitch," I say, rolling my eyes.

"You're welcome," she muses. "I'll be your bitch anytime." She gets up and brings our mugs back to the kitchen while I grab my coat. "Now go find out if he's for real."

"Thanks, I will. Wish me luck!" I say as she opens the door to let me out.

"I'll be texting you!" she yells after me. "You'd better text back. I want to know all the details, you hear me?"

"I will," I yell. "But first I have a man to catch."

She winks. "Whip out that fishing pole, girl!"

CHAPTER THIRTY-THREE

When I arrive at my house, I find Leo's limo parked right outside my house.

With furrowed brows, I stare at it while parking my own car in my driveway. As I step out, Leo does, too.

"What are you doing here?" I ask.

"Waiting for you," he muses, smiling.

"You were here all this time?" I frown.

He walks toward me, tucking his sunglasses into the hem of his shirt. "Yes. I didn't leave."

Wow, this dedication is kind of awe-inducing. "Why? I was away for like an hour or something."

"I know. I don't care," he says, casually strolling toward me. "I'll wait as long as I have to."

"Okay …" I gulp.

"Can we talk? Because I think we left off on the wrong foot."

"Yeah, that was pretty much the moment you mentioned that you were Mr. Awesome."

"About that … I have a very good reason."

"Tell me then," I say, turning toward him. "If you care so much about me, prove it."

He cocks his head. "All right. If you want me to spill it all here out on the street, I will. For you."

I swallow from his comment. Now I feel bad for making him do this. However, I want to know why he went on to the app and played along for so long, knowing it was me.

"I didn't go on the app to find girls. I went on the app to find you."

I frown, shocked. "To find me? So you're telling me this wasn't about getting laid?"

"Well, it was, but I only wanted you." He hides a smile, his skin flushing a bit. "If you mean that I went after girls before you, of course I did. Any man does that. All men want to get laid, but they want a girlfriend, too."

"Right … that's not making this any better, Leo. I don't understand why you'd want to connect with me on the app. You've been ignoring me all the time that I've worked for you."

He holds out his hand in defeat. "That's because I didn't know what to do with myself." He sighs. "Okay, hear me out. When you applied for the job, I couldn't believe my eyes. Physically, you were everything I love. And when you opened your mouth, I fell in love with your voice. I wanted to hear that potty mouth talk every day. When you accepted the job, I thought I was dreaming."

I don't know what to say. My jaw drops; I'm flabbergasted.

"But I knew it wasn't right," he proceeds. "You work for me. How would that look? A CEO dating his employee? Everybody would talk. They'd accuse you of trying to get higher up. They'd accuse me of favoring you for a job because of sex. It's taboo."

"I know, which is why I don't think this is a good idea," I add.

I don't know why I'm saying this. Maybe I'm just being chicken shit, but sweat is literally dripping down my back.

"That's what I thought, too. But I couldn't stop staring at you. When you talked to me, I didn't know what to say. I didn't want to make it look like I was hitting on you, so I opted for nothing at all. Besides, it would make it easier. At least, that's what I thought."

"It kind of hurt my feelings, you know."

"I know, and I'm sorry. I'm sorry that I couldn't stay away, either. And you know what else? I'm sorry for finding out you were on that dating app."

"How did you find out?" I ask, tilting my head, curious for his answer.

He places his hand on the back of his head. "I went through your email."

My jaw drops again. "You went through my private files?"

"Technically, they're company files."

"Not if you're looking at my emails!" I yell.

"Right …" He bites his lips, frowning. "I know it's bad, I just couldn't resist. Once I knew, I made an account there, and next thing I know, I was chatting with you as Mr. Awesome. Talking to you without the stigma, without all the fuss … it was addictive." He clears his throat. "I couldn't stop. Especially not when I found out that you love to be dominated. My cock had a will of its own when that came out. It was like a match made in heaven."

"So, you went to that app because of me? To talk to me and seduce me?" I repeat.

He licks his lips. "Yes … it was meant to be something casual, innocent. But I kept wanting more and more. Then the incident in Las Vegas occurred and I had to turn to you to be my fake wife. That's when I knew I couldn't resist the temptation anymore."

"So that's why you suddenly started showing interest …"

He takes a step closer. "Sam, I've never *not* been interested."

"But you weren't allowing yourself to take the step."

"Exactly," he says.

I look down at the ground. "But … that doesn't change the fact that it's still wrong because I work for you."

"It doesn't, but I don't care anymore. I *have* to have you. Even if that means facing legal problems."

I take in a much-needed breath, feeling overwhelmed by what he just told me. If it's true, then … wow.

"Do you believe me?" he says.

I nod. "I think so, but it doesn't make it any less … scary." I turn around and walk toward my door.

"Scary how?" he asks, following me.

"Well, the fact that my boss knows how I truly feel about him, coupled with all the dirty details about my sexual appetite, makes it kind of shameful."

"That's nothing to be ashamed about. I actually admire how you express your sexual freedom. I haven't met many girls open and willing to do those things." He leans in as I turn the key in the lock. "That's why I like you. You're not afraid to do what you love and speak your mind."

"I might be afraid… a little," I say.

"Of me? There's no reason to be. I won't hold anything against you. I won't tell anyone. It can be our dirty secret." His finger gently strokes my arm, causing goosebumps to scatter all over my body.

"I don't want a dirty secret, Leo …" I say. "I want something real. Something I can feel in my heart, not just in my vagina."

He chuckles, coming even closer until his arm is around my body, his hand resting on my belly. His head is near my ear, and he whispers, "Why do you think I don't want that?"

"Because of what you do … you tease … you seduce …" I mutter.

"To prove to you that I am what you want," he says, his hand still caressing my arm, making me shudder. "What you've been looking for on that app as well as in real life."

"What do you think I want? Have you asked me?"

"You've told me many times. You want a relationship. Someone you can trust. Someone who gives you what you need. Someone who makes you laugh. I'm sorry if I missed a few points there, but let me prove to you that I *am* that man."

"Or you're just trying to get into my pants again," I say.

When I try to open the door, he pulls the handle, closing it again. I whimper, feeling his body so close to mine.

"You're right, I am. I won't deny that. I think about having you every day … in my bed, in yours, on the couch, on the table, in the kitchen, on my desk, under the shower, in the bathroom of that cafe we went to."

I slam my lips together to prevent a giggle from escaping. I can actually imagine us having sex at all of those places and more. Does that make me dirty? Or just honest?

"I know you thought about it, too. We want each other so badly we hate each other for it. But why? What's the point?"

I sigh. "I don't know. But I won't admit it."

"Because you think it makes you weak?"

"Because I'm afraid I'll get hurt if I do." There, I said it. It's the truth.

"I can't promise you that I won't hurt your feelings every once in a while. Sometimes that shit just happens," he says. "But that doesn't mean I won't try to make you as happy as you can possibly be."

"You want me … How do I know it's not just temporary?" I say.

"I've always wanted you, and it won't stop. Not just now, but every day, I want you near me. I want to touch you, I want to hear you, taste you, everything. I want you, Sam. I *need* you. Not just for a day. That's the truth. And I know you want me, too. You turned to the app to find someone who could fulfill all your needs. I *am* that guy."

"Not just sexually," I add, sucking in a breath when he breathes hot air into my ear.

"Would any man try this hard if he wasn't out to claim a girl's heart?" he muses.

"I don't know … I'd take you for a panty whore."

He chuckles. "Only when it comes to your panties." He sniffs my neck, making me laugh. "You always smell so nice."

"You're such an animal, sniffing and groping me."

He growls, "Just for you, Princess."

I shiver when he calls me that.

He turns me around in his arms, placing one hand on the door and the other on my face. His thumb gently strokes my cheek, an appreciative smile adorning his face. "I love you."

"What …?"

"I love you, Sam. I always have."

I can't believe what I'm hearing. Is this real? I feel like I could scream, cry, and jump him all at the same time. His thumb brushes along my broad smile, and before I have time to say anything back, he leans in and presses his lips to mine.

CHAPTER THIRTY-FOUR

His kiss takes my breath away, as well as my brain. I can't think. His lips consume me, take over my body, and make me latch onto him. I wrap my hands around his neck, pulling him closer. His mouth is devouring mine with a need I can feel zing through my veins. By the time I get to catch a quick breath, my lips are raw and pink and desperate for more.

"God, I love you so much," he murmurs.

He loves me? I almost can't believe it; it's too good to be true. The more he says it, the more I want to grab him and never let go. His words have an effect on me that I simply can't ignore. I'm falling, hard. And oh, that tongue of his, fuck me. The way he kisses makes my heart throb.

I fumble with the handle, and when the door opens, we stumble inside my home. He kicks the door shut while keeping his eyes solely on me. He can't take them off me, and it makes me feel good. I don't know why I want this so badly, but I'm swept away by his kisses.

His hands are all over my body, ripping and pulling at my coat to get it off. It drops to the floor and off go my shoes. In a frenzy, he rips off my shirt and unbuttons my pants, tearing it down until I'm in my bra and panties. His eyes take in my body, his tongue swiping across his lips before he ravages me again.

His kisses are tantalizing, hypnotizing me as we stumble backward until I bump into my kitchen table. I squeal when he lifts me onto the table, but he devours my sound with his mouth.

A moan leaves his lips. "Fuck, I want to fuck you so hard right now."

He bites my lip and tugs, growling. His lips are everywhere, on my neck, my chin, my collarbone, down to suckle on the mound of my breast. I'm lost in delirium.

"Do it," I say. "Fuck me."

"Uh-uh, Princess, you know that's not how it goes," he muses, flipping my breasts out of their holsters. When he sucks on my nipple and pinches the other, I'm silenced by my own moan.

"You do what I want," he says, seducing me with half-mast eyes as he returns his attention to our sort of conversation.

My lips part. "What?"

He cocks his head. "Do you want me to pleasure you, Sam?"

I frown. "Is this a trick question? I don't think I know what I'm getting myself into," I say, regretting it already.

"Just answer the question, Sam. Yes or no. It's not that hard. Only two possible answers. One is the truth, and the other is a lie. Simple."

"Are you calling me a liar?" I ask.

"No, I'm simply telling you to own up to your desires. It's time you gave in and stopped fighting," he muses.

I take a deep breath. "All right. Yes."

A smile slowly builds on his face. "So you admit that you want me right now."

"Fine, yes," I say, sighing.

He laughs. "I'm glad we can finally both agree on something."

"Oh, stop it," I say. "Just kiss me already."

I purse my lips, but he places his finger on my lips. "Not yet, Princess."

"Princess?" I gasp.

"Yes, Princess. My princess."

"That's what ..."

"What *I* called you, yes. And I won't stop now. You like it when I do because you *are* my Princess."

I blush from that comment, and he places his finger underneath my chin, tipping my head up. "Do you know what I want right now?"

"No," I say. "Well, I could guess. It has something to do with your cock."

"I want to fuck you," he says gruffly. "Not just with my cock but with my hands and my mouth as well. But I need you to do something for me, too."

"What?"

"What I want is for you to call me …" He stops talking, purses his lips, and waits, as if he wants me to finish his sentence. I already know what he wants. It's perfectly clear. He's Leo King, but he's also Mr. Awesome. I just have to put one and two together. He loves control, and he's not afraid to take what he wants … which is me.

All I have to do is give in.

"Sir …" I mumble.

"Exactly." He gives me a peck on the neck. "And how do you ask for something?"

"Please, fuck me, Sir?" I muse, chuckling a little.

A smirk builds on his face. "Good. That's what I like about you. You're a quick learner, always eager to please me."

He caresses my cheek, brushing his lips against mine, tempting me.

"You're such a dirty, bossy asshole," I say.

"And you like it," he whispers, blowing hot air across my lips.

A smile spreads on my lips, and before I know it, we're kissing again. I just can't get enough of him; he's like some kind of drug, or better yet … chocolate. Just as sweet and delicious, but oh so addictive.

"Fuck," I hiss.

"What, Princess? Getting wet for me?" He licks his lips while his fingers travel down my body to rub my pussy. My panties are getting soaked as he circles my clit with his thumb, and my breath comes out in short gasps.

"You want me to fuck you, Princess?"

"Yes …"

He playfully slaps my breast, causing me to squeal. "Try again."

"Fuck me, please, Sir," I moan, as he tugs on my sore nipple.

"Oh, I will, but first, let me taste that pussy," he says, grinning.

He reaches behind my back and releases my bra clasp, dropping it to the floor. Cupping my breasts, he squeezes and pinches them, making me moan out loud. Suddenly, he places his hand on my chest and pushes me down.

"What are you—"

"Shh. It's playtime now, Princess. You follow my rules and do as I say," he says, placing his finger on his lips.

I shudder, taking a short breath when he rips down my panties, too. For a moment, he just looks at me, biting his lip, as if he's enjoying the view. His finger gently strokes down my pussy, setting me ablaze. I buck when his finger leaves again, wishing he didn't stop.

"Patience, Princess," he muses.

Then he walks around the table and unbuckles his belt, pulling it through the holes with a lot of noise. He grabs my hands and wraps the belt around my wrist.

"Now, the safe word is pear, just like last time. Remember it."

"Yes, Sir," I say. "Pear. Got it."

"Although I don't think you'll need it ..." he muses, the left side of his lip quirking up into a devilish smile. "After all, you must be dying to let me lick you."

"Oh, yes ..." I moan.

He pinches my nipple and tugs so hard that I squeal. "It's Sir to you. Don't forget, Princess."

"Ah, yes Sir!" My heart is beating like crazy, and all my nerves are on fire. His possession of me is crazy, in a good way. It's not pain, it's excitement, and I love the way it feels.

"Hands above your head. I don't want to see them move an inch," he says.

He places them above my head and then walks back to my legs. Standing between them, he nudges them apart with his hands, leaning forward to blow hot air onto my pussy. I wriggle underneath him, desperate for him to touch me.

"Oh, so sensitive," he muses. "Don't explode too soon, Princess. I want to enjoy tasting you."

His tongue dips out to playfully stroke my lips, giving me a taste of what's to come. He's being a tease, and he knows it; I can tell from the smug look on his face. He loves torturing me, and I can't say anything or I'm sure he'll punish me. He's waiting for me to do it, waiting for an excuse to spank me. Any other day I would misbehave just to make him do it, but now all I want is his mouth on my pussy.

And oh Lord, when he licks my clit, I'm lost in him.

What he can do with his mouth is insane. He kisses my mound, licks me like he's hungry, and presses his mouth to my pussy like he wants to eat me whole. He has crazy skills, and the way he swipes his tongue up and down makes me writhe.

I'm dying to hold onto him, but my hands are bound. With a flat hand, he holds me in place, spreading his fingers across my belly while driving me insane with his tongue. His other hand digs into my thighs, pushing apart my legs as I attempt to wrap them around him.

"Open up for me, Princess. No closing your legs for me," he murmurs against my pussy.

He licks up my wetness and probes my entrance with his tongue, thrusting inside a few times. I'm moaning hard, holding onto the belt like it's my only lifeline because I'm about to drown in ecstasy.

"You wanna come, Princess?" he whispers, circling his tongue around my clit again and again.

"Oh, God, yes!"

"Sir will suffice," he jokes.

"Can I come, please, Sir?" I ask because I know he loves it. I don't even know why I want him to allow me to. Maybe I'm just addicted to this game of domination. Or maybe I'm just addicted to him.

"Not yet, Princess," he muses, still licking and kissing me senseless.

I'm about to explode, but I know I can't. Somehow, just knowing I'm not allowed to stops it. As if my body *wants* to obey his every command.

He comes back up and zips down his pants. They drop to his feet, and then he lowers his boxer briefs. His cock springs out already erect and bounces up and down, catching my attention. I lick my lips at the sight, and a cocky smile appears on his face when he sees me.

"You ready for me, Princess?" he says, stepping out of his pants and boxer briefs.

"Oh, yes," I whimper, staring at his hard-on. I realize right now that for the first time I'll fuck Mr. Awesome while knowing it's him, something I've been dreaming of, which is now a wish come true.

"I'm clean. You're clean too right?"

I nod.

"Condoms spoil the fun," he says. "I want to feel your tight, wet pussy wrap around my cock." He groans as he rubs his tip against my entrance, teasing me to the limit.

"Oh, please …" I mumble.

"Please what?" he says.

"Please, fuck me, Sir," I murmur. "I want it."

"You want this?" he says, pushing in just a little.

I moan, feeling the pressure rise. I'm so close that I could burst right now.

"Don't you come yet, Princess. I want to fuck this pussy first." He gives my mound a playful slap, causing me to buck. "Mine," he adds.

My senses are aroused, and goosebumps scatter on my body as he pushes inside.

"Oh, it feels so good," I say, as he fills me completely.

"Open your legs, Princess," he says. "Show me how much you want it."

I part my legs, and he takes out his cock to thrust back in again. The feel of him inside me is heavenly, and all I can think of is having him deeper and deeper. He holds my waist while he dips in and out slowly, almost to the point of torturing me. I think he's enjoying the fact that I'm on the edge. There's a certain gleam in his eyes that gives it all away, and that smile of his … damn, I can't decide whether I want to tell him to fuck me harder or to give him a big, fat punch in the face for teasing me like this.

"You want me to go hard?" he asks gruffly.

"God, yes, please," I murmur.

He slaps my inner thigh, causing me to moan and twitch.

"What do we say?" he growls.

"Yes, Sir," I say.

"Good."

He thrusts harder, moving the table with him. He bites his lip while watching me, and I can almost feel his stare penetrate my skin as he watches my boobs bounce up and down. He moves his thumb to my clit and circles it as I desperately claw at the table. The belt around my wrists makes arousal course through my veins, and his groans and rough handling pushes me to my limit.

"Oh, fuck me," I say. "Harder, Sir."

"Gladly." He pumps into me with fervor, digging his fingers into my thighs as he toys with my clit. When he hears my whimpers, he says, "Not yet, Princess."

"Please …" I moan. "Oh, Leo …"

"You want to come that badly, Princess?"

"Yes, fuck yes," I moan. "Please, let me come, Sir."

He thrusts into me so deeply I gasp. "Come all over my cock,

Princess. I want you to milk me."

"Can I?"

"Come, now!" he growls, thrusting in me with everything he has.

And then I explode. My entire body convulses, lust rippling through me like waves. His cock becomes more rigid inside me as my muscles clamp around him, every nerve in my body awakening. A loud roar bursts from his mouth, and then a hot jet of seed spurts into me. Again and again he thrusts, filling me up to the brim.

Panting, my head drops to the table as he takes out his cock while he's still groaning. "Fuck, I needed that."

"Ha, so did I," I mumble.

"But I'm not done yet," he growls.

And then he pulls my legs. I squeal as he hauls me off the table, onto my feet, and grabs the belt to pull me with him. "Come."

"Where are we going?"

He gazes at me over his shoulder, a wicked grin spreading across his lips. "The question you should be asking is 'what am I going to do with you?'"

CHAPTER THIRTY-FIVE

Leo pulls me into my own bedroom and closes the door, locking it behind him. I swallow, seeing him tower above me.

"Lie down," he says, pointing at my bed.

I do as he says, sliding onto the bed while he takes off his shirt. My eyes are glued to his delicious body, his ripped muscles tightening with every pull. I love watching him get naked, especially with that dirty grin on his face.

With a confident stride, he walks to my closet and opens a drawer. "So, tell me where you hide that lovely pink dildo."

I part my lips, but nothing comes out. My cheeks heat up like a lightbulb, and I'm sure he finds it amusing to watch me flush. I point at the bottom one. "That one."

He slides it open, rummages through my underwear until he finds it and holds it up to inspect it.

"Peculiar thing. So this is the one you used when you sent me those pics?" he asks.

"Yes, but it's not the only one I have."

"What else?"

"The bullet ..." I clear my throat because somehow I feel kind of exposed with him going through my underwear and pulling out my dildos. It's weird, to say the least.

"Oh ... *that* thing." He glances at me over his shoulder. "You know, there are better ones out there."

"Oh, and how would you know?" I retort.

"Tsk, Princess. Language, please." He flicks his finger. "Just because we're talking, doesn't mean you shouldn't call me what you always call me."

"Sorry … Sir."

He smiles. "And about your question, yes, I do know because I test them regularly."

"Test? On who?" I ask. "And why?"

He cocks his head. "For the magazine, of course." He bends my dildo with his thumb and index finger as if he's testing the material. "Being a CEO of a woman's magazine means knowing what your readers want. What they need. I can only learn by trying things out myself." His lips curl up into a smile. "But don't worry, Princess. I won't be using them on anyone but you from now on. We'll have plenty of testing time … and playtime."

I laugh. "I don't know whether to be scared or excited."

"Both." He grins. "Are these the only two you have?"

"Yes," I say. "Is that bad?"

"No, it just means I'll have plenty of toys to buy for you." He smirks. "Don't want my Princess to run out of things to pleasure herself with, especially not when I'm watching."

I bite my lip, suppressing a giggle. I can't help but think about the conversations on the app. It's still a bit surreal.

He walks toward me and says, "Spread your legs, Princess."

He places the dildo between my tied hands and turns on the buzzer. Then he grabs a pillow from my bed and tucks it underneath my head. He walks back to a chair near my door and sits down, his legs wide open, his half-erect cock dangling between. While his left hand lies on the armrest, his right hand starts to stroke himself.

"Pleasure yourself, Princess. Think about how I licked your pussy, how I filled you up with my cum. Show me how much you liked it. I want you wet and moaning out loud, Princess," he says.

I move my hands to my pussy and slide the dildo up and down. It's hard to do with bound hands, but it adds to the intensity of this game. The pillow allows me to watch him as he pets his hard-on, biting his lip. The look in his eyes is ravenous, almost animalistic. It makes my pussy flutter with need, seeing him want me that much.

"I see your red cheeks, Princess," he suddenly says. "You're blushing. Why?"

"Well, it's pretty obvious."

"Then it should also be pretty obvious to you that you shouldn't have to."

I swallow away my nerves.

"Enjoy what you're doing," he says. "Have fun, that's all that matters."

"But I feel exposed. And you're ..." I look at his cock, which looks so yummy, but it feels so wrong to have him watch me like this, knowing that he's my boss. Oh, Lord.

"Stop thinking. Turn your brain off. I want you to focus on the here and now. You and me. *My* pussy and my cock."

"Yours?" I repeat.

"Yes because that pussy is mine now," he says with a smirk. "And I will do everything in my power to please it every day from now on." He sinks back into the chair and starts jerking himself with no inhibition. I love it. I love how carefree he is. How much he's into me. I love how he says 'every day' as if this will be the norm. As if he doesn't intend to ever want someone else again.

I'd like that. It makes me want to please him more and forget about our misunderstandings. Forget about everything we said and did, and focus on the fact that he's sitting right in front of me, watching me play with myself and enjoying every second of it.

With the dildo, I spread my slickness everywhere and moan when I touch my own clit. The cum that's still inside my pussy acts like a great lubricant, and I love how this feels with him watching me the way he is. The buzzer is amazing, although I do wonder now what else he knows about these things. Who knows, I might be missing out on something amazing. Somehow, my mind can't stop wondering what it would be like to do this with a different one each day, and him watching me each and every time. It's different from the app. No pictures but a live performance instead. It's exhilarating, to say the least, and I'm getting horny so quickly that I can't help but utter his name.

"Oh, Leo ... this feels so good," I mumble.

"I know, Princess. Give that pussy the attention it deserves. I want to watch you come," he says with a gruff voice.

Chills run through my body as he caresses his cock while watching me pleasure myself. It's thrilling, the way our eyes and bodies seem to connect on an almost ethereal level. I feel lost in him, his eyes, his presence. It's all that I need right now, all that I can think of. Nothing else matters but us.

His cock is growing harder again, and the sight of it makes my mouth water. I part my lips as another moan slips out, caused by the buzzing against my clit. With his eyes boring into me, I'm skyrocketing to the next orgasm.

"Oh, dear God … I think I'm going to come again," I whisper.

He jerks off his now fully erect cock even quicker when I say that. "Ask me nicely and I'll allow it."

"Please, Sir, can I come?" I moan, flicking the dildo like crazy.

Blood pumps through his veins, making his cock bounce up and down in his hand, and it makes me want to receive what he has to give. Anywhere, anything. My mouth, my pussy, even my ass. Nothing is off-limits to him. He's turned me into a submissive goddess, which isn't something a lot of men can do. I'm drunk on his control, and I need more of it. I want it all.

"Yes. Come for me. Do it now and look at me, Princess. Look me in the eyes while you fall apart."

My eyes zoom in on his like a hawk, and then I come apart at the seam. My breathing stops, a loud moan escapes from my mouth, and my thighs squeeze together from the delicious orgasm.

"Keep those legs wide open, Princess. I want to see it all," he growls.

The way he strokes his cock makes my orgasm more intense as I watch him, pure lust coursing through my body. He groans with me as I twist the dildo against my clit, desperate to feel more. The pressure of the belt strains my wrists, but I won't stop. It feels too good to ever stop.

"Good girl," he says.

Panting, I drop the dildo to the floor, unable to hold onto it any longer. Leo stands up and walks toward me, his cock bouncing up and down as he stands in front of the bed.

"On your knees," he says with a smooth but authoritative voice.

I suck in a breath as I sink off the bed and to my knees.

CHAPTER THIRTY-SIX

He grabs his cock and pushes it down while his other hand tips my head forward. He brings my face to his hard-on, and I open my mouth automatically. He doesn't have to ask. I know what he wants, and I want to give it to him so badly.

As his length slides onto my tongue, I close my eyes and enjoy his fingers clenching around my chin. He hisses and licks his lips. "So willing."

"I can do this all day," I say.

"I bet you could," he muses. "My Princess should love my cock as much as she loves to come."

"I do," I say, but then he plunges into my mouth and silences me.

"Shh … don't talk. Let your tongue do all the work." His hand moves to caress my cheek while I swivel my tongue back and forth across his length. "Good girl. Spoil me. Make it nice and wet."

I suck and lick as hard as I can, wanting to taste his delicious cum. I can't hide the fact that I adore this; that I love to be wanted. It's a sort of power rush that I crave.

"I remember you saying you loved my cum," he groans. "Show me how much you want it."

I take him deeper with every stroke, my hands dangling between my legs while I give him head. He seems to revel in the fact that I love tasting him because he cups my face with both his hands and thrusts in and out, each time quicker than before. His cock pulses in my mouths, my saliva coating his length, making it easier for him to slide down my throat.

"Do you know how horny that made me? Watching you tease yourself on the bed?" he growls. "Horny enough to make me want to come all over you."

The salty taste gets me going, my pussy thumping again. I love how he feels against the back of my throat, releasing all his need in my mouth as if he wants to claim it as his own. No-holds-barred, he's fucking my face, and I love it. Even if I wanted to, there's no way to stop him. My hands are tied and his body is so close I can smell the lust dripping from his skin.

He groans. "Hmm … those lips, Princess. I just want to cover them with my cum. Would you like that, Princess?"

I nod while he gives me some air to breathe before plunging back in again.

"Fuck, you're making me wanna come down your throat," he growls.

"Hmhm," I mumble. When he takes his cock out, I say, "Do it."

He tilts his head, his hard-on bouncing against my lips. "Remember the rules, Princess."

"Do it, Sir?" I repeat, biting my lip.

He smirks. "Cheeky girl. Biting your lip won't make me go easy on you. It only makes me want to fuck you rougher." He bends over to look me in the eyes. "I like it when you play hard."

"I know, Sir."

"Hmm …" He smiles. "Keep that tongue wrapped around my dick. I'll give you my cum if you can ask nicely. Now open up."

I part my lips and in he goes again. My pussy is soaking wet, and I can feel it running down my thighs as he fucks my mouth. God, I've never been this horny in my entire life, and I've never loved sex as much as I do now. This man knows how to push my buttons, the good way.

When his dick leaves my mouth for a second, so I can breathe, I say, "Please, give me your cum, Sir."

"Oh, you want it that badly, huh?" he says. "Even sacrificing a bit of air for it."

He plunges back in again, thrusting with everything he has. My back is strained against the bed, and he holds onto my head like he wants to go even deeper. I can feel him push himself to the limit, his cock pulsing inside my mouth.

"Please, give it to me," I say, heaving as he comes out again. "I want to taste you, Sir."

"Fuck, I'm going to come inside your mouth, Princess," he growls, and then he pushes in so far, I feel him explode on the back of my tongue. Cum squirts into the back of my throat, streaming down, and I swallow it all, the taste amazing. He comes and comes, and it seems like there's no end to it. It fills my mouth to the point of it overflowing my lips and dripping onto my chin. After a few seconds, he takes his flaccid cock out, panting heavily.

"Fuck, that felt good," he murmurs, wiping the tip. He brings his finger toward my mouth and circles around my lips, pushing all of his juices into my mouth. "Don't let a drop spill on the floor."

"I won't, Sir," I say. "I love it." And I do. I love every taste of him I can get, even though I sometimes despise his personality. It's a sort of love-hate relationship—difficult to define, easy to accept.

"Hmm …" He grabs my cheeks and caresses them softly. "I know you do, which is one of the many reasons I adore you."

His words have me smiling a bit, feeling good about myself and what we just did. He doesn't feel ashamed of loving my dirty side, so neither should I.

He grabs my hand and helps me up from the floor. Then he slowly unties the belt around my wrists. "These must feel sore," he says, rubbing my hands. "Do you have any hand cream stored somewhere?"

"Yeah, in the cabinet," I say, pointing to the other drawer.

He goes and gets it and smears some of the white stuff on his hands before gently rubbing it into mine. The way he holds my hands, so carefully and full of love, takes my breath away. It feels so good to have his hands warm up mine, for him to massage the cream into my hand with delicateness. He's putting the utmost care into doing it as perfect as possible. I'm a bit flabbergasted. He really cares; something I did *not* expect from Leo fucking King.

We're standing naked in my room, he's rubbing my hands, and all I can think of is that I don't want him to stop. Ever.

When he's finished, he places the pot on the cabinet and focuses his attention on me. He grabs my hands and rests his forehead against mine. "Come lie down with me."

We step backward until we both tumble onto the bed, and I let out a big sigh. "Wow …"

"Hmm … indeed," he says.

I laugh. "So … what now, *Sir*?"

He turns his head to look at me. "Playtime is over," he quips. "For now." The foreshadowing in his voice makes me giggle as I turn to him.

"So no more Sir."

"Well, you can say it if you like. I like the way it sounds, especially coming from your mouth."

"As opposed to coming out of some other girl's mouth," I jest.

"No, as opposed to the app," he retorts, rolling his eyes. "Stop thinking there are other girls in my life. There aren't. I have enough on my plate with you."

"Hey!" I punch his arm.

"I meant it as in 'you are too good for me,'" he adds, grabbing my arms.

"Of course you did," I say, narrowing my eyes. "Liar."

"I told you, I like how difficult you are." He winks. "That makes it more fun."

"I don't know whether to take that as a compliment or an insult."

"Pick the first, that puts me in a better light," he says, smiling with that cute smile I can't resist. Goddammit.

I poke him, he pokes me back, and then it's a game of poking and laughing. I don't know when it ends, except I feel happy. That's all that matters.

When the laughing subsides, he wraps his arms around me and pulls me close to him.

"I love this," he says.

"What?"

"You. Me. This. Us. Whatever it is."

"Yeah …"

"You think so, too?" He narrows his eyes, which are sparkling with curiosity.

"Uhm .. I don't know?"

"You don't know if you like me?" He laughs. "Well, that's kind of late to find out now after we had sex."

I shake my head, chuckling. "No, you know I don't mean it like that."

"Well, you'd better decide fast."

"Why?" I frown.

"Because I'm not letting you off the hook if you're not clear enough. I don't do vaguely."

"Dude, you're always vague."

"I know, that's my thing, don't steal it," he jests. "One of us is enough."

I roll my eyes at him. "You're such an asshat."

"I know, and that's why I also know you *do* like me. You're just afraid to say it. That's okay, I'll wait."

I sigh, not knowing how to respond. He nuzzles my neck, leaving kisses everywhere, making me feel all warm and fuzzy inside.

I like him. I just don't like how he treated me. How he lied to me. But maybe that could all change. At least, he said it would. Can I trust him with my heart? I don't even know if I trust myself with my own heart. Last time I gave it away, it was crushed, and I was left to pick up the pieces by myself. I don't want to go through that again.

Oh Lord, what am I going to do with myself?

"Hmmm ... I spoiled that pussy of mine well," he murmurs against my skin. "You can thank me again later."

"I'm not the only one who got pleasured, if I recall correctly," I retort.

"Such feistiness ... I love that about you," he says. "I love everything about you. Although that doesn't mean we can't be grateful for pleasing each other."

"Oh, stop it," I say, blushing.

He grabs my chin and makes me look at him. "I mean it. I like how you struggle. How you keep resisting me."

"I don't," I say. "Look at us." I laugh.

"Backtalk. See? You like to be naughty. You like to be fierce, and I like that about you. You aren't easily persuaded to do something, especially not for me."

"True."

He leans in. "That's exactly what I need. A girl who pushes back. You didn't fall for me. You ran from me instead, but I managed to catch you anyway. It took a lot of effort, but that only makes it worthwhile."

"What do you mean?" I ask.

"I thought I enjoyed it when girls used to lay down at my feet, but it turns out I appreciate it much more when I meet someone who actually fights my advances, so that I have to work for it. I have to earn your love."

"Love? Hold on, I never said anything—"

"You don't have to say it. You and I both know you're feeling it," he says, lowering his eyes. "Stop denying it. You keep coming back to me, you keep letting me back into your life, even after lying to you, even after everything I did. You still want me. Don't think I didn't notice … you can't resist me." The smug look on his face makes me want to slap him.

"If you'd only admit it, this would be even more fun. We could do this on a daily basis or even hourly …" He muffles a laugh. "I know you want to. I can see it in your eyes. You've always hated me because you couldn't stand how much you fantasized about this. You loathe being dependent, being vulnerable." He grabs my hands. "But I won't hurt you. I promise. At least, not your heart and mind. I can't promise anything about your ass."

That comment makes me giggle.

"Being submissive means giving everything to your partner, and I want you to give everything to me so I can give you everything in return. Think you can do that for me? Can you trust me with your heart?" he asks.

I swallow away the nerves. "It's going to take some work. Some adjusting," I mumble.

He smiles at me. "I'll do it all. Nothing will stop me from having you, Sam. Even if it means working my ass off. Or yours," he says, chuckling. "In the end, working hard to gain your love only makes it that much more valuable. Something to cherish."

Oh, my God. What am I supposed to say to that? Nothing I say will even remotely come close to how sweet that was, so I opt for not saying anything at all. Instead, I wrap my arms around his body and hug him tight. He doesn't know how much it means to me to hear those words. To have someone fight for you instead of just walk away. He wants me, nobody else, and he'll fight to have my love. There's nothing more romantic than that; nothing that can make me feel as good as he just did.

Not even rum-filled chocolate. There, I said it.

And make no mistake, chocolate means the world to me. I mean, if it ceased to exist, I would jump off a cliff so I could go to heaven where there is plenty of that shit.

However, I couldn't even do without Leo.

Not in this world, or the next.

Leo is my chocolate now. My chocolate-eyed, chocolate-hearted, Doritos-loving, bossy asshole.

CHAPTER THIRTY-SEVEN

A few weeks later

I'm writing on my laptop when Leo gets a call from his lawyer. I only manage to catch half of the conversation because I'm too busy penning my experience down. It's still about Leo because, once I started, I didn't want to stop. It feels so liberating to write about him and what he made me feel.

He doesn't know that I'm writing this, and he doesn't need to know. I mean, it's just something too personal. Like he'd look into my mind or something, and I have enough of him sneaking around in my life as it is.

Words stream out of me like a waterfall from a mountain as my fingers skid across the keyboard. And not all of it is bad. I mean, this isn't to ax him. I just want to get it out of my system. There's a lot of the good and sweet stuff in there, too ... okay, maybe not that much because there's not much that doesn't get on my nerves, but that's why I like him, too. We're like two magnets attracting and pushing each other away.

However, when I hear him yell, I don't think I can write anymore.

"Seriously? Again?" he says, crushing his phone in his hand. "You have *got* to be kidding me."

"What's the matter?" I ask.

He looks at me but doesn't speak. Instead, he starts yelling into his phone again. "Fuck her. Fuck her and her wishes and her life."

I frown, hearing that. It must be about that Marilyn woman. I wonder what she's done now.

"She only wants to sign it if I meet *those* criteria? No, no, no, absolutely not. Tell her to go jump off a building for all I care. No, I am not kidding. She is screwing me over big time, and expecting that I'll just fucking bow to her. Fuck her. No. Find something else. Do it, I don't care what it takes. Just make her sign the fucking paper. I don't care how. I want you to solve it. Now!"

He takes the phone from his ear, smashes the button, and then throws the phone so far it makes me squeal. Luckily for him, it lands on the couch.

"What happened?" I ask.

"That bitch," he growls, letting out a roar. "I can't believe she pulled that card."

"Is it that bad?" I ask, frowning.

"She's asking me to dump you."

"*What?*" I sit up straight.

"Exactly my thoughts. She's gone insane." He starts pacing through the room.

"But why? What does the company have to do with me?"

"Nothing, she's just jealous and wants you out of the way. Apparently, she found out what we have is more than purely professional."

I swallow away the lump in my throat. "When? Oh, God, was it because I went to your house when we were ..."

He nods. "She texted me in the morning, just after you left, that she had seen us coming out of the bar. Turns out, she even followed us to my home. That woman is crazy. I'd have her arrested for being a stalker if it wasn't for the fact that I have no proof ... and let's not forget that I'm fucking married to her." He lets out a long drawn-out sigh, rubbing his face. "She wants me to end it with you. It's the only thing that'll get her to sign the divorce papers."

I make a face. "I can't believe she's trying to do that. I thought she was over you already."

"Apparently not. It seems the company isn't all she wants back from me."

"She never had you in the first place," I say, standing up. I don't know if what I say is true, though. Maybe he did like her once. "Right?"

He cocks his head. "Well, I might have flirted with her, but I never made a move. I learned quickly that she wasn't my type at all, so I never pushed further. I didn't want to," he says. He comes to me and holds my hand, pressing a kiss to the back. "I love you."

"But she's trying to drive a wedge between us, Leo. She won't divorce you unless you do what she wants, and she wants me gone and you back in her claws. How can this ever be okay?"

"Don't worry, I will handle it. If she doesn't go one way, I'll make her go the other way."

"What about us? Is there even an us?"

"Of course, there is." He leans his forehead against mine. "I don't want anyone else but you. Nothing will change that fact. Not what she does, what I do, or even what you do." He smiles. "I'll make this work, I promise."

"But you want to divorce her, right? More than anything?"

With his index finger, he tips up my chin. "No. What I want more than anything is you, and I'd do pretty much anything for you."

I smile, my cheeks flushing with heat. "I … I don't know what to say. I'm a bit shocked."

He chuckles. "I know it's hard to believe after everything I put you through, but it's the truth. I've been trying to resist you for too long, and now I've given up."

I laugh. "Well, I'm sure glad you didn't give up the fight."

"You are?" he asks, and somehow that little trickle of insecurity about my love for him sparks a fire in my heart.

I nod, and he comes close to press his lips on mine. Just the touch of his fingers on my cheeks, his lips on my lips, his body against my body … this is bliss.

CHAPTER THIRTY-EIGHT

When he takes his mouth off mine, I can still taste him, and it makes me want to pull him close again. Staring into his eyes is equally mesmerizing, though.

"What were you doing on your laptop?" he asks, looking sideways over my shoulder at the couch I was sitting on.

"Oh, nothing. Just a few notes."

He narrows his eyes. "You don't want to tell me."

My eyes widen, but then I laugh it off like there's nothing going on. I don't want him to read it. At least, not yet. Maybe in a couple of years. Maybe when we're fifty. Or never.

"You're lying …" he draws out, a sly smile appearing on his face.

"No," I say.

"Your red cheeks give you away," he says.

"Oh, fuck off," I say, shoving his shoulder.

He cocks his head. "No, I want to know what you're doing."

"Why? Is it important to you?"

"Yes," he says, smiling sweetly. "I want to know what keeps you busy. You know, what you like to do when you're not working for me."

"Well, not a lot, since I have so very little me-time anyway," I scoff, trying to divert the conversation.

He narrows his eyes again. "If you want more me-time, all you had to do was ask."

"You weren't so keen on giving me anytime before, why now?"

He puts his hands in his pockets. "Because you deserve it."

I snort. "Good one. Just like that money you still owe me."

"Well, technically, I can deduct some money off that since you spent it on lingerie."

"Oh, you're pulling that card now?" I say. "Asshole."

He laughs. "That's me. Always an asshole at your service."

"Do me a favor and don't be at my service," I retort.

"I wish I could do that, but unfortunately, this asshole has his eyes set on you." He raises his brows playfully, making me shake my head.

I sit down on the couch again. "Oh, you're such a weirdo."

"Yep, and you know you want it." He comes closer as I start typing away again. "So, what are you doing?"

I look up from my laptop and then close the damn thing. "None of your business."

"Oh, c'mon. You're not even going to tell me a little bit?" He sighs. "How am I supposed to work with this, huh?"

"I don't know. Ask something else."

"There's plenty of time for that. I want to know why you're typing so quickly. Is it something important?" he asks, sitting down right behind my laptop.

I quickly grab it and put it on the table behind me before he can snatch it away. "I just like to write."

"Hmm ... so you write often?" he asks. There's a hint of curiosity in his eyes that make me believe it's not all just fun and games with him. Maybe he is actually interested.

"Yeah. I mostly write down my thoughts. I like writing things down. Gets the thoughts out of my head and onto the paper. I used to dream about writing articles for a newspaper or a magazine, but that was long ago, when I was still in high school." I smile, thinking about all the memories. "I used to write some articles for the high school newspaper. God, that was fun."

"Why don't you write more and submit them then?"

"What? You mean like for real?" I ask with furrowed brows.

"Yeah." He shrugs. "Why not?"

"I don't know ... "

"Well, you should," he says. "If you love it, you go for it. Nothing's stopping you except you. Just try it sometime. It's worth a shot."

For a moment, I'm flabbergasted. It's just amazing how easy it all is to him, how he just loves to jump into things and doesn't have a care in the world. Except for me. He cares about me, worries about me and his chances with me. Only now do I realize that means a lot coming from him.

Then his buzzing phone distracts me. He takes it out of his pocket and reads a text before jumping off the couch.

"Where are you going?" I ask.

He walks off and grabs his coat. "I have to go to the office. Have to solve this shitty crisis right now."

"You mean Marilyn?" I ask.

"Yeah," he says, pressing a peck to my forehead. "I want to nip this in the bud before she starts a fire I can't extinguish."

"Let me help you," I say.

"No." He furrows his brows. "I don't want you to get involved more than you already are."

"Why not? I can help."

"I appreciate the thought, Sam." He caresses my cheek with his thumb. "But I don't want you to get hurt. She's rather vicious. If she catches onto the fact that you're trying to help, who knows what more she'll ask from us. From you. She's trying to hurt you, and I won't let her."

"But she'll hurt you, too," I say as he walks to the door.

"I don't care. I'm a big boy." He gives me a wink and a sly smile that makes my heart beat faster. "I can take it."

And then he closes the door behind him, leaving me with a dreadful feeling. I know this isn't going to end well. She won't give him anything unless he gives up on me or his company completely. I won't make him choose. I have to do something.

But what?

What can I do to fix this impossible situation?

The only thing I can think of that might work is to ruin her chances to even get the company. That's the only thing she wants, next to Leo, whom she obviously can't have. The only way to do that is to make her seem like a terrible replacement CEO. And the way to do that is ...

Public exposure!

I suck in a big breath and immediately jump behind my laptop again. There aren't a lot of things I can do to help Leo, but there is one thing. I know how to write. And I know how to create a story worth reading. How about a story about a man who had his assistant play his fake wife because his real wife wouldn't divorce him due to his money after his whole family found out he got married?

A big grin spreads on my face. The media will eat this up.

I just hope Leo can forgive me.

CHAPTER THIRTY-NINE

A few days later

I'm still trying to wrap my head around the fact that Leo is Mr. Awesome, but it's getting better every day. He's right; it is the perfect solution because Mr. Awesome gave me what I needed sexually, but not emotionally and physically. Now that Leo is he, those two problems are solved. The only one left is the fact that he's still a giant asshole sometimes, but I think I can live with it ... after all, if I'm as feisty as he proclaims, we do indeed make a good couple.

Just thinking about it gets me all flushed and giggly. I don't know why. Maybe I actually do believe we have a shot at this. That I could be more to him than just a girl ... his girl.

These past few days I've been helping Leo with making appearances as his fake wife for the few business associates of him who asked about it. Sometimes I made a fool out of myself, but Leo never seemed embarrassed. On the contrary, there was a huge smug smile on his face the entire time I was with him, and I couldn't help but feel flattered, even though he still wanted me to hold up the façade. Luckily, there aren't many that we need to visit. I just hope the deal with his real wife ends soon.

After having finally received the money Leo owed me, I'm back to working for him as his assistant. Nobody on the work floor knows about our 'relationship' (it hasn't been defined yet), which is perfect because there would probably be a riot if they knew. They'd want to get raises, too. No, if they are ever to find out, which I'm sure they will, it'll have to be after I no longer work for him. And I don't expect that to be anytime soon. After all the shit that went down between us, we're finally in a good spot. I could even say I'm in the best spot I've been in a long time, so I don't want to spoil it.

Except, right when I'm working on a statement for him, I hear some noise coming from his office. When I glance over my shoulder, Leo shoots up from his chair, throws his phone on the table, and barges toward the door.

Oh, shit.

Oh, fucking hell.

The livid look on his face and the thunder in his eyes are enough for me to want to pack my bag and run out of the door.

I know why he's mad.

He knows what I've done.

"Samantha …"

"Yes?"

"In my office. Now." The way he says it, with that grated growling undertone, has the hairs on the back of my neck standing up.

I tiptoe behind him as he storms back into his office, waiting for me to enter before slamming the door shut behind me and walking back to his desk in complete silence. I stay put near the door, not moving an inch as he sits down in his chair, collecting his calm by blowing out long, hard breaths. His entwined fingers rest on his desk as he stares me down, but I'm not opening my mouth first.

I've been dreading this moment for weeks because I knew it was coming. Once I submitted the article to a prominent tabloid and promised them exclusivity on my story, I knew shit would hit the fan when he found out. I guess that day is now.

On his desk is today's newspaper, and the page it's opened to clearly shows his photo with the headline "*W* magazine's CEO King's secret marriage." My eyes widen and I suck in a deep breath.

"I'm sorry, Leo. Let me explain, please," I say, gazing back and forth between his penetrating stare and the crucifying newspaper. "I did it so they could see what a wicked bitch she is. I didn't do it to hurt you, you have to believe me."

He frowns, parting his lips, but nothing comes out. Instead, he just sits there quietly, listening to me.

"I put the focus on her so she'd get all the blame. This way the media will side with you, and then she won't be able to steal *W* magazine from under your feet. They hate her now; she'll never be accepted as CEO, let alone in a high position anywhere else. This'll ruin her chances. And I have more where that came from. I doubt she wants it out there in the world. She'll probably want to hide now so I expect her to sign the papers soon." I take a few breaths. "Please, you have to believe me. I did it for you."

When it's quiet for a few seconds, I don't know what else to say. I had my reasons, and I hope he understands they came from a good heart.

"Are you done?" he asks.

I'm taken aback by his cold-heartedness. "Say something ..."

I'm not sure I want to hear it because I know he's pissed off, and rightfully so. It's just hard to swallow, knowing that I did it for him, for us, but it hurt him. I don't want to hurt him. I wanted to get rid of her so we could be together, and this was the only way. It can't get any worse than this, right?

Wrong.

"You're fired."

My jaw drops and my eyes almost bulge out of my skull. I can't believe what I'm hearing. "What?"

"You heard me," he says with furrowed brows, his eyes glistening.

Tears well up in my eyes. "Is this some kind of cruel joke?"

"No joke. Please just ... pack your things," he says, looking down at his desk. "I'll make sure any stuff left will be sent to your home."

My lips quiver as I fight the urge to let the tears run loose. "You can't even look at me when you say it."

"Please ... don't make this harder than it already is."

"Is this it? Is this my punishment for trying to help?"

He doesn't respond as he keeps his eyes on the desk, his fingers twiddling with each other to the point of turning red. His inability to deal with this like a man makes me so angry.

"Fine." I turn around and barge out of his door. "Good-bye."

CHAPTER FOURTY

A few days later

My supply of chocolate never went down the gutter quicker than now. Or rather, down my stomach and onto my fat ass. I've been drowning myself in it, as well as Doritos, coffee, and the occasional martini while sobbing with Stephanie. Every sip was another sentence to tell, and every time it got too much, I just took another sip to quell my anger and sadness.

These past few days I've been camping out in Stephanie's house, not able to sleep in my own bed because it smells like him. Everything in my house reminds me of him; the laptop he snooped at, the couch he sat on, the coffee mug he drunk from, the carpet he walked on ... even the fucking air smells of him. I can't take it.

I hate him.

I hate that I love him.

I hate that he pushed me out, just like that. As if it didn't mean a thing to him.

I crush another pencil with my hand. "Goddammit."

"Sam ... you gotta try to calm yourself down," Steph says as she grabs the laundry basket.

"I can't. Every time I try to write a single word, that asshole crosses my mind and he screws everything up." I get up and throw the pencil in the garbage so I can grab a new one.

"Then stop writing," she says.

"I can't. I need to write *something*. This is going to be my new job. I don't care how hard I have to work for it, but I will goddamn make it work."

I grab a new paper and start penciling down a few keywords for my next idea. I refuse to use a laptop because it'll only tempt me to check my email, which is filled with emails from him. I've gathered many since I started working for him, so much that I don't know where to start to clean up this mess and ban him from my life forever. It's like spiders; you can never fully get rid of them. Better to just burn your house to the ground.

"That's fifteen pencils already. If it continues at this rate, I can go buy a new packet every day," she says.

"I'll pay you for it," I say with a grumpy voice.

"Sam ..." she sighs. "You can't go on like this."

"Sure, I can. I just have to ignore it and keep working toward my goals. I'll forget about him. You'll see. It won't take long."

"I doubt that. You've never been this hung up on a guy before."

I groan, but it sounds more like a growl. "Biggest mistake ever."

"You say that because he hurt you, but you don't mean it."

"Yes, I do."

She puts the laundry down so hard, the sound makes me jolt up in my chair. "That's not true. I refuse to believe that you hate him as much as you say you do. You would never fall for a guy if he was as much of an asshole as you say he is. You're hurt, Sam. And that's okay, it happens, but don't let it stop you from finding happiness."

"I'm not. Look. I'm finding happiness in my writing," I say, holding up the paper.

"No, you're avoiding what it's really about, which is him. You've been avoiding him, you've avoided talking about him, and you've even avoided thinking about him. You have to face what's bugging you, Sam."

"No, that'll only make it worse!" I say, slamming down the pencil.

She puts her hand on her side. "Maybe he fired you for a reason."

"Yeah, to get rid of me." I sigh. "I should never have put that story about us and what he did in the newspaper. God. How could I be so stupid to believe that it would make all our problems go away?"

Stephanie cocks her head. "Honey, don't be so hard on yourself.

You tried to get rid of the bitch, you meant well."

"But I hurt him with it." I frown, grinding my teeth. "And then he hurt me back. Fuck him. Just because I did something to help us out doesn't mean he can just hurt me like that. Why did he have to retaliate the way he did?"

"Those we love hurt us the most, sweetie," she says, stepping closer to wrap her arm around me and pull me in for a hug. "You both loved each other so much; you ended up hurting each other badly."

"I just wanted to fix it. I wanted her gone. And I want him to myself ... I should've known that he couldn't cope with the public exposure on this. It was too embarrassing. Of course, he wanted to fire me. What boss in their right mind wouldn't fire an assistant like that?" I sniff, hiding my tears in her shirt. "God, I'm so fucking stupid."

"Now, now. Tell you what, I think you need some good old fashioned shopping with good ol' me. What do you say?" she asks, smiling at me.

"If that means getting an extra-large cup of Starbucks coffee, I'm in. I need some caffeine to wash this self-pity away."

We both laugh a little, but then her phone buzzes. She takes it out of her pocket and frowns, staring at the screen.

"What?" I ask, wiping my face with a clean towel.

She turns the cell phone toward me. "It's from Leo."

I snatch the phone from her hand. Now that the digital revolution is in my reach, I can't help but succumb to it. It's bad, no excuses, but I can't help myself.

Like coffee, I ingest the text.

Please tell her I'm begging her to forgive me.
I love her.

Leo King

My hands are clenched around the phone, desperate for more, but there isn't any. Stephanie literally has to pry my fingers loose one by one in order to get it back.

"How did he get my phone number?" she asks.

"Beats me. He must have gone through my computer at work. I

didn't have time to delete everything."

"Stalker," she says, chuckling a little.

"He's trying, though …" I sigh.

She rolls her eyes. "I know what you need. Fresh air, away from this vicious spiral." She grabs my hand. "C'mon."

She pulls me to the door where we put on our coats, and she opens the door. Right when I step outside, the newspaper boy cycles by and hits me in the face with the newspaper.

"Motherfucker," I mumble, pulling the paper off my head. "Fucking kid."

"He always does that to me," Stephanie says. "Sorry, I should have warned you. I never step outside without something to protect myself, but I wasn't thinking."

I laugh. "That dipshit does that to every girl. I think it means he likes us."

"Aha, weird. Especially because he's like … twelve."

I chuckle. "Yeah, I know. Men."

We shrug and laugh, but then I look at the newspaper and my heart stops beating for a second.

"What?" Stephanie asks as she steps closer.

I read the front-page title. "CEO of *W* magazine tells his side of the story."

"Oh, what does it say?" Steph asks.

I read out loud, trying to make sense of it, but it's not his side of the story at all. It's a letter.

Everything you read about me in the newspaper is true.
I am an asshole.
I asked the girl I secretly admire to pretend to be my wife just so I could keep my reputation intact. My family, my friends, my colleagues, even my clients had to be kept in the dark.
I did some pretty bad things for the sake of keeping my image clean. I thought I had a good motive. I was wrong.
The woman I was really married to had baited me into marriage for the sake of stealing everything I love, including W *Magazine. She wanted the position I currently hold, and she wanted to ruin me. I couldn't sit by and let her get away with it.*
Which is why I'm coming forth with this.
In an attempt to rid myself of the woman who soiled everything I stand for, I

hurt the woman I truly love. Samantha Webber. If you're reading this, please know that I love you and that I am begging you to forgive me.

I want to tell you so much, but the newspaper wouldn't allow too big of an article. That, and if I truly told them how I feel about you, half of it would be X-rated, and in a family friendly newspaper those things just can't appear.

I do hope you read this, Samantha, and that you'll allow me to apologize to you in person.

I owe you that much … and much, much more.

Please give me a chance.

I love you.

Leo King

CHAPTER FOURTY-ONE

My hands quiver as I stare at the paper, unable to utter even a single syllable.

"Oh, my God …" Stephanie mutters. "Did he actually write that?"

I nod, my jaw still wide open.

"What are you going to do?" she asks. "You *have* to do something, Sam. You can't just stand here and wait."

I look at her over my shoulder, not knowing how to respond.

"He's begging for your forgiveness, Sam. You can't just let this pass. If he's not the one for you, I'm going to swallow my own fucking cell phone," she says chuckling. "That's how sure I am that you two belong together. All that fighting only means you care about each other. This is the proof." She points at the newspaper, which still shakes in my hands.

"Go!" she yells. "Fucking go after him, you idiot!" She pushes me forward across the pavement. "Go get your fucking man back."

I drop the newspaper as I walk away from her house. "I can't …"

"What 'you can't'? Do you want me to come with you and hold your hand? Because I swear to God, I will. He's worth it, and I will not let anything ruin this moment," she says.

"No, I just … I have to get away from here. Right now. Alone," I mutter.

My mind is going crazy, thoughts about how he fired me spinning through my head, his letter ... I have to escape it all. Too many emotions punching into my gut. I need some of my favorite coffee because it feels like I have no energy left.

I just walk out of Stephanie's neighborhood and make my way to the nearest bus stop. I don't think I even said goodbye. I'm so confused right now; I don't even know what I'm doing, except running. Running away from whatever it is that I'm feeling. I don't want to hurt anymore.

I quickly catch a bus and sit down on a seat in the far corner, trying to blend in. I just want to get to the city center where all the people are and where I won't feel so cramped. Plus, I really need my Starbucks right now. Like, I think I might die if I don't quick-start my body with some caffeine.

Staring outside, I try not to think about anything at all. Even that is impossible because on all the bus stops we pass there is a digital advertisement ... and it's not showing an ad. Instead, it's showing Leo's face with the words 'I'm sorry, Sam' written below.

With eyes wide open and my hands in my pockets, I jump out of my seat and walk toward the exit of the bus.

"Excuse me, can you open the door? I really need to get off."

"Um ... sure," the driver says, and the bus slowly comes to a stop.

"Thank you," I say when the door opens, and I jump out.

I run far away from the bus stop to the nearest train station, which we luckily just passed. I buy a ticket and get on the train, thinking I'm safe here. Taking a big breath, I sit down on my seat and don't look out the window at all. Better safe than sorry.

Except, the video on the display that normally shows the times the train arrives at the next station, suddenly shows a clip of Leo King apologizing to me in front of the world.

Shocked, I stare at the display, wanting to scream.

I don't know what to do.

What to say.

Where to go.

So I opt to leave the train at the next station, which is not too far from the city center.

I walk the rest of the way to the mall. It's quite cold outside, but the perpetual motion of my body keeps me warm ... and all these confessions warm my heart. I don't know if it's a good thing, but at least I'm not shivering.

When I arrive at the mall, my first instinct is coffee, of course. So naturally, I make my way to Starbucks and order something different than usual. A Double Chocolaty Chip Crème Frappuccino; another favorite of mine, but only reserved for days I need it the most … like now.

But even *here*, in my haven, I'm not safe. The moment I take a sip from my cup, the television hanging in the corner changes channels, and on comes a guy standing on a square outside a very familiar mall. The mall I'm standing in right now. And it's not just some guy … it's Leo. I shouldn't be surprised, but I am. Who in the world does this? How? And why?

Blinking, I stare at the screen.

"This is for Samantha. You know who you are. I love you, and I won't let you go. Not ever. And if that means begging for your forgiveness day in and day out, even if you won't talk to me, or even see me, I'll do it with pleasure," he says, staring at the camera that's taping him. I feel like he's watching me, and maybe he knows that I am, too.

"Sam, I'm sorry. I'm sorry for everything I did. I want to tell you so much more, but words fall short when I try to describe what I feel for you. I want to apologize for hurting you. Please come outside the Starbucks you're standing in."

My eyes widen. He knows. He knows that I'm here? How?

"You must be wondering why I know where you are. I didn't have anyone follow you, trust me. I'm not that type of guy." He muffles a laugh. "But I know you well enough to realize where you'd go when you're hurt. What you want when you're sad. What you do to cheer yourself up. That, and I texted your best friend, who wasn't all too keen on helping me … but she did it anyway. Provided that I'd beg for your forgiveness *and* accepted the consequence of hurting you again, which was a smack in the face from her."

The people in the Starbucks laugh, but I'm the only one whose jaw feels screwed loose.

"I deserve every inch of your wrath, so please come and give it to me. I'm in the mall, right in front of the Starbucks you're in. Will the beautiful redheaded curvy girl come outside."

Now all eyes zoom in on me, and I can feel my cheeks heat up. My head drifts toward the window, peeking through the mass of people to spot Leo standing there in his suit with a huge bouquet of red roses in his hand.

With my lips slammed together and a whole bunch of eyes watching me, I make my way through the Starbucks crowd and step out of the door. My heart is beating like a drum as we walk toward each other. Everyone's looking, not just the people in the Starbucks, but half of the people in the mall have stopped shopping to watch us.

As I stand in front of him, I don't know what to say when he smiles at me without saying a word. He holds out the roses. "These are for you."

"Thank you ..." I mutter as he hands them to me and gives me a peck on the cheek.

"I didn't want to come empty handed," he says.

"You certainly made a big entrance," I say, chuckling. "Everybody is looking at us." Just thinking about it makes my body heat up with embarrassment.

"Let them stare." The look on his face has turned completely serious. "I only care about you."

I don't know what to say to that. It's all a little overwhelming.

"How ..." I mutter.

"How did I find you? Well, I've been trying for days, but I guess you already noticed that." He chuckles. "I'm not one to give up easily."

"I saw you everywhere, on the bus, on the train," I say.

"Yes. What a few advertising companies can do, huh?" He puts his hand behind his head as if even he doesn't know quite what to say.

"Wow ... all of that ... for me?"

"Anything and everything, Sam. I really meant it when I said that I loved you. I even went as far as to harass your friend so she'd tell me if you were still at her place. The moment she texted me that you were out on your own, I knew I had to set the plan into motion."

"Oh ... holy shit ..." I say, blowing out a huge breath.

He smiles, looking down at the floor. "Yeah, I'm quite crazy." He glances up at me from under his eyelashes. "Crazy about you."

I sigh, smiling and shaking my head at the same time. "Leo ..."

"I know, I know what you're thinking ... that I can't come here and just say stuff like that, but it's the truth. And I made a promise to a certain someone that I'd stop lying for good."

"Hmm ..." I make a face because somehow I find this all a little hard to believe. I wonder what he's up to. "So … why did you want me to come and meet you outside?" I ask.

"Well, for starters, let me just apologize for the way I behaved in my office. It was harsh and unnecessary. I didn't want to brush off like that."

"But …?"

"There is a reason," he says, licking his lips and taking a deep breath. "I *had* to fire you."

"*Had* to? Why? I thought you said you didn't care about what anyone thinks, and that you wanted me more than anything else."

"I did, and I still do. And yes, you're right, I don't care what they think. However, I was forced to fire you."

"Who forced you?" I ask with furrowed brows.

"Marilyn did."

CHAPTER FORTY-TWO

My jaw drops. "What?"

"It was her final demand for her to sign the papers."

"And you did it? So you'd get out of the marriage? You used me again then." I fold my arms.

"It's not like that. We were on the phone when I found out about that article you sent to that newspaper."

"Oh ... so it *is* about that. I told you why I did that, and it wasn't to hurt you. But you didn't have to retaliate like that, Leo."

"It wasn't my intention to get back at you," he says. "When I read that article, I knew we were fucked. I was angry, yes, that my reputation had gone down the drain within a day. However, hers was, too. Once she noticed, of course she realized that she had no more options. Nobody would take her on or would want her to be CEO of any corporation. So in essence, what you did was good."

"You tell me that now, *after* firing me. Where's the logic?"

"It was the only way to get her to sign the papers and to finally be rid of her. If she felt like she had just a little bit of control over the situation, it would go much smoother than if I would have smoked her out, so to speak. She had to do it, thinking she'd won."

"So you fired me so you could annul your marriage with her ..." I say.

"Yes."

"You couldn't have just said that? Why didn't you just tell me this from the beginning?"

"Because she demanded that she hear everything. She wanted to hear me fire you over the phone, so she knew for sure that I'd do it. If I told you what was going on, she would have heard it and wouldn't have accepted the deal."

Staring at him, everything finally clicks into place for me. "Is that why you were so abrupt with the conversation?"

"I just wanted to get it over with as fast as possible. I knew I couldn't say much, if anything, because she was listening in to our conversation."

"No wonder ..." I say, grinding my teeth.

He leans in to grab my arm, and the sudden touch makes me aware of how good it felt to have him near me.

"I'm sorry, Sam. I really am. Please believe me. I didn't want you to get hurt the way you did."

"But she did," I add.

"Yes, she wanted us both to hurt. She even told me that she wanted to see me in pain after that article in the newspaper. She felt ruined."

"Good," I hiss, a little too vicious.

His lips curl up into a smile. "You seem to enjoy ruining her."

"I do because she ruined my life, too. Because of her, I had to pretend to be your wife. *And* she got me fired!"

"And she made me lose you. Again," he says, looking down at me as he steps closer and grabs my hand. "But I'm not letting you go, Sam. Even if I'm the one to blame for all this mess, I'll take it. I'll take whatever punishment you want to give me, as long as it means I'll get to keep you in my life just a little longer."

I swallow away my nerves. "I don't know what to say ..."

"Say you'll forgive me. I didn't want to fire you, although I have to admit it wouldn't have worked if people found out you and I were a thing."

"I don't like the past tense you're using," I say.

He laughs. "Me neither. I'd prefer this to still be a thing. And more ..." He raises his eyebrows. "Even if you're not my assistant anymore, I still want you ... more than ever."

"But what am I supposed to do now? I lost my job."

"I've got the perfect solution to that. You love to write, right? Well, I can now offer you a permanent column in *W* Magazine."

My jaw drops as I blink and stare at him. "What? Are you serious?"

"Dead serious. I'm not taking no for an answer," he says with a smirk.

"But what about Marilyn? She won't like this; it's basically circumventing the deal."

"What's done is done; she has no control over me now. She and I made a deal that I'd fire you, and I did. She got what she wanted. She already signed. The marriage is over."

I suck in a breath. "So you're a free man?"

"I'm as single as can be." Suddenly, he wraps his hand around my waist and pulls me close. "Not that I want to be ... I much preferred the fake marriage life."

I can't help the smile that forms on my lips. "So you're basically just screwing her over by giving me a whole different job?"

"Yep, big time, and I don't regret a thing." He grins. "Like I said, I always get what I want, and what I want is for you to be happy."

"Does that include a certain asshole in my life?" I ask, tilting my head.

"That depends ... do you want him to be there? Because, if not, he'll still happily take the column writer. The two don't have to be connected, and I won't hold it against you if you choose not to want to continue with me, but do want to write for *W* Magazine."

I mull over it a bit, and then a wide grin spreads on my face. "Nah. That's like asking me to choose between chocolate and Doritos. I like to have them both."

He smiles broadly, resting his forehead against mine. I place the bouquet of red roses on a small ledge and wrap my arms around him, hugging him tight. People behind us are still staring and some are even whistling, making me laugh.

"I love you," he says. "I love you more than anything in this world, and that says a lot coming from me."

I chuckle. "Yeah, it does, actually. You're such an asshole."

"I know, that's why you love me," he muses.

I poke him in the side, and he flinches. "God, you piss me off so much. Sometimes I just can't stand you. And you hurt me like no man ever has before. I think I hate you more than anyone else."

"There's a thin line between love and hate, Princess," he muses, winking at me. "The people you despise the most are the people you feel the most for. Otherwise, they wouldn't be able to hurt you."

"Maybe ..." I say.

"Maybe what?" he says with a soft voice.

"Maybe I do love you."

"You know, I was hoping you'd say that," he says.

"Why?" I ask.

"Well, I want the fake marriage to stop being fake."

I frown, confused. "You said she signed. Aren't you going to tell your parents?"

"I'd much rather tell them nothing at all and just keep things as the way they were," he says.

"No, why? I don't want to live a lie."

"You don't have to," he says. "I was hoping we could turn it into something real so we don't have to pretend anymore."

He unwraps his arms but holds onto my hand.

And then he goes down on one knee.

"Will you marry me, Samantha Webber?" he asks with a huge smirk on his face. "For real this time?"

CHAPTER FOURTY-THREE

With my jaw dropped, I stare at him as he fumbles in his pocket and takes out a little box. When opened, a sparkling diamond ring flashes in the sunlight.

"What do you say?" he asks, cocking his head to the side.

I go for the first word that springs to my mind. "Yes!"

And then I jump him. I literally jump on him, wanting to hug him so badly that I smother him with my breasts. My added weight makes him tumble over and fall ass-first to the ground with me lying on top of him.

The entire crowd behind us is cheering and clapping, making a lot of noise. My cheeks flush as I wrap my arms around him and he coughs from the lack of oxygen.

"I guess that's a definite 'yes,'" he says, laughing.

I giggle as I climb off him and help him up. "Sorry."

He pats down his pants and then takes the ring from the box, grabbing my hand. "I didn't expect such enthusiasm, but I'll take it."

With care, he slides the ring onto my finger. Looking at it makes me feel like I'm dreaming. I must be, right? I mean, Leo King just asked me to marry him for real. It's like a fairy tale, only I'm not a princess in need of rescuing, and he's not Prince Charming, although he is quite handsome. But who gives a shit, I'll take him over any man I met before this day, even if he acts like a douchebag sometimes. He's *my* douchebag.

He smirks. "Like it?"

"Yes, I love it, but …" I hold up a finger. "You'd better keep your promise, Mister. Don't ever lie to me again."

He smiles. "I promise I won't hurt you ever again. With Marilyn out of the way, there's nothing stopping us from doing what we want, and what I want right now is to have and to hold you forever."

He pulls me close and growls possessively, which creates goosebumps all over my body. Leaning in, he tentatively purses his lips, waiting for me to allow him to kiss me. However, he doesn't need my permission. He can kiss me anytime, anywhere, no limits. No doubts. Nothing standing between us.

I feel the incredible urge to throw the bouquet of red roses into the air, but that would ruin them, so I opt to smash my lips into his instead. I can never have enough of his taste, his sweetness, his harshness, and all of it combined. Our kiss is an instant hit to my heart, which almost knocks out of my chest. I'm so happy right now; I could fly.

"So, you're not changing your mind anymore, right?" he asks between kisses.

"No. Never."

"Are you absolutely sure? Because once you say yes, there's no going back. This is it. I won't let you go. Ever."

I smile against his lips. "I already said yes. I'm yours, Leo."

He smiles but then kisses me again, and I can't resist the urge to kiss him back. Our lips entangle in a furious fight for love, and I wouldn't have it any other way. I was already his a long time ago. From the moment I first stepped into his office to apply for a job to all the time I spent with him writing his statements and making calls for him. All the talks we had on the airplane and in our homes, and all those little moments between.

I was always his.

EPILOGUE

A few months later

The new assistant takes my coat without saying a word. She does give me a weird look, as if she's scared because I'm her boss' fiancée. She's rather skittish, not at all like me, and I get the feeling she's going to have a handful with Leo, not to mention the fact that she'll probably be overwhelmed in a matter of days.

Oh well, I guess I'll have to help smooth things out for him. After all, I am not just his fiancée, but also his trusted advisor when he's at home with me and in need of guidance. Once an assistant, always an assistant. I might not be paid in money, but I get enough reward by having him in my bed every day.

Talking about reward … it's time I delivered this new article I wrote and receive my payment.

As I walk toward his office, I get the sense not all of his staff are used to the idea of him and me being together. It's like their eyes are burning a hole into my back. I try to ignore it for Leo; he told me not to pay any attention to the looks we'd get. He wants me confident and proud so that's what I'm going to be. I love the way he looks at me as I knock on his door and he sees me. That sparkle in his eye … it's like I make his day.

It makes me happy seeing it, although I always know why he's so happy to see me. Now that I no longer work for him, we have all the freedom in the world to do what we want, when we want it. Including having sex all over the place. In his car, in the park at night, and even here in the office. I admit, we're dirty, disgusting perverts, but it's made my life so much more exciting.

As I open the door and step inside, a smile appears on his face. "Finally, you're here."

"Sorry I'm late," I say as I close the door behind me.

In his eyes is a certain gleam that makes me shiver in place. "Love that outfit."

I look down at my short black skirt and tucked in red blouse. Along with my high heels and this bun on my head, I look like a real secretary. Except, I'm not ... not anymore, but that doesn't mean I can't pretend to be one. Just for fun.

Seductively, I walk toward him and place my article on his desk. "Here it is."

"Hmm ..." He glances at it briefly, but his eyes can't help but drift to my boobs and then up to my face. "You know I love your work, but you said you'd deliver it one hour ago."

"I know, but it was so hard to find the right words." That's a lie, but I like what he does when I don't follow the rules. What can I say? I'm a naughty girl.

His eyes narrow and his fingers spread on his desk. "No excuses. You know what happens when you disobey."

I purse my lips. "I'm sorry."

His chair scoots back and he stands up. "It's Sir for you."

"Sorry, Sir," I say, hiding a smile.

"You will still have to be punished for being late." He walks to the windows and closes the blinds so nobody can see what we're doing.

"I understand," I say as I spread my legs and place my hands on the desk. "Punish me, Sir."

A wicked grin spreads on his face, one I'm all too familiar with and which I've come to adore.

He steps away from his desk and circles around me. Suddenly, I feel his hand on my thigh, sliding up underneath my skirt. "I can't resist you when you're wearing this. I hope you understand the consequence of dressing the way you do."

"Yes, Sir," I say, my voice hitching when his hand comes down on my ass. Oh, I understand the consequences all right, and it was all intentional. We're both dirty fuckers, looking for any excuse there is to turn things bad … in an oh so good way.

"You come into my office late, bearing a half-assed article, hoping that it's good enough. Well, I want more. And I want you to give me everything I ask. Understood?"

"Oh, yes, Sir," I moan when he slaps my other cheek, my nails digging into the desk.

"Good because if you're going to dress like a secretary, I'm going to treat you like one." He muffles a laugh. "Something I've always dreamed of doing."

"Now you have the chance," I say. "I want to please you, Sir."

He smacks my ass again, and this time I feel it zing through my entire body. God, I'm getting all rosy again. I love it!

"And how do you intend to do that?" he asks, rubbing me sensually.

I lean back to touch his pants with my ass, where I can clearly feel something bursting.

"Hmm …" I smile. "I want to crawl under your desk where no one can see how I'm going to suck you dry." He hits me again. "Sir!" I squeal.

"Fantastic idea, Princess. Let's start now."

He pushes up my skirt and rips down my panties. Not even a second later, his fingers are slipping down my pussy, spreading my wetness everywhere.

"But first I'll take your pussy across my desk, and then I'll take your mouth while I sit in my chair. No questions asked."

"Oh, yes. Fuck me, Sir," I murmur as he places a kiss on the back of my neck.

A zipper is pulled and then his cock teases me until finally he thrusts in and takes me completely.

This is it; this is what I need, what I desire. What we both wanted all along.

There's no reason to fight it any longer. He is mine, and I am his. Just like it should be. And right now, we're making all our dreams come true.

THANK YOU FOR READING!

If you enjoyed this book, please leave a review on Amazon or Goodreads. It would mean the world to me. Thank you so much for reading my stories!

Be the first to see cover reveals, read exclusive chapter previews and even to win cool gifts! Your information is safe and sound with us and will never be sold or released to third parties.

Don't worry - we hate spam just as much as we hate a story without a happy ending so emails will be kept to a minimum.

Sign up here: http://bit.ly/Newslettercoco

TALK TO ME!

I love hearing back from my fans. You can contact me on my website, http://www.cococadence.com, or leave me a message on Facebook: https://www.facebook.com/authorcococadence.

ABOUT THE AUTHOR

Coco Cadence is an erotic romance writer, who loves cocky heroes and smartass heroines. She adores happy ever after's as much as her fans do, and she will never stop writing them. In her free time she enjoys reading a good book, playing with her cute dogs, and spending quality time with her soon-to-be husband, but you can always find her drifting off into her mind to think of new stories.

Connect with Coco:
Website: http://www.cococadence.com
Facebook: https://www.facebook.com/authorcococadence

Made in the USA
San Bernardino, CA
21 May 2018